DEATH AND THE SINGLE KILLER

BY

RANDALL J. FUNK

ALSO BY RANDALL J. FUNK

Death is a Clingy Ex

Death Lives Across the Hall

Death Wears a Big Hat

Death is Sleeping with My Wife

Death Stole My Ride

Death and the Fanboy

Death is a Real Killer

Death, You Jabroni

Death Stalks the Retirement Party

Death is the One That Got Away

Death Will Be Brief: Joe Davis Mystery Tales, Volume One

Published in the United States by Ghost Light Press, LLC

www.randalljfunk.com

ISBN: 979-8-9997285-1-7

Cover design by Ann McMan

First edition

Special Thanks to:

Beatrix Funk, for her consultation on firearms and vehicles

Ann McMan, for her usual awesome work on the cover.

Michelle Hughes, for being the first audience for the book and my sounding board.

Everyone who has bought the previous Joe Davis books and helped me along on this adventure.

For Paul Reyburn, the biggest Deirdre I have.

PART ONE

ONCE UPON A TIME IN MINNESOTA

CHAPTER ONE

The office looked out over Fifth Avenue. A corner suite. Empty. Most recently owned by a dot-com millionaire whose stock was now toilet paper. The view was all that mattered.

Miles looked through the open window. Kept the rifle low, out of sight. His eyes were on the hotel across the street, twenty floors down. A doorman in a gray uniform. An approaching car. A bike messenger coming. A skinny kid, bag slung over his shoulder, shifting in the saddle. The kid was nervous. The timing had to be right.

Pat Vitti walked out of the hotel. Silver suit, salt-and-pepper hair, gold-rimmed shades. Mafiosa R Us. He chatted with the doorman, waited for the car. The kid on the bike closed fast. He reached into his bag. Vitti's bodyguards didn't pay attention. No wonder Vitti needed outside help. Miles brought the rifle up, watched through the scope.

The kid's hand came out of the bag. A Glock 19. He sat up in the saddle. Aimed.

Miles shot him in the chest.

The kid's body snapped back. Miles put a second one through his forehead. The kid tumbled off the bike, gun clattering on the sidewalk, bike rolling and falling. The bodyguards came to life, pieces out, blocking Vitti. Welcome to the party.

Cars slammed on their brakes. People screamed.

Miles closed the window. He disassembled the rifle, stowed it in a metal valise. Left the office in about ten seconds, He slipped off his gloves, checked his pulse. Normal. So much for adrenaline.

He stepped off elevator, into the lobby. Dress shoes clacking on the marble floor. Movements precise, not hurried. Sunlight poured through the windows. People stood shoulder to shoulder with fake plants. Chaos on the street. Police there. Ambulance sirens in the distance. Miles went unnoticed, a handsome guy in a black suit. He didn't stand out. He exchanged looks with the woman at the security desk. She shrugged. So much for crack security.

Miles stepped into the street. The ambulance was there. Cops had the crowd under control. The kid's body was under a sheet. Witnesses being questioned. One couple pointed toward the office, high above. Vitti was nowhere in sight.

Miles slipped on a pair of shades, disappeared into the crowd

***

Once upon a time, Miles refused to take jobs in whatever town he was living in. "Don't eat where you shit" was how his old man would have put it. New York was different. He loved the anonymity, the lack of

3

connection. People were killed on a regular basis. Most of them had it coming. Who was going to notice one more?

His apartment was in Brooklyn. He took the subway home. A few shady types eyed the suitcase. One look from Miles and they backed off. He walked home from the station. Kids played in the street. People called down from windows. The noise went away the second he closed the front door. He tossed his keys on the table, said, "Hi, honey, I'm home." The room was empty.

He hung his black suitcoat and tie in the hall closet. Undid the top button on his black shirt. Dropped onto the sofa, kicked off his shoes. He looked over the books and DVDs on the shelves. What to read. What to watch. Same old, same old.

The adrenaline ebbed. It was barely there in the first place. Once, it would take hours. Usually, it required aid. A good run, a movie, booze, sex. Now, he didn't want to do anything. He'd read this was a sign of depression. His old man's voice rang in his head. What the hell do *you* have to be depressed about? *(Hearing his old man's voice was never a pick-me-up.)*

His cell phone rang. It was Shane.

"Mr. Vitti has paid in full," Shane said.

"That was quick."

"He didn't want to drag things out. He adds his deepest gratitude."

"I'll remember that when somebody hires me to take him *out."*

4

Shane was tapping a keyboard "Might have something else. You heard of Michael Santana?"

"Cartel guy. Out of...what? Phoenix?"

"That's the one. He wants a meet."

Miles rummaged around the coffee table for the remote. "What do you know about him?"

"Runs a good chunk of the southwest. Arizona, New Mexico, Colorado. Whatever business they can pick up in Utah."

"Not So-Cal?"

"They don't trust him. Too big a market, and he's too big a fuck up." Shane wheezed, moving his bulk around. "His uncle runs the cartel."

"Don Pedro?"

"The same. To these guys—fuck up or no—he's close to a Made Man."

"Incompetent and untouchable. That's somebody I want to get into bed with."

"No harm in listening."

"True." Miles gave up on the remote. "What the hell? Beats hanging around the house."

"I'll send you the info."

Shane rang off. Miles tossed the cell phone on the coffee table. He got up, looked over the movies on the blonde wood shelf. Maybe a John Woo flick. Hong Kong days, not Hollywood. A Better Tomorrow looked good. He popped it in, stretched out again. Tried to find a comfortable position.

***

The meeting was in Phoenix. Miles flew coach. He bought two seats, guaranteeing some privacy. He read a John Irving novel. Rented a silver compact car at the airport. Checked into a hotel in Tempe. Santana's people called, said they would send a car. Miles sat on a sofa in the lobby. A blonde woman in a cream skirt and sleeveless blouse walked past. Gave Miles a once-over. Maybe she liked what she saw. Maybe she wondered what ninny wears all-black in this heat.

A red Toyota Land Cruiser pulled up. A thick Latino dude got out. He wore shades. His bald head gleamed in the sun. Blue suitcoat likely covered a shoulder holster. He ignored the woman in the cream skirt. Miles stood to greet him. The thick guy didn't offer a handshake.

His voice was flat. "Victor."

"Miles Slayne."

Victor led Miles to the Land Cruiser. Miles parked himself in the backseat. The driver was a Latino dude with a ponytail and a mustache. He didn't greet Miles. Didn't look at him.

The drive took them out of Phoenix, into the remote hills. Arizona didn't interest Miles. Sand and more sand. He saw enough of that in Kuwait. Santana's house was on a hill. Spanish colonial, beautiful view of the cactus. Victor led Miles through the house. It was clean. Frida Kahlo prints on the walls, decorated pots on the tables and shelves. They stepped through a sliding glass door, out to the pool area. Santana sat at a glass table. An umbrella threw shade.

"This the man?" Santana said. It took him two tries to get out of the chair.

Michael Santana might have been good-looking once. Those days had passed. His face was lined, his dark hair was going gray, a second chin was developing. His Hawaiian-print shirt was half unbuttoned. A gold chain slapped against his hairy chest. He wore a pair of tan cargo shorts and flip flops. A bottle of tequila sweated on the table, shot glasses on either side. Santana gave Miles a broad smile, offered his hand.

"Michael Santana," he said.

"Miles Slayne."

Santana dropped into his chair. His eyes were bright, unfocused. Miles kept his shades on. Santana poured himself a tequila.

"You don't get hot wearing all-black?" Santana asked.

"Heat doesn't bother me," Miles said. Santana reached for the other glass. Miles put his hand over it.

"Little early for me. I'll take some coffee if you have it."

Santana snapped his fingers at Victor. Victor disappeared into the house. Santana knocked back the shot, poured himself another.

"Miles Slayne," he said. "That your real name?"

"No. I made up the Miles."

Santana laughed and drained most of his tequila. Victor set the coffee in front of Miles. Miles thanked him. Victor didn't reply. He returned to his place by the sliding door. The coffee was dark and rich. Michael Santana was a fuck up, but his coffee was excellent.

7

Miles's eyes drifted toward the large pool. A woman lounged in a deck chair. Her dark hair splayed out. She wore a blue bikini. It did sterling work showing off her figure. A pair of shades covered her eyes. Miles nodded her direction.

"That the Mrs.?" he asked.

Santana's smile faded. "Just a friend."

Miles was tempted to ask if Santana's wife knew about this budding friendship. He said nothing. "How can I help you?"

Santana set his tequila down, kept his hand on the glass. "Got a problem. Hoping you can help me with it. This guy who does the books. One of the front companies. He's figuring out where the money comes from. And he's been talking to the feds We think he's going to turn. I need him taken care of."

"Not using your own people?"

"Don't want my guys involved." *His thumb rubbed the sweat on the glass.* "This guy's a civilian. Feds might go ape shit. We need...ah, what the hell do they call it? When you can really say you didn't do something?"

"Plausible deniability."

Santana slapped the table. "That's it! That's what we need. That's why I'm talking to you. How much this gonna cost me?" *Miles named his price. Santana sucked in air through his teeth.* "That's pretty steep."

"I'll need half up front."

"Shit." Santana blinked away a bead of sweat. "They say you're the best."

"It's not a competition. But I'm pretty fucking good."

They shook hands, sealed the deal. Chitchatted while Miles finished his coffee. His eyes, hidden by the shades, occasionally drifted to the woman in the bikini. She glanced his direction, sucking on the stem of her sunglasses. Her eyes were brown, her expression cool. Miles sensed curiosity but not attraction. Or maybe she was being discreet.

"I assume she can't hear us?" he asked.

"She can or she can't. Doesn't really matter to her." Still, Santana barked her direction. "Ali! Why don't you go inside?"

Ali gave Santana a teenager-ish scowl. She tossed the beach towel over her shoulder, made her way toward the house. Miles kept an eye her. Built like a brick shithouse. She passed Victor at the sliding door. Neither acknowledged the other.

Santana drained his tequila. "How long do you think it will take?"

"Got to look at the situation first," Miles said. "How interested are the feds in this guy?"

"He hasn't committed to anything, or they would've put him in witness protection. Victor can give you the guy's address and anything else you need."

Santana's eyes drifted toward the upper portion of the house. Probably picturing Ali getting out of her bikini. Miles sensed it. Because

he was picturing the same thing. Best to end the meeting now. Miles set his
empty coffee cup aside.

"If there's nothing else you need…"

Santana's eyes were still on the upstairs window. He offered a
hand. "Nice to meet you, Miles Slayne. Victor will give you a ride back.
Look forward to hearing from you."

The drive back to Tempe was silent. When they got to the hotel,
Victor handed a file over the backseat. Miles thanked him. Victor said
nothing. Miles grabbed the door handle.

"Not thrilled to have me in on this, are you?" Miles asked.

"Just get the job done."

Miles stepped out of the Land Cruiser. It took off the second the
door was closed.

***

The target's name was Robert Stewart. Early forties, married,
two teenage kids. Stereotypical accountant: medium height, paunchy,
brown hair, bald spot. Twenty years as a CPA. Smart enough to figure
out he was cooking the books. Not smart enough to know he was in over
his head.

The Stewarts lived on a cul-de-sac in Scottsdale. The street was
lined with palm trees and other vegetation, native or not. The same cookie-
cutter made all the houses; single story, flat roof, covered porch. Robert
Stewart drove a green Lexus. His wife was tall, blonde, and pretty. The
son was a younger version of the father, the daughter a younger version of

the mother. The wife drove the kids to Chaparral High every morning, picked them up every afternoon.

Miles bought a used Geo Metro. Hired someone to stencil the name of a real estate agency on the side. Pure bullshit. The phone number was a dummy. Shane would answer it. Miles cruised the neighborhood, following Stewart's movements.

Complications arose. Miles didn't want to do the job near the family. Stewart didn't have a life outside of work or home. Office on the third floor of a gray building. Came and went by an underground parking garage. Miles considered a sniper shot. The buildings in the neighborhood didn't give him a clean look. Stewart kept regular hours. Usually came home in rush hour traffic. No chance to hit him without witnesses.

Poisoning was an option. Quick and clean. No witnesses. Use the right shit and the cops might not even suspect foul play. He mentioned it to Santana. Santana wouldn't hear of it. Robert Stewart had to die violently. A message to other rat bastards.

The lack of logic chapped Miles's ass. Santana's idea of plausible deniability. We don't want anyone to know we did it. But we want everyone to know we did it. *But he had half of Santana's money. And a reputation. The customer is always right.*

Miles felt tired. He'd felt this way for a while. A lack of enthusiasm, aggravated by dealing with idiots. He wasn't much past thirty. Felt like he'd lived longer. He didn't know how to do anything else. Hadn't much wanted to. Before now. Retirement crossed his mind. Followed by, "And do what?" He tried to push it away. Concentrate.

11

The house across from the Stewarts was empty. The backyard screened off by trees. A high wooden fence. No security system. An easy break in. Picture window in the living room.

They kept the shades open. Miles watched them. They ate meals together. The kids' achievements were taped to the refrigerator. The parents helped the kids with their homework. Robert kissed them before they went to bed. They laughed a lot.

Miles hadn't had that life. Maybe fleeting moments. Whiskey sometimes made his old man agreeable. When it didn't, Miles took refuge at his aunt's house. She made gingerbread cookies. Talked to him about books and movies. At home, it was a blur of screaming, fists, and broken furniture. The Stewarts lived on a different planet. They were happy. Could Miles take that away from them?

It was disturbing. When Miles thought about consequences, they were his *consequences. Would he get fucked on payment? Would there be any blowback? But the people he eliminated? Fuck 'em. Killers, mobsters, drug dealers, gunrunners. Not a knight errant in the bunch. Miles did his job, slept like a fucking baby.*

What was the problem now?

***

I'll be honest: sometimes I'm confounded Minnesota even exists. Keep in mind, I love the place. I've lived in various parts of it for the entire thirty-six years I've been dragging a crank around this planet. But I think about the pioneer days and imagine settlers coming here, not knowing what they were in for, dealing with a winter of endless gray vistas, deathly cold temperatures, boogers freezing in your nose, your face growing heavy and numb with the cold and then *choosing to stay.* They persevered so that wusses like me can enjoy their radiators and suffer only on walks between the car and the apartment.

My name is Joe Davis. That stray thought will eventually wind up in one of my columns. And I'll get paid for it, thank you very much.

Right now, I'm truly suffering the Minnesota winter. It's a cold February night (as if there's another kind), and I'm negotiating the erector set of decks and stairs behind my Summit Avenue apartment building. Said building is a converted brownstone and the aforementioned decks and stairs were not part of the original design. As a result, they frequently creak and groan as if they're about to step away from the building and go into business for themselves. This is particularly true in the winter. I'm forced to move carefully, both for my own safety and the precious cargo I'm carrying.

I make my way across the deck and shove open the backdoor to my apartment. My cats are waiting in the hall. They're littermates, and they run my household. Lenny is a butterscotch tabby whose appetite and sense of decorum would have fit right into Nero's Rome. Squiggy is the nervous former runt of the litter, whose black-and-white coloring and obsequious manner puts me in mind of a butler. As such, he's always ready to apologize for his brother's gaucheries. As soon as I'm through the backdoor, Lenny makes a beeline to his food dish while Squiggy remains behind and seems to say, in a deep, English-accented voice *Thank heaven you've returned, sir. The guests have grown restless.*

I scratch Squiggy's ears and follow him down the hall to the main room, passing my one bathroom and one bedroom as I go. I set the to-go order on the breakfast bar that separates my thin kitchen from the living room, then drop some kibble in the cats' bowls. My friend Carol is stationed at the breakfast bar, looking resplendent in a wine-colored blouse and black slacks. My other friends, Lars and Mike, are in the living room. They hop up as soon as they smell the food, trailing the aroma like the big dogs they're only a few chromosomes away from being.

"About time," Mike grumbles, his big bulldog head looming over the grub.

"You're lucky to be getting anything," I tell him. "Fong rescinded your lifetime ban after less than a year."

Mike chews his goatee, halted but not chastened. A quick explanation: Fong's is, for my money, *the* best Chinese restaurant in the St. Paul. Mike was their top delivery man for a few months, but he started getting pushed by Ron, another delivery driver who mastered all of Mike's tricks. Mike let his competitive streak get the better of him and Ron was lucky to escape with his life after Mike sabotaged his car. This led to Mike's firing and his ban from Fong's. (After that, whenever I ordered, Fong himself needed a guarantee I wouldn't share any of his delicacies with my idiot friend.)

Mike waves away my admonishment. "It's just because Ron and Fong's daughter are engaged."

Carol unloads some chicken fried rice from the bag. "After Biyu had been dating you, Fong must feel like he dodged a bullet." She mumbles, "I know how he feels."

Mike narrows his malevolent brown eyes. He and Carol dated for about a year. It's been over for a while, but the occasional recriminations and bitterness remain. Still, knowing his daughter moved on from Mike has caused Fong's cup of mirth to bubble over.

I fetch the square plates and the utensils from the cupboard while Carol finishes laying the food out on the breakfast bar. Lars heaps chicken fried rice onto his plate, grabs an eggroll the size of his head, and sashays into the living room. (You'd think this much food would burst his scarecrow frame, but he's a noted trencherman.)

"We should have our next production meeting at Fong's," he says. "It might create the right atmosphere."

Or give us indigestion. Nearly a year ago, Lars came to me with an idea for an independent film. He'd hoodwinked two rich kids and their father into bankrolling it. I've loved film since I was in college and decided, against my better judgment, to write the script, as long as I could also be a producer. Since then, I've done about three hundred rewrites, a director was fired, and many potential crew members have been alienated. Lars has taken over as director and fashions himself as a new Quentin Tarantino (with all of the ego and none of the actual talent). Even mentioning the film threatens to ruin my appetite.

"You can mention it to Fabio and Frankie," I say.

Fabio and Frankie are twins and the aforementioned rich kids backing for the film. I wonder if they regret getting involved with this clambake as much as I do. Lars reclines on my futon and drapes his long legs on my coffee table (even though I've told him a hundred times not to do that).

"Speaking of the next production meeting, I have an idea for a scene," he says.

"Is this another sex scene idea?" I say.

"Yes. And it's necessary."

Dear Lord. The man has been coming up with sex scene ideas for the last couple months. He's not only displeased with the way I write them, but he chafes when told the actors might not go for them. Our previous director, Ollie, was singularly good at coming up with ridiculous action scenes. I now regard those as the good old days. I dish up some Orange Peel Beef and try to keep my tone calm.

"What does this sex scene involve?" I ask.

Lars talks with his mouth full. "We're going to have two characters doing it atop a speeding train."

"A train?"

"Indeed. You've seen Keaton's *The General*?"

"Several times."

"Not to mention the way Spielberg effectively ripped it off for *Indiana Jones and the Last Crusade*?"

"Yes."

"Well, why can't *we* rip it off? But with hot, naked action."

I put a couple potstickers on my plate. "We *are* still making a vampire/heist film, right?"

"Of course," Lars says, adjusting his cardigan sweater. (He tends to dress like The Dude in *The Big Lebowski*, only less fashionable.) "But the train is the essence of action and the sex is the essence of the vampire. Why can't we combine the two?"

"Offhand," I say, "talent, vision, budget. Talent."

Lars uses a flipper-like hand to bat aside my suggestion. "Dust in a windy street, my friend. We have to buckle down and make it happen."

"Lars—"

"I don't want to debate the matter. Just put it in the script. Simple as that."

Sadly, I've gotten used to having discussions shut down by Lars's dictums. (Heavy on the *dic*.) It's doubly frustrating because this is so out of Lars's character. I can only offer weary acceptance.

"Fine," I tell him. "I'll get to work on it."

Mike joins Lars on the futon, leaving Carol and me at the breakfast bar. Once upon a time, she might have been dainty about putting food on her plate, but she's known us all long enough to dispense with such formalities. There's a concerned look on Carol's face. I lower my voice.

"Everything okay?" I ask.

"It's Fabio," she says. "He's not taking the breakup well."

Oh boy. I could see this coming. Last fall, Carol started—how can I put this politely—bumping uglies with Fabio. I didn't give the match my full-throated endorsement. While it was nice to have Carol manipulate Fabio for our benefit, I knew the match was doomed. Fabio is a good-looking kid but not what you'd call intellectually gifted. He wasn't going to hold Carol's attention for too long. She would be into the relationship until she wasn't. We reached *wasn't* about two weeks ago. I haven't dealt with Fabio much since then, though there has been a melancholy tone in his monosyllabic emails.

"What's going on?" I ask.

Carol spoons some Slayer Stir Fry onto a square plate. "He keeps calling me and asking to get back together. Wonders what he did wrong. He'll be different if I just tell him what I want. That sort of thing." She stops dishing up. "I feel bad. Fabio really didn't do anything wrong. He's just...who he is."

Ouch. I've had that a few times, asking *What can I do differently?* and being told *Literally nothing.* "Are you still going to be involved in the film?" I ask.

Carol was made an associate producer after she started knocking boots with Fabio. "Not at all," she says. "If I don't want to see Fabio, I sure as hell don't want to see his sister."

Frankie didn't approve of the relationship, either. I think she resented anyone other than her having influence over her brother. And there might have been some jealousy involved. I don't know. Fabio and Frankie have a weird dynamic, and I'm not deeply interested in exploring it.

"Too bad," I say, putting half my heart into it. "I enjoyed working with you."

"No, you didn't," Carol says, checking her appearance in the hallway mirror. "You never used any of my suggestions. You and Lars have totally lost the plot. It's like you don't even know what movie you're making."

"It started off as a vampire/heist film. Now it's a combination of those things and the entire Playboy Channel library. But somehow...less."

We join Mike and Lars in the living room. I let Carol have the comfy chair while I drag my desk chair over from the corner of the room. I'm grateful to have the position closest to the radiator. Frost gathers on the arch windows at the front of the apartment, obscuring the view of Summit Avenue, one of the main arteries in St. Paul, (once called by F. Scott Fitzgerald *A museum of architectural failures* and yet, we celebrate his bitter, drunken ass in this part of the woods, so provincial are we).

Mike's cell phone rings. He wipes his hands on his jeans and checks the caller ID. He speeds down the hall to answer. Carol and I look at each other and shrug. Lars stares at the floor, lost in his thoughts. Carol nudges him with her foot.

"Something bothering you?" she asks.

Lars's long face falls. "Got a situation with Chuck."

Oh boy. Lars's friend Chuck is a walking situation. He's a frequent partner in Lars's various get-rich-quick schemes. While Chuck doesn't do much legwork, he provides plenty of ideas and advice. The problem, sadly, is that his ideas are universally bad, and his advice is completely worthless.

"Trouble in paradise?" I ask.

Lars runs a hand through his quasi-pompadour. "Chuck is engaged."

Carol and I sit up. She ventures forth. "This woman wants to…spend her life…with Chuck?"

"It's true," Lars says, sadly. "I'm amazed he was still on the market, too. Sorry, Carol. But we all feared this day would come. I'm worried this engagement will distract him. How can he concentrate on our business? We'll be ruined."

"Don't think me insensitive when I ask this," I say, "but what fucking business?"

Lars ignores me. "This could be a complete calamity. I don't know what I'm going to tell our investors."

"Again: what investors?"

He rolls on. "I have to talk sense into Chuck. But how do you talk sense into a man in love?"

Carol adds, "Or Chuck, under any circumstances."

"I'm not sure what to do," he says.

This puts Carol and me in a difficult position. We generally act as mom and dad to our little dysfunctional family. Lars needs some decent advice. He won't take it, but it must be offered. I let Carol do the honors. She power-rolls her brilliant blue eyes.

"Have you met this woman yet?" she asks.

"I have not."

"So, maybe meet her before you make any judgments. See what kind of influence she's going to have on Chuck."

Lars scratches his beard. He hates to go with the simple solution when the expediency of hiring a contract killer to take this woman out might also be available. But this is one of those rare occasions when common sense gets the upper hand.

"Maybe you're right," Lars says. "I should meet her first. Then I'll consider hiring a hitman and having her taken out."

See, I told you he'd get there.

Mike returns from the hallway. He tosses his cell phone on the futon, runs a hand through the brush of brown hair atop his oversized head, and digs back into his Kung Pao Chicken. I set my fork down.

"Everything okay, Chumley?" I ask.

"Fine," he says. "Just something about a meeting."

Carol raises her perfectly trimmed eyebrows. "About what? A job?"

Mike focuses on his food. "I can't get into it right now."

I ask, "Why not?"

"Because I can't. Let it go at that."

Great. It's like putting on a ski mask, picking up a gun, and saying you're going to the convenience store, don't wait up. Why would I find that suspicious? What's worse: this isn't like Mike. Reticence is not his strong suit. I set my food aside.

"You got something going on?" I ask.

Before Mike can answer, Lars jumps in. "Hey, brother, the man said he can't provide details. The least you can do is honor his request." He turns to Mike. "We trust you."

"Thanks, man," Mike says.

"No sweat." Lars lowers his voice. "You're going to tell *me* about it, right?"

This prompts Mike to move to the breakfast bar. Lars lets it go. We eat our meal and eventually wind down for the evening. I put the leftovers away and load the dishwasher. Lars glides out the front door, heading for his apartment downstairs, taking many of the leftovers with him. Carol and Mike bundle up for a trip out into the cold. Fortunately, neither lives too far away (assuming their cars start). I'm about to say goodnight when there's a knock at my backdoor.

Everyone stops. Someone coming to the backdoor is never a welcomed thing. The parking lot is off an alley and largely hemmed in by the carriage house behind the building. It's not a high-traffic zone.

"I should probably get that," I say.

"We'll hang around for a minute," Mike says.

I walk down the hallway, up the single step, and peer through the peephole. The guy on the other side is tanned, and his brown hair is swept back. He wears a dark overcoat (possibly cashmere) and a white scarf (possibly silk). I recognize him, though I don't know how glad I am to see him.

"It's Jim Street," I say.

Mike and Carol don't seem comforted, either. I last saw Jim Street about a year, and it was on a night like this. He wasn't bearing good news then and I'm not certain he'll be bearing it

23

now. (Street and I are not on a social call basis.) I flip open the door.

"Officer Street," I say, "welcome to the party."

The look on Street's face concerns me. Normally, he's got a smirk that offsets the intensity in his blue eyes. Now, he looks subdued. He speaks with a slight drawl.

"You got a minute?" he asks.

"Sure," I tell him. "Come on in."

I let Street into the hallway. Mike and Carol don't seem thrilled, but they move on. Street stops beside the breakfast bar. I step past him and grab a seat.

"What brings you by?" I ask.

"You heard from our friend lately?"

Our "friend" is a contract killer named Deirdre. I last saw her a year ago, and I sincerely hope that's the *last* I'll see of her. Street currently works the Minnesota Bureau of Criminal Apprehension, but he's worked for other law enforcement agencies in the past. Deirdre is a favorite target of his (one might say *obsession*, but I'm not going to tell him that). His being here is unnerving but his asking about Deirdre is more so.

"I haven't heard from her in a year," I say, "Is she back?"

"In a manner of speaking," Street says. "She's dead."

Okay. I guess I don't have to worry about bumping into her again.

CHAPTER TWO

Miles stopped at a place called the Thirsty Pelican. It looked as classy as the name. But he needed a beer and a shot. He pulled into a parking space. His phone rang. Victor, Santana's righthand man.

"Stewart's still alive," Victor said. It wasn't a question.

"For the moment," Miles said.

"What's the hold up?"

Miles swallowed his resentment. Interrogated by Santana's dumb muscle. "Haven't found the opening yet."

"The feds protecting him?"

"Not that I can see."

"So again: what's the fucking hold up?" Victor's voice was flat, menacing. Trying to rein in the inner thug. Not quite succeeding. "Secret Service ain't working this, are they?"

"That's cute. Look who bought himself a Milton Berle joke book at the dollar store."

"I ain't fucking around, homes."

"Good. Because I'm not someone you want to fuck with. Homes"

A beat. Maybe Victor was angry, maybe he was amused. "Get the job done. You don't want it, we'll take care of it."

He rang off. Miles slipped the phone into this pocket. He walked to the bar. The night was cool. A hint of rain.

The Thirsty Pelican wasn't promising. English-style pub. Brick arched entrance. Paneling. Wooden tables and booths. Stained glass fixtures. Low lighting. Peanuts on the tables. Crappy adult contemporary on the PA. A large stuffed pelican over the bar. Miles grabbed a beer and a shot of whiskey, He found a corner table.

There were a handful of regulars. The usual sad sacks. Miles knocked back the shot, sipped the beer, wondered what the hell was wrong. Victor was right, much as that chapped his ass. Robert Stewart should be gone. Miles should be back in Brooklyn, parked on his couch, watching a spaghetti western or a John Ford film. Instead, he was hiding in an empty house, watching the Stewarts night after night.

He had dreamt about them. Nothing distinct. A lot of movement. Yelling and screaming. The parents disappeared. The kids were crying. Their faces covered in blood. Miles woke, couldn't get back to sleep.

It wasn't as if Miles didn't dream. But he rarely remembered them. Rarely thought about them. Was never bothered by them. What changed?

A woman walked in. A knockout. A blue dress glided around her legs, hugged her figure. Dark hair flowed past her shoulders, perfectly framed her face. Her lips were full, her mouth turned down. She sat at the bar. The dress slid perfectly into position. The bartender greeted her. She was a regular. The other regulars gave her appreciative looks. She didn't pay attention.

Miles recognized her. Ali. Michael Santana's. . .friend.

He picked up his beer, walked to the bar. He had no idea why. Nothing good would come of this. But what the hell? Why not run a risk? Otherwise, you're just a dipshit drinking beer at the Thirsty Pelican. He took the place next to her.

"Of all the gin joints in all the towns in all the world," he said.

She half-turned his direction, ready to dismiss him. Another mouth-breather whose reach exceeded his grasp. Something stopped her. Her brown eyes were warm, and her mouth hung open a bit.

"Excuse me?" she asked, her voice smoky.

"It's from Casablanca*," Nothing in response. "Humphrey Bogart? Ingrid Bergman?* Play It Again, Sam? *Although that line is never actually said in the movie." Still nothing. "Your name is Ali, right? I saw you at Michael Santana's."*

A spark of recognition. "You're Miles Slayne. I should have remembered the suit. And I prefer Allison. Only Michael calls me Ali."

"Allison then. Okay if I join you?"

"Sure."

The bartender set a martini in front of her. Miles tapped the bar. "Put it on my tab."

"Very good, Mr. Tuttle," he said, scurrying away.

Allison's fingers rested on the rim of her glass. "Mr. Tuttle?"

"As far as Visa knows. Can't be too careful."

27

"Is Tuttle your real name?" she asked.

"No."

"Is Miles Slayne?"

"No."

Allison sipped her martini. "Thank you for the drink, Mr. Whoever You Really Are." She caught her reflection in the mirror behind the bar. She looked away, turning Miles's direction. "I'll skip the question about what brings you to Phoenix."

"Probably for the best. Does Michael talk business with you?"

"No. But I see things. Your outfit screams contract killer."

"And I was hoping to keep it down to a dull roar."

She seemed amused. Didn't laugh. Miles wondered if she ever laughed. Maybe that coolness went all the way to the core. Debating it caused Miles to gaze at Allison longer than he meant to.

"Don't get any ideas," she said.

"I'm smarter than that, darling."

"When people ask, what do you tell them?"

"I'm a businessman. Which is true. Viewed from a certain angle. How about you?"

"I'm in customer service. Which is true. Viewed from a certain angle."

"Michael takes care of you."

"He pays for the house I live in. He pays for the car I drive. He pays for my clothes and food. All he asks from me is…companionship."

"And you're okay with that?"

Allison took a healthy sip. "You kill people for money. You okay with that?"

"I am."

"How do you get there?"

"It's not hard. The people I eliminate have it coming. Besides, it's the job. It's not me."

"Easy once you make that choice, isn't it?"

Miles finished his beer, ordered another. He liked Allison. She was too smart to be with Michael Santana. But too smart to turn down what Santana was offering.

"You see any future in being with Michael?"

"I don't think about the future. Do you?"

"I have lately."

"That's a bad habit."

"Don't I know it."

Allison finished her drink. Miles bought her another. When it arrived, she didn't drink. Her eyes fell on the face in the mirror.

"This is what I've chosen, right?" she said.

"Doesn't mean you can't change your mind."

"You think it's that easy? 'Hi Michael, this has been great, but I think it's time I moved on.' He'd probably hire you to come after me."

"Assuming I haven't chucked it all and moved to Tibet."

"Besides, what would I do? All this stuff I have now? It's not going with me if I leave. And Michael's not a bad guy. He's sweet in his

own way." She looked at Miles, a few strands of hair falling across her face. "What makes you think I'm not happy?"

"Because you're working awfully hard to convince me. And maybe yourself."

"You ask yourself those questions. I don't."

"So be it."

They were quiet. Miles wondered why he pushed her. What the fuck was it to him if she was Michael Santana's kept woman? Maybe it was his own crisis. Maybe he was projecting. Maybe it was because she was off-limits. Fucking with her as an alternative to actually fucking her. He didn't know. He didn't seem to know anything these days.

"If you're curious," Allison said, "this isn't what I wanted. Not to start with."

"What did you want?"

"To be an actress."

Miles could see it. She was attractive enough. She had a brooding quality. Gave you a sense something was going on. Something she wouldn't let you in on. All the Golden Age actresses had that. But here she was. In the Thirsty Pelican in Scottsdale.

"What happened?" he asked.

"Nothing. L.A. is cold. I was there long enough to know it wasn't going to happen. I got involved with Michael." She stirred the martini with the olive stick. "What about you? What did you want to do?"

"Kill people for money."

Allison rolled her eyes. "Have you always been a smartass, or did you become one when you took this job?"

"Come by it naturally." He rested his arms on the bar. "I am serious. Growing up, I had no friggin' clue what I wanted to do. My father worked in a factory. It put a roof over our heads, gave him the chance to get drunk, remind us how much we owed him and if he could do it all again..." He drained his beer. "That didn't look appealing. Didn't want to work an office job. Didn't want to be an actor. No offense. Thought all athletes are douchebags. Delivering pizzas looked like fun but not for a living. So, I went into the army."

"Why the hell did you do that?"

"I don't know. I figured I might find a skill. And I did. Just...maybe not the one I expected to find. Anyway, that's how I got here. I was good at this and could make a good living. I didn't want to do anything else."

"Until lately."

"Maybe."

Allison took a gulp of her drink. She cradled the glass. Miles tapped the bar.

"You need a ride home?" he asked.

"I'm fine. I stop myself after two. If I have another, one of Michael's guys can pick me up."

"You trust them?"

"I'll be all right."

31

Miles called for his tab. He used the John Tuttle signature. The bartender thanked him. Looked discreetly at the large tip. Miles stood up, buttoned his suitcoat.

"It was nice meeting you," he said.

Allison pushed her glass aside. "Why did you come over here?"

"I wanted to talk."

"You didn't want anything from me?"

"I did. To talk."

She brushed the hair out of her face, looked up at him, a smile swimming below the surface. "If this was another time and place…"

"Wouldn't that be cool?" He turned away. Stopped. Took a card from his billfold. Slid it over to her. "That's how you can get ahold of me. If you ever need help with something. Or if you want to talk."

She slipped the card into her purse. "It was nice meeting you, Miles Slayne."

"Best of luck."

"Sure."

Miles walked to the door, looked back at Allison. She stared at the bar, her brows knit. He knew how she felt. Deflated. Waiting for something to make her feel better. He stepped back into the night.

***

I'm wondering if I've had too much merlot. Something is frozen inside me and, for once, it has nothing to do with the cold. This feels surreal, like I'm in a dream. (A sweet dream? A nightmare? Hard to say.)

"Deirdre's dead?" I ask. "How do you know?"

"The Brooklyn Point police. They found a woman dead in an abandoned store up there. The description matched Deirdre."

"Are you sure it's her? You said you've never seen her."

"We got Deirdre's DNA on file. It's a match."

I slump against the breakfast bar. "What was she doing in Minnesota?"

"That's what I came to ask you, Slick. Last couple times she's been here, she was hanging out with you."

"I wouldn't exactly call it hanging out. She threatened to kill me both times. Actually tried it once."

"She was a contract killer. It was her...what do they call it? Love language?"

"That's what they call it, but I don't know if the term applies." I sit up, my elbows resting on the bar. "Last time I talked to Deirdre was on the phone. She skipped town after..."

"Killing Kendall?"

"Yeah."

It's not a pleasant memory. Deirdre had been hired to kill the CEO of a local corporation. When she attempted to do so, she discovered the guy had already been killed, and she had been set up. Kendall was part of the corporation and part of the set up (though, strangely, not part of the killing). Deirdre asked me to solve the murder to help clear her. Well, *asked* is a little strong. She threatened to kill me if I didn't do it. Along the way, I thought maybe she would find some redemption if somebody showed her kindness. I solved the murder, but Deirdre went scorched earth, killing Kendall in the process. She spared me. Sometimes, in unguarded moments, I realize I contributed to a woman's death. It's what makes my reaction to Deirdre's demise so mystifying. Why am I bothered?

"Somebody had to have hired her," I say. "That's the only way she'd be in Minnesota. Especially this time of year. She hated it here."

"I get where she was coming from," Street says. I've always assumed he's not native to this part of the world. "I talked to the interim chief in Brooklyn Point."

"Hank Maxwell?" I ask.

"You know her?"

"Ran across her a few years back. I can't believe she's still an interim."

"African American woman in a tight-ass suburb? They're not gonna roll out the red carpet, Slick. At any rate, Chief Maxwell said they haven't had anything unusual going on, other than Deirdre turning up dead. Nothing to indicate why she was here. I thought maybe she was in touch with you."

"No such luck. If *luck* is the word I want." I cock my head. "Why do you care? This sort of cleans the slate for you."

Street leans against the breakfast bar. "Doesn't feel clean. You chase someone long enough, you want a decent conclusion. And…I don't know, Slick. You feel close to them. You didn't want it to end like this."

"You wanted to be the one who took her down."

"Maybe. I don't know."

I walk over to the liquor shelf in the living room and grab a bottle of whiskey. I find two lowball glasses in the kitchen and pour a couple fingers. I hand one to Street.

"To Deirdre," I say.

Street joins me in a toast. He downs most of it in one shot, sporting the requisite whiskey grimace. The cats mill about, but Street ignores them. He sets the glass on the breakfast bar. A thought occurs to me.

"What happens to the body?" I ask.

"No one to claim it," Street says. "No family, no known associates."

I swirl the whiskey in my glass. "She mentioned someone named Emily. Someone who handles her business."

"You got any idea how to get ahold her?"

"No. I wouldn't begin to know that."

"Nice idea anyway, Slick." Street finishes the whiskey. "Guess that's the end of that."

He puts the glass in the sink (gaining my eternal gratitude, as I like to keep my apartment neat as an operating theater). He walks down the hallway, his tread heavy. I set my glass on the breakfast bar.

"What happens now?" I ask.

"Not sure," Street says. "I don't know anything. You don't know anything. Brooklyn Point PD doesn't know anything. Not a lot we *can* do. You have a good night, Slick. Thanks for the drink."

A chill rolls down the hallway as Street opens the backdoor and leaves. I sit in the silence of the apartment. For some reason, it's never felt more silent than this.

***

"In pure storytelling terms, our path is clear," Lars says. "We need more sex."

I try not to let my head hit the table. (It's a Herculean effort, believe me.) If we add any more sex scenes, we're going to have to put in a call to Ava Addams's agent. (Oops, I'm not supposed to know who that is.) I look at the other members of the production staff. Frankie, her large brown eyes shining, seems intrigued. Kyra, our new production coordinator, cannot keep the look of disgust off her round face. Fabio, his dark wavy hair, his metrosexuality and his orchestra, stares toward the picture window. I don't think a word of this has registered with him. I'm forced to stop playing hangman in the margins of my script in order to deal with this nonsense.

The Tav is the local watering hole of choice for my friends and me. I'm concerned the the memory of these production meetings will forever taint the place. It's on Selby Avenue, just down the street from the St. Paul Cathedral and a stone's throw from downtown St. Paul (if anyone hung out after hours in St. Paul to throw a stone). The Tav is a combination pub and sports bar, featuring a lot of quaint decorations, high top tables and big screen TVs. It draws both the blue collar and artistic denizens of the Cathedral Hill neighborhood. We're on the restaurant side, which is distinct from the bar area. On this end, there are cloth napkins and tablecloths. The staff wear white dress shirts and black slacks. The lighting is brighter. It's a slow night, and we're tucked into a fairly private corner. I set aside a plate containing the remains of my Chicken Dijon Sandwich.

"I think the sex scenes are getting a little numerous," I say. "Not to mention graphic."

Lars tosses his white scarf over his shoulder and straightens his beret. "It's a vampire/heist movie. You can't tell a vampire story without sex."

"Sex, yes," I say. "A *little* sex. Some seduction. Right now, we're running a cinematic knock shop."

"Joe, we have to meet the audience's expectation," Lars says. "When they see a movie called *Whore of the Vampire*, they're going to expect some emphasis on the horizontal."

Everyone exchanges looks. Kyra glares at Lars over the thick frames that normally hide her sharp blue eyes. She speaks in a voice that contains absolutely no B.S. whatsoever.

"We're calling the movie *Whore of the Vampire?*" she asks.

Lars tosses his head back. "Nobody suggested anything. I thought it high time we had a title."

I push my script aside. "This is just a working title, right?"

"Working and final, yes."

We need to take this to higher (God help us) authority. Krya is clearly opposed to the title but lacks the authority to kill it. My vote is cancelled out by Lars. This leaves things up to Frankie and Fabio. Frankie narrows her eyes, giving the title some thought. Fabio is still in a stupor. I have to reason with them.

"We can't call the thing *Whore of the Vampire*. Unless we're planning to sell it straight to Pornhub." (Sorry, I'm not supposed to know what that is, either.)

"It gives it the right flavor," Lars says, and I genuinely hope he's not going to expound on what that flavor is. "When you hear a title like *Whore of the Vampire*, what do you think of?"

"How grateful I am porn theaters aren't a thing anymore."

Lars slaps the table. "I'm not in a mood to discuss this, Joe. You don't understand my vision for this film, and you've never tried."

I hold up my hands, trying to stay calm. "Okay, leaving the title aside, can you explain to me how the ménage a trois scene fits into your vision?"

"It's a metaphor," Lars says, adopting his most condescending tone. "All the sex in the film is a metaphor."

"A metaphor for what?"

He thinks about it, then shrugs. "Fucking."

I put a hand over my face. Kyra shoots a look toward Frankie and Fabio, her severe ponytail whipping around behind her. Fabio says nothing. He might be drooling at this point. Or dead. Frankie toys with one of her gold earrings.

"I think it's an awesome idea," she says. "Who wants to look at old-timey vampires for two hours?" She drops into a pale imitation of Bela Lugosi. "I vant to suck your blood. Blah!" She purses her lips. "That would be so boring. We need something to heat it up."

Fabio remains silent. Two to one, with one abstaining (and possibly comatose). The ayes (to say nothing of the dipshits) have it. I fold my metaphorical cards.

"I'll do what I can," I say.

Lars bows, satisfied. Kyra buries her face in her hands. We move on to other subjects. I listen with only half an ear, knocking back some merlot and entertaining thoughts of getting the hell out of this project. While I'm doing that, something in the bar area gets my attention.

Mike is talking to a middle-aged dude. It's somebody I don't recognize. He has dark, slicked back hair offering a good view of his receding hairline. His face and body are puffy. He wears a gray suitcoat and black slacks, both likely purchased at Target (probably on sale). Is this the meeting Mike mentioned? I turn to the others.

"Are we about done?" I ask.

Lars gives us a regal nod and grandly flips his folder shut (sending papers flying across the table). Frankie looks to Fabio. A moment passes before he realizes what's going on.

"I'm sorry," he says. "What were we talking about?"

I get up from the table, leaving the others to explain, and make my way toward the bar. Mike sees me approach but doesn't acknowledge me. That's weird. It's even weirder when our buddy Stoner materializes in front of me.

"Evening, Joe," he says, his voice smooth and unhurried. "How are they hanging?"

Matthew Riley Stone, known as Stoner to his friends and family (yes, even his family), has been a buddy of ours since college. Back then, he managed his best friend/mortal enemy Robbie in drinking contests (twenty-seven wins, no defeats, three hospitalizations), conducted a variety of floating gambling games, and from his dorm room, ran a criminal empire that would have been the envy of Michael Corleone. His winnings were such that he repaid his student loans right after graduation. These days, he works at FedEx Express and avoids any kind of shady activity. As far as I, or anyone in law enforcement, knows.

"Who's Mike talking to?" I ask.

He remains obstinately and jovially in my way. "Fraid I can't let you in on that."

"Why not?"

"Fraid I can't let you in on that, either."

I put my fists on my hips while Stoner lazily runs a hand through his brown hair. Mike has refused to look my way, even though he must know I'm here. Given that I've known these guys for all of what passes for our adult lives, it's not hard to realize they're up to something.

"What's going on?" I ask.

To his credit, Stoner realizes a reply of *Nothing* will not only fail to allay my suspicions, it will also prolong this conversation. "What if I told you we're working on something, and we can't let you in on it?"

"I'd still want to know what's going on."

"What if I offered you twenty dollars, and told you we're working on something, and we can't let you in on it?"

I give it a moment's thought. "I'd be okay with that."

41

"Fine. I'll take it up with Mike, and if he's cool with it, we'll get you the money."

Stoner gently puts a hand on my elbow, as if he's going to escort me away. I plant my feet.

"Stoner, you said *you* were going to give me the money."

"No. I said I was *offering* you the money. I didn't say the payment was coming from me."

"That's what you implied."

"I am not in charge of how you interpret things, Joe. All I know is that we have a verbal contract stating you will receive twenty dollars, and I will arrange to make sure you get the money. That good?"

"Not particularly."

"What if I told you the thing we're working on concerns T.J.? Would that help make up your mind?"

Hmm. T.J. is another of our college buddies. He's currently the only one employed in what you'd call a respectable job. He's middle management at some company that makes doohickeys of a variety. (I said it was respectable, not memorable.) He's also the most decent guy among us. What kind of trouble would T.J. have that the extras from *Animal House* would have to bail him out?

I look toward Mike's friend. "Is this guy part of the solution or part of the problem?"

"Problem. That's as much as I can tell you. But we need you to stay out of sight. We don't want the guy to recognize you."

"Why not?"

"You'll know when the time comes."

So glad I have that to look forward.to. Still, Stoner has worn down my resistance. I let him move me toward the door. He makes sure to position himself between me and the bar. He glances back to the table where the production staff is wrapping things up.

"How did the meeting go?" he asks.

"About as well as could be expected," I say, knowing Stoner's interest is polite at best, self-serving at worst.

"Couldn't help noticing one of your producers is a real hottie."

Oh boy. I need this, right? I follow his eyes. Frankie is in conversation with Krya. I have to admit, with the white sweater hugging her chest the way it does, Frankie is very worthy of ogling. Still, there are conflicts of interest to consider.

"I assume you mean the one with the curly dark hair?" I say.

"Definitely not her short, round friend," Stoner says. (What he lacks in tact, he makes up for in...y'know what? Let me get back to you on that one.)

"That's Frankie," I say. "She's one of our angels."

"Excellent," Stoner says. "You mind if I go over there and ask her to fuck?"

I spin toward Stoner. It's not as if he doesn't have a healthy libido, but the crass approach is more Robbie's style than Stoner's. "Yes, I would mind that very much."

"I'll just talk to her then. Let the fucking be her idea. You have a good evening."

He claps me on the shoulder and makes his way over to the table. I take another look at Mike in his meeting. I walk out into the cold, fighting the temptation to lie down in the snow and stay there.

***

The Tav is only a handful of blocks from my apartment building. On any halfway decent night, I'm willing to walk it. This, however, is not even a halfway decent night. My car, a Saturn Ion, consents to starting but protests every other activity it's asked to perform.

The Deirdre thing still bothers me. Maybe I thought she was invincible, and it's hard to believe someone murdered her. Maybe something feels unresolved. I wanted to believe she could be a better person. That underneath everything, she was a human being and not just a killing machine. Maybe I hated to be wrong. I don't know.

There's also the matter of what the hell she was doing in Minnesota. Who hired her? What was she doing in Brooklyn Point? Like I told Jim Street, I *do* know the interim chief up there. I could always ask her. But for once, I'm in a mood to stay the hell out of it.

I park in the lot behind the building and scale the erector set of decks and stairs. I'd run, but the footing isn't great since the lazy ass building superintendent (i.e. Lars) hasn't salted the steps. I'm half-frozen by the time I get to my backdoor. The warmth rushes over me once I'm inside. I walk down to the kitchen, basking in the cocoon of warmth.

Until somebody clobbers me from behind.

CHAPTER THREE

Miles ran into Robert Stewart's daughter in a convenience store. He didn't see her coming. He had grabbed a movie magazine, was getting a bottle of iced tea out of the cooler. She materialized in front of him. She was pretty. Honey-colored hair in a ponytail, bangs falling around her face. A white soccer uniform with black shorts. Miles reminded himself she was fifteen or sixteen. She had a bottle of red Gatorade in her hand. The heel of one foot rested against the ankle of the other.

"I've seen in you in my neighborhood," she said. "Did you just move in?"

Nothing suspicious in her tone. Her face was open, her eyes pretty and blue. Miles slipped off his shades.

"I'm just looking at some real estate options," he said.

"You're new in Phoenix?"

"Why do you ask?"

"People usually don't wear black around here. At least, not during the day." She looked at the magazine in his hand. "You like movies?"

"I do," he said. "This one has an article on Ozo."

"Ozu? What is that?"

"Yasujiro Ozu. He was a Japanese filmmaker."

"Oh. I'm sorry, I've never heard of him."

Miles figured it was a reach. He could ask her about an insipid romcom at the cineplex. Probably get chapter and verse. He kept the eyeroll inward. Looked over her uniform.

"You have a game today?" he said.

"I'm just on my way." She held up the Gatorade. "Gotta stay hydrated." She looked over her shoulder. A green Lexus was visible through the picture window. "My dad is driving me."

"Nice that he could make it."

"He comes to all my games. He's the best."

His dream came up. The girl. Her face covered in blood. He closed his eyes, pushed the image away. She looked toward the front window.

"I've got to go," she said. "Can't be late."

"Good luck."

"Thanks. Good luck with the real estate."

She paid for the Gatorade, ran outside. Kissed her father on the cheek. They got in the car, chatted as they pulled out of the lot. Miles approached the counter. The clerk frowned.

"Will that be all?" the clerk asked.

Miles's eyes were on the Lexus. "That's about it."

∗∗∗

Miles spent two more days thinking about it. He could quit the job, send the money back. His reputation would take a hit. He could live with that. It wouldn't solve everything. Miles could free himself from Michael Santana. Robert Stewart couldn't. There'd be another killer, one not having an existential crisis. Could Miles drag his feet? Did Robert Stewart have anything the feds wanted? Would they put the family in witness protection? Would Santana wait that long?

Miles grabbed some In-and-Out Burger, drove to the house he was using. He broke in the back. Set the food on the kitchen counter. Looked out the front window.

A red Land Cruiser was parked outside the Stewarts' house. Miles recognized it. Four guys getting in. The driver had a ponytail. The car blasted away from the curb. Tires squealing. The door to the Stewarts' house hung open.

Miles ran out the front door. Fuck his hiding place. He crossed the street. Ran into the Stewarts' house.

Smoke from the gunfire. A rotten egg smell. Robert Stewart sprawled in a chair at the dining room table. Head and torso ripped apart by bullets. His wife facedown on the floor. A track of bullet holes up her back. The son in the living room. Chest blown apart. Lying in the remains of the glass coffee table. No sign of the daughter.

Miles closed his eyes, took a breath. Coldness at his core. Engage the brain. That's The Discipline. He slipped on gloves, moved through the house. Furniture overturned. Knick-knacks decimated. Bullet holes riddling family photos.

No sign of the daughter's body. Did she get away? No. The doors were closed. She wouldn't stop to do that. Maybe Santana's men didn't know about her. They broke in, shot Robert Stewart and anyone else in the room.

Sirens any second. The neighbors wouldn't walk outside if they heard gunfire. But they'd sure as hell call the cops.

A room at the end of the main hall. Posters of boy bands. Stuffed animals on the bed. Had to be the daughter's room. Milee looked under the bed. Nothing.

Then he heard it. A whimpering, barely audible. Coming from the closet. Miles yanked it open. A walk-in closet. A pair of legs retreating behind a line of clothes. He pushed the clothes aside.

The daughter screamed. Huddled against the wall. Practically burrowed into it. She covered her face, cried hysterically. Miles knelt. Held his hands out.

"I'm not going to hurt you," he said. "I promise."

Miles remained still. This wasn't his specialty. There was nothing comforting about him. And the girl needed a fucking saint to calm her down. He had to get the fuck out of there. He couldn't leave her. No panic. Keep the brain engaged. The daughter removed her hands. Her face was red, mottled. Her hair disheveled. Eyes shiny from the crying. She gulped air, trying to find words.

"What is happening?" she asked.

"Some men came."

"My family…"

49

There was no good answer. "I'm sorry."

She put her face in her hands and sobbed. Miles ignored the sick feeling. The cops were coming. He couldn't be here. Too many questions. No good answers. He'd have to abandon the rental car. No big deal. Let the police find it. A car rented to Jeffrey Lebowski of St. Louis Park, Minnesota. Not much of a lead.

What to do with the daughter? She had relatives. They could take her in. Santana would figure out his men missed someone. Maybe she was a witness. Santana wouldn't take the chance. Relatives couldn't keep her safe. The feds wouldn't do much. Robert was valuable. She wasn't. Local yokels wouldn't fuck with the cartel. The girl was screwed. No time to debate it.

"You need to come with me," Miles said. "I know that's hard. You don't know me."

"You were at the 7-11."

"That's right. I know the men who did this. I'm not with them, but I know them. They're going to come for you."

Her hands fell away. "The police..."

"The police can't help you. These men won't stop until they get you. I need you to trust me. And come with me."

Miles offered his hand. The daughter's arms were folded, hugging herself. Moments passed. She wiped her eyes. Her voice was small.

"You can keep me safe?" she asked.

"Yes."

He held his hand steady. They were running out of time. He couldn't push her. She took his hand, tentatively.

"Good." Miles helped her to her feet. "What's your name, hon?"

"Christina."

"Okay, Christina, we need to go. Now."

"My stuff," she said.

"There's no time. You leave it behind. You leave everything behind."

Christina let Miles guide her out. He stopped in front of her.

"I need you to stay close to me, Christina. Close your eyes and don't look at anything in the room. It's nothing you want to see. Do you understand?"

Her eyes filled. Sirens could be heard. He put his arms around her, kept her head buried in his chest, unable to see. They moved through the living room. She was trembling.

"Just keep going," he said. "Don't look at anything. You're doing good, darling. When we get out, I'm going to run. I need you to take my hand and try to keep up. You understand?"

Christina nodded. She clutched Miles. He got the backdoor open. No fence in the backyard. Just trees for privacy. Nothing they couldn't sprint past. Sirens rang. Flashing lights approached.

"Okay, Christina, it's time to run. You ready?"

Her voice was shaking. "Yes."

Miles let her go. Took her hand. She looked back at the house. Turned to Miles, squeezed his hand.

51

They ran, disappearing into the darkness.

***

I'd love to tell you this is the first time somebody has broken into my apartment and clobbered me. Sadly, it's gotten to be a frequent occurrence. This one doesn't knock me out. In fact, it doesn't knock me off my feet. I crash into the breakfast bar. The cats are nowhere to be found. (Thank heaven for small favors.) The apartment is dark. Light filters through the windows.

My attacker comes down the hallway, moving with a pronounced limp. (I didn't do anything to him, so I assume he came with the limp.) He's a little shorter than me but spends a hell of a lot more time in the gym. His hair is slicked back, and there's a sneer on his face. He wears a black leather jacket, black jeans, and a black t-shirt. His only concession to the cold is a pair of black gloves, and I don't think warmth is their main purpose. Despite the limp, his movements are casual. There's a gun in his hand, held loosely at his side.

"Joe Davis?" he asks. His voice is gravelly, and there's an accent. Latino?

I may be putting my life in danger by answering truthfully, but: "Yeah."

"I need Grace Jelinski."

You ever have one of those dreams where you're taking a test (even though you haven't been in school for years) and, for whatever reason, you have not prepared at all? You wonder how you could have possibly pissed away the time until zero hour. I have that same feeling now. Because the gunman's bug eyes bore into me, and I have only one answer for him.

"I don't know who that is."

"Bullshit. Deirdre was working on it. You know Deirdre. You gonna tell me she didn't let you in on anything?"

My heart beats in my ears. My breath is in short supply. "I'm sorry, but that's exactly what I'm going to tell you. I haven't seen Deirdre in a year. I was hoping to never see her again."

"That the case? Fine. You don't have to thank me."

Weirdly, I have an impulse to fire back at the guy. But that would only make a bad situation worse. (Not that I've let that stop me in the past.) I hold my hands out, palms down, trying to be Mr. Reasonable.

"Can I ask who you are?" I say.

"You can ask, but I'm not going to fucking tell you."

Frankly, my hopes weren't high. The trouble is I don't have any information to give him. This conversation probably isn't going to end with him saying *I can see I've wasted enough of your time. Good evening to you, sir.*

"I don't know what Deirdre was up to," I say. "I've never heard the name Grace Jelinski before now."

53

The gunman takes a breath through his nose. "Then you aren't any good to me, are you?"

He raises the gun. I hold my hands in front of my face, knowing full well they won't stop a bullet. My knees go weak. Then the front door flies open.

The movement distracts the gunman. It's enough to let me dive out of the way (temporarily, at least). He aims at whoever is coming through the door. Only to find a giant fucking forty-four staring back at him.

The gunman backs up, stumbling down the hall. The backdoor opens and closes. The owner of the forty-four comes through the front door, closing it behind him. It's Old Man Albertson.

Mr. Albertson lives on the first floor. He's anywhere between seventy and three-hundred years old. Word on the street is he hasn't left the building in a couple decades, minimum. I've seen nothing in my eight years living here to contradict that. Even seeing him out of his apartment is an event. He's tall, thin, and craggy. His gray hair bears a military cut. He wears a scowl, and his eyes have a permanently suspicious look. He's completely comfortable with a gun in his hand.

"Looks like you had a visitor," he says.

"Not one *I* invited," I say.

He helps me to my feet. "What was that all about?"

"I'm not sure," I say. "It had something to do with a contract killer I used to know." Old Man Albertson's permanent squint relaxes, telling me I've surprised him (for a change). "It's a long story."

"You might want to give the police a call."

"I'll do that." I take a breath, hoping an infarction isn't nigh. "Thanks for bailing me out."

"Don't mention it. Not the first time. Probably won't be the last." He goes to the front door. "Long story, huh? You'll have to tell it to me sometime."

"Sounds good."

Assuming I'm around to tell it.

***

I *do* call the police. In fact, I call them twice. One is the standard 9-1-1 call. They send a couple uniformed cops who ask me a series of questions about the break in. They say they'll look into it, and that's probably the last I'll see of them. The other call goes to Jim Street. He agrees to meet me the next morning.

I choose Glacier's Coffee Shop for said meeting. It's in my neighborhood, near the looming St. Paul Cathedral. It's my creative home away from home; a converted café with checkerboard tile floors, brass rails and picture windows. It draws the young and artistic types from the upscale side of Cathedral Hill. Things are fairly busy at the moment, since

55

every poseur needs their morning shot of java. A couple is in deep conversation near the window. A guy is talking on the phone, pretending he's working on the laptop in front of him. Another couple appears to be practicing a scene from a play. The woman's acting is visible from the other side of the room (which defeats the purpose of acting, I think).

I find a table far from the door and sip my French roast. While I wait, I doodle in a notebook, scribbling ideas for future columns. Street and his partner, Ric, finally arrive. Street wears the same dark coat and white scarf from the other night, this time accompanied by a dark blue suit and a yellow shirt. Ric, a short, balding Latino gentleman with bug eyes and a poker face, wears a gray overcoat and a gray suit. His blue tie is askew. He presents a sharp contrast to his boss, and I can't help wondering if this is by design. They sit opposite me.

"Sounds like you had an interesting night, Slick," Street says.

"That's one word for it," I say.

Ric drops his hands into his lap. "Better it's us dealing with you than St. Paul Homicide."

That sends a shiver through me for three reasons: one, we're talking about my possible demise; two, it's cold in here; and three, if St. Paul Homicide handled my murder, it might be assigned to Sergeant Frank Pike, a cop I've dealt with many times in the past, and who would, on some level, be disappointed he was investigating my murder rather than having committed it.

"Tell me the story again," Street says.

He's heard it once, but I suspect he's listening for new details. I do as he asks. Ric goes to fetch coffee. Street drapes one arm over the back of his chair and rests the other on the table.

"What did this guy look like?" he asks.

"Latino, I think. A little shorter than me. Craggy face. Black mustache. Black hair, pulled back in a ponytail. Voice was kind of gravelly. He walked with a limp."

Street hasn't written any of this down, but I'm sure he could repeat it verbatim, even hours from now. Ric sets down a pair of to-go coffees. Street toys with the cup.

"We'll look into it," he says. "We might have you come down and talk to a sketch artist. Depends on what we find." He picks up the coffee. "Anything else we need to know?"

"Grace Jelinski," I say. "The guy is looking for her. Gave me the impression it had something to do with what happened to Deirdre. Does the name mean anything to you?"

"Doesn't ring a bell. How about you Ric?"

"Nope. Looks like we'll have to check that out, too. We love it when civilians give us more work."

I ignore him. "If Deirdre was involved with this Grace Jelinski, I have to assume Grace is up in Brooklyn Point."

"Excellent idea, Slick," Street says. He turns to Ric. "The kid knows his stuff."

"I'll recommend him to the academy," Ric says.

"Be nice," Street says. "He doesn't need that kind of grief."

These guys are a regular Abbott-and-Costello, if they just played nursing homes and elementary schools. Luckily, we have nothing left to talk about, so I'm spared further exposure to their notion of witty repartee. Street thanks me for the information and says they'll be in touch. He and Ric get up from the table. Something occurs to Street.

"You *are* going to let this go, right?" he asks. "You don't need any more people breaking into your place and slapping you around. You understand what I'm saying?"

"I do," I say. And I let it go at that.

Street doesn't seem convinced. Much like the aforementioned Sergeant Pike, he knows me too well to believe I'll mind my own business. I give him my blandest face and hope he believes what I'm telling him. I'm not sure he does, but he chooses not to pursue it.

"See you around, Slick," he says.

A few moments later, they disappear out the front door. I pick up my cup of French roast and begin plotting to go back on my word. I have many an ex-girlfriend who would be willing to commiserate on that score.

***

"Look, I love your apartment," Carol tells me. "But if this keeps up, you might want to seriously consider moving."

I pick up the cup of coffee she's poured me. "I could do that, but I'm pretty sure this crap would just follow me."

We're hanging out at her place. Carol is doing a work-from-home day, something she admits she doesn't do frequently enough. We're both, in a general sense, in the same line of work. Carol is an ad writer, one of the better ones you'll come across. Though she often expresses disdain at my ability to work a few hours then spend the rest of the day goofing off, she seems to have her own pronounced ability on that score.

Her place is a one-bedroom number, like mine. It has beige carpeting and walls. Carol has done her best to brighten up the place. It's clean and comfortable (the heater works better here). A large curio cabinet dominates the living room. The walls are decorated with a copious amount of antique store artwork, most of it featuring women in various states of undress; the sort of thing Carol can get away and the rest of my friends wouldn't dream of trying. It's early afternoon, and she's taking a prolonged lunch. She closes the laptop sitting on her kitchen counter and returns to the living room to join me.

"Deirdre's really dead?" she asks, sitting across from me on the deep, burgundy sofa.

"That's what I'm told," I say. "And I'm getting it from a number of sources."

Carol lounges in the corner of the sofa and contemplates that. She's dressed down a little today. A comfy blue sweater and a pair of designer jeans. Her hair is even up in a ponytail. She's embraced the sort of sartorial flexibility that's marked most of my adult life.

"You don't sound sure," she says.

"It's hard to believe. You don't think of the Angel of Death as having a limited lifespan."

Carol twists her mouth to one side. "What are you going to do next?"

I recognize that tone. *You're not going to stick your nose in this, are you?* Carol has never approved of me getting involved with things best left to the police. I studiously avoid eye contact.

"A dude came into my home and wanted to kill me," I say. "I'm not exactly comfortable being a bystander here."

"You'd rather trade a *chance* of getting killed for an almost certainty?"

I remind myself Carol is just concerned. Still, I'm a thirty-six-year-old man, and my parents live four hours away. I don't need to get lectured. I should be allowed to screw up with impunity.

"I just want to find out a few things," I say.

Carol doesn't find this comforting. "How are you going to do that?"

"You remember Hank Maxwell? The chief of police up in Brooklyn Point?"

"Of course. We met her when you had that thing with your cousin Micky."

"Deirdre was found up in Brooklyn Point. It's worth talking to Hank, at least."

"And that's all you're going to do?"

"That's everything on the agenda." I let the *For now* go unspoken.

Carol raises her hands in surrender. "All right. Just know that if you get killed, I'm going to mad at you for the rest of my long, natural life."

"I would expect no less."

I glance toward the window, trying not to be wistful. Being stuck in the middle of winter makes me long for warmer weather and the ability to have coffee or adult beverages in the great outdoors. There isn't even snow flying past the window. Just frost and the vague sense of chill that comes with single digit weather in February. Carol perks up.

"I had a date last night," she says. "It went really well."

Normally, Carol's announcement of a new date stirs mild interest from me. Occasionally, it causes concern, such as how Mike will react and how Carol will remind him they've been broken up for years, and Mike will deny being bothered by it, though only a neon sign overhead saying *Jealous Ex-Boyfriend* would be more obvious. This time, though, I have another cause for concern.

"That's nice," I say, hoping I'm covering well (though I'm almost certainly not). "Who is this guy?"

"His name is Jeff. He's a former client. We bumped into each other at a bar, got to talking, and he invited me out for dinner. It was really nice."

"I'm very happy for you."

"You don't seem very happy."

Shazbot. I should have known Carol is too bright to buy my line of well-intended horseshit. She keeps her eyes laser-focused on me. I scratch the back of my head.

"I was…wondering how Fabio might take it," I say.

Carol lets out a cluck of disgust. "I don't care how he takes it. Fabio and I are finished. He just won't accept it."

"I get that, but—"

"I will not sacrifice my dating life so you and Lars can make this ridiculous film."

"It's just—"

"Fabio is a sweet guy, but he's going to have to learn he doesn't get everything he wants in life. He's had it too easy up to now. His parents have given him everything. They seem stern, but they indulge their kids. Fabio and Frankie have never had to grow up. They haven't even moved out of their parents' house, for crying out loud. Face it, that indulgence is why you and Lars are getting to make this movie."

"Oh, I'm grimly aware of that."

"He's a sweet kid," Carol says. "But still just a kid."

I can't argue with her. Fabio has been decent to me, but there's an air of entitlement about him that I've always found off-putting. Still, I'm in the middle of an ugly situation; one that's bound to get uglier.

This bit of pleasantness is interrupted by my phone ringing. It's Mike. Normally, I might ignore it. But with his recent activities, my curiosity has been piqued. I get it on the third ring.

"Seattle Seven Headquarters," I say. "This is The Dude speaking. But that's, just, like, your opinion, man."

This sort of thing usually gets an exasperated response. Now, Mike is all business (whatever business that may be). "Are you at Carol's?"

"How did you know?"

"I didn't. I was guessing." He takes a quick breath. "Someone is coming by with a package. They're going to drop it off for Carol. If they come to her door, I need you to stay out of sight."

This brings up any number of questions, but I confine it to one: "Why?"

"Don't worry about it."

"This is the thing with T.J.?"

"You got it. You want to help him out, don't you?"

The answer, naturally, is *yes*. There's an air of command in Mike's voice that's not normally there. I'd admire it if I didn't hate taking orders from people generally and idiots specifically. But Mike will keep hammering me with the T.J. thing until I agree to help. So be it.

"Does Carol know what's going on?" I ask.

"She knows as much as she needs to know."

That's a big help. "I'll be expecting a decent explanation somewhere along the way."

"If we pull this off, I'll give it to you. Meantime, do what I say."

He rings off before I can spit out a comeback. I'm tempted to chuck the phone through the window, but that would just cost me money. I slip it in my pocket.

"Mike said some guy is coming to your door?" I ask.

Carol nods. "He texted me about it. I'm supposed to let him in."

"Any idea *why* he's coming here?"

"To give me a book."

"What book?"

"I have no idea. I think it's supposed to be a rare volume or something. Mike told me to take the thing and thank the guy. No questions asked. Don't worry if the package is already opened and the guy tried to cover it up. In fact, that would be for the best. That's all Mike said."

Carol's phone rings, indicating somebody is at the front door of her building. She buzzes in the visitor and shoos me toward her bedroom. I feel like a moron here. I slip inside, keeping the door open, and trying to ignore the painting of the nude maiden bathing in the moonlight. A minute later, there's a knock at the door. Carol answers promptly. A gruff voice carries across the apartment.

"My name is Lyle Wills," the voice says. "Your brother asked me to drop this off."

Somehow, Carol maintains her composure when presented with the idea of Mike being her brother. (It's wrong on a number of levels.) "Thank you so much. He said you'd stop by."

Maybe Lyle is waiting to be invited in. I doubt Carol would do that, even if I weren't here. I position myself so I can get a quick look at Mr. Wills. I nearly slip on the doorframe. He's the guy Mike was talking to at The Tav. Okay, he meets with Mike, and now he delivers a book to Carol. What in the blue hell is going on?

"Thank you for dropping this off," Carol says. "I really appreciate it. It's an important book to me."

Wills's piggy eyes regard Carol suspiciously. He mumbles, "No problem."

He disappears from my view. Carol doesn't hesitate to close the door. I emerge from my hiding place.

"What was that all about?" I ask.

Carol hefts the package. "I have absolutely no idea."

I take the package from her. It's a weighty tome, whatever it is. "Should we open it?"

A couple pieces of tape barely hold the wrapping in place. It appears they've been pulled away and hastily stuck back on. "Looks like Lyle already did that for us," Carol says.

"If the seal's been broken, there's no harm in looking."

I strip off the wrapping for this rare book. It's a Webster's Dictionary, probably at least a decade old. (Who the hell *owns* one of these anymore?) Carol takes it from me.

"What the hell?" she says. "I thought this was supposed to be a rare book."

"You know Mike. For him, a dictionary *is* a rare book."

"And for this, I had to pretend I'm Mike's sister?"

"You're helping out a friend, remember?"

"Not one of my friends."

"Nice attitude," I say. "Clearly doesn't run in the family."

***

It's time for a drive out to Brooklyn Point. It's a first-ring suburb directly north of Minneapolis. Main Street is filled with shops and antique stores, many of them with striped awnings. The streetlamps are actual lamps. The street signs are four-dimensional placards. If the library on the corner wasn't designed by Frank Lloyd Wright, I'll eat my hat. Everything is clean and retro, like Doc Brown just stumbled out of the DeLorean. The recent snowfall adds to the charm. The police station is a squat cement building near the end of Main Street. You half-expect a couple of lion statues to flank the steps out front.

The main office is to my left as I enter. The floors are marble, and there are exposed wooden beams in the ceiling. It's as clean as the Beverly Hills Police Department (at least as clean as it was during the *Beverly Hills Cop* era). An overweight, balding cop eyeballs me as I enter. This guy was working the same job the last time I was here. So much for upward mobility. I ask to speak to Interim Chief Henrietta Maxwell.

"Regarding?" the cop says, giving me the stink eye.

I try to keep my tone pleasant. "Please just tell her Joe Davis would like a minute."

The look on the cop's face makes it clear I'm a pain in his ass. Nonetheless, he moves down the hall to the chief's office. He waddles back several seconds later.

"Go ahead," he says. "Office is at the end."

I thank the cop, who merely grunts in response. I walk past a series of offices before arriving at the end of the hall. The chief's is a reasonably large office with a small desk at the far end. It's carpeted, and there's a hanging light fixture rather than the fluorescents favored in the rest of the building. The only decoration is a print painting of an African woman with wide-set eyes and what appears to be rain dripping down her face. *Girl in Blue* by Lionel Smit, if I recall. Interim Chief Maxwell is seated behind the desk as I enter.

"Mr. Davis," she says, her voice slightly deep and her tone playful. "It's good to see you again. Not surprising but good."

Hank Maxwell looks very much the way I remember her: chocolate-colored skin, dark hair in a ponytail, cool eyes, and a mouth with a definite *Don't fuck with me* set to it. The leather jacket and black jeans she once wore have been replaced by a dark suitcoat and slacks. She rises and greets me with a handshake. Her movements are smooth and panther-like. I look around the office.

"Almost two years and you're still the interim chief?" I say.

"Stuck in purgatory," she says. "Too good to replace. Not the right type to make permanent."

Hank says it with an air of resignation. Brooklyn Point isn't the kind of suburb that's anxious to make a gay African

American woman its top law enforcement officer on a permanent basis. Hank may have accepted that, but I reserve the right to be pissed.

"This town needs to get its head out of its ass," I say.

"I'll mention that to the mayor the next time I talk to him." Hank invites me to sit in the little chair across from her. It's an uncomfortable straight-back. She sits on the edge of the desk. "I'm guessing the murder is what brought you out here?"

"How did you know that?"

"There's nothing else that would have gotten your attention."

"Ah."

"And Jim Street from the BCA called to let me know you might be coming out."

"Oh."

On the bright side, I really didn't think I'd fooled Street. It's still a little frustrating to know he's a step ahead of me. Now it's just a matter of how cooperative Hank will be.

"Okay if I ask about it?" I say.

"You can ask."

Hank has a smirk reminiscent of Street's. I cross my legs, trying to find a comfortable position in the chair.

"The victim's name was Deirdre?" I say.

"That's what I'm told. She had a Missouri driver's license on her. Only thing in the system was her DNA. Far as the grid goes, the lady barely exists. Except she's lying in my morgue right now."

"She was found in an abandoned store?"

"An old arcade. Eli's. Big ass place. It's been empty for years."

"How...uh...?"

"Gunshot wound to the chest. Can't say if death was instantaneous, but I don't think she lasted too long."

"You have any suspects?"

"None. No witnesses. No video footage. Victim had no local connections. Jim Street told us she was a contract killer, and you've had some dealings with her."

"I haven't seen her in a year. I was honestly hoping I'd never see her again."

"Looks like you got your wish."

Careful what you wish for, I guess. "What can you tell me about Eli's Arcade?"

"Not much. It was big, back in the day. Started as a little place in a mall out by the freeway. Owners decided to go big or go home, so they bought a warehouse space and brought in all kinds of bigger games. Went out of business before I got here. I guess it was a major pain in the ass after it closed. Kids breaking in, having parties, busting the place up. Cops were going out there practically every weekend."

"Is it still like that?"

"No," Hank says. "Somebody bought it a handful of years ago. Cleaned the place up. Tightened security."

"But it's still abandoned?"

"It is. New owner isn't required to do anything with it. They just need to keep the place from becoming our problem."

"Any idea who this owner is?"

"Fitzgerald Investments. Contact person is named John Tuttle. I called the number and left a message. No one's gotten back to me."

"Is that unusual?"

"Not if they're absentee owners. It's more a courtesy call than anything." Hank returns to the chair behind her desk. "There was something else Jim Street told me. He said if you came out here, asking a lot of questions about the murder, I should remind you the police are handling it."

"Message received."

"But not agreed to?"

I'm not sure how to answer that. Both Hank and Street know me well enough to know I'll handle a warning the way I've handled *every* warning I've ever gotten, from parents to teachers to bosses to girlfriends: I'll nod, smile politely, and do whatever the hell I want.

"I'll take it up with my staff," I say.

"Street had one other request. Don't know if you're going to like it, though."

71

"What is it?"

"He wants you to look at the body."

Glurk. The last time I was in Brooklyn Point, I was asked to look at a dead body. It didn't go well (though it turned out worse for Lars). I have to stop coming to this place.

"Why does he want me to do that?" I ask, hoping this is Street's idea of a joke.

"Because you've met Deirdre in the flesh. You're in the best position to identify her."

Lovely. Deirdre: the gift that keeps on giving. Strangely, though, I'm not entirely averse to this. It's been hard to believe Deirdre's really gone. Maybe it's a desire for closure or maybe it's just morbid curiosity. But I'm surprised to hear myself saying, "I'll do it."

Hank rises from the desk. She leads me down the hall to the elevator. The elevator takes us to the basement, where the morgue is located. Our footsteps echo on the marble. An uneasy feeling stirs in my stomach. Hank senses it.

"How well did you know her?" she asks.

"I saved her life once. She saved mine a couple times. Not sure how well I *knew* her."

"But you'd recognize her if you saw her."

"Yeah, we were that close at least."

The morgue is a plain, square room with drawers along one wall. The contents of those drawers cause me to fight back a shiver. The room itself is just as I remember it: not dank, just clean and antiseptic. Even the floors are gleaming. Hank crosses to a drawer that sits about waist high. She throws open the metal door and pulls out the sliding tray containing a sheet-covered body. I step to the other side of the tray.

"You ready?" Hank asks.

I'm unable to find my voice. Hank gently moves the sheet. I stare at the body, trying to both take it in and distance myself from it. A clinical part of my brain looks over the honey-colored hair, now matted down, and the full lips, faded against the bluish skin. The other part of my brain realizes the corpse is naked and still. This part processes this whole thing as a violation. I take a quick breath and look at Hank.

"It's her," I say. "It's Deirdre."

CHAPTER FOUR

Miles got Christina out of Phoenix. The first night, she was in a numb state, barely aware of what was happening. They drove back to New York. She looked out the window. Said nothing. They got to Miles's apartment. He set her up in the second bedroom. She slept twelve hours. Cried in her sleep.

Michael Santana hadn't ordered the hit. *His guys went off the reservation, created a big fucking mess. The killings were all over the news in Arizona. The feds went ripshit, dropping the hammer on any cartel guy who got so much as a parking violation. Miles's rental car was impounded. It went nowhere. A few neighbors saw someone going into the house after the shooting. A nondescript white guy in a black suit. Fuck all to go on. The cops didn't waste time on it. Miles was the man on the grassy knoll.*

Miles met with Shane. The place was Java Bob's. A neighborhood joint. Bob always let Miles use the meeting room in the back. (He was friendly and accommodating, blissfully unaware Miles had screwed his wife at least three times.) Miles was at the conference table, sipping a skinny latte. Shane waddled in, carrying a large mocha, extra shot. He wore a tent-like blue t-shirt, a brown leather bomber jacket

74

purchased many years and many pounds ago. He lowered his bulk into a chair, pushed up his glasses.

"What the fuck happened in Phoenix?" he asked.

"I ate at an In-and-Out Burger," Miles said. "You ever tried it? Highly overrated."

"Miles, I love you. But this isn't a good time to be funny."

"Any time is a good time to be funny. It's a survival mechanism. Believe me, I know."

Shane looked over his shoulder. "The girl still at your place?"

"She doesn't have anywhere else to go." Miles set his latte aside. "What are they saying about her?"

"The shooters grabbed her, had their jollies, left her in the desert."

"Good. Let them go on thinking that."

"What are you going to do? Adopt her?"

"I didn't plan that far ahead. There wasn't exactly time." Miles sipped his coffee. "Santana buying that story?"

"No. He knows the girl is still alive. But he's not going to look. He's got enough heat as it is."

"Do Santana and I have a problem?"

"He wasn't happy. But, like I said, he's got badder fish to fry." Miles's eyes zeroed in. "Who ordered it?"

"No one's saying for sure. Probably Santana's right hand. Victor Merced."

"Makes sense. Victor looked hungry. And he's smarter than Santana. Then again, so's that doorstop over there. If the feds are crawling around, that's going to weaken Santana, maybe set him up for something."

"I thought he was protected."

"His uncle can only do so much. Especially when the feds are involved." Miles sipped his latte. "At the same time, it could be someone else in the cartel, making a play for Santana's territory. Using Santana's own guys to set it up."

"Not our problem, though, right?" Shane toyed with his coffee cup. "You never answered my question about what you're doing to do with the girl."

"Christina. She's got a name. I'll keep her safe. Set her up in school here. She'll graduate in a couple years."

"And then what?" Shane asked. "There isn't exactly a statute of limitations on wanting someone dead. Santana's guys know they didn't get her. When all this shit with the feds blows over, they might come looking."

"One step at a time."

Shane's eyes lingered on the bakery counter. "You told her what you do for a living?"

"I told her I'm a businessman. That's all she needs to know."

"You gonna tell her the truth?"

"If I had told you the truth when I hired you, would you have taken the job?"

"Probably not."

"There you go. Sometimes, it's best to keep things on a need-to-know basis."

Shane rested his beefy arms on the table. "You told me once that you don't like loose ends. They get you killed. What is this girl—Christina—if not a giant fucking loose end?"

Miles wasn't surprised. Shane was good. He made a fuckload of money, more than he ever would have in I.T. But—irony of ironies—Shane had no stomach for complicated shit.

All he said was, "I can handle it."

Shane shrugged. How to say You're the boss *without saying it. Maybe he didn't have confidence in Miles. Miles couldn't blame him.*

He wasn't sure himself.

***

Miles's existential crisis had come to a sudden fucking halt. His moment of weakness created chaos. It hadn't done much for his reputation. He hoped time and no further cockups would solve that. He was open for business.

Miles bought Christina a new wardrobe. He got a store recommendation from Shane's wife. Christina picked out her own clothes. She made some remark about not wearing black all the time.

Miles enrolled her in a private high school. Shane built a fictional background. Miles gave the school a big donation. They wouldn't look too closely into Christina's past.

"You're going to need a new name," Miles told her. "Got one you'd prefer?"

Christina sat in the breakfast nook. Miles poured milk on her cereal. Put the bowl in front of her. She didn't respond. Miles started to repeat the question. She looked at him.

"I like Kara," she said. "That was my best friend's name. Back home."

She looked out the window again. Miles wasn't going to give her the I want you to think of this as your home *bullshit. Home was what she left. This was a refuge. Nothing more.*

"Kara, it is," Miles said. "I'll tell Shane to get it done."

She ignored her breakfast. Miles didn't know how to engage her. He wasn't a parent, had no desire to be. He was her caretaker. Nothing more.

"Eat your cereal," he said. "You don't want it to get soggy."

Christina picked up the spoon and ate. It was perfunctory. Miles sipped his coffee. They sat in silence.

***

For Christina, the numb state was easy. Nothing in Brooklyn resembled home. It was crowded, scurrying, humid. No desert sand, yet it felt dirtier. Neighbors passed without acknowledging her. It felt like a different country. A different planet.

But there was comfort in that. Unfamiliarity made the grief bearable. Slightly. She navigated each day, concentrated only on the next thing. Tried not to think or feel. But she couldn't guard herself when she slept. The nightmares would come.

Some were specific. A door being kicked open. Screams from the living room. The drum of gunfire. The dark of the closet. Then the unearthly quiet. Trying not to cry, to even breathe. Footsteps. Words in Spanish.

Some nights, her father came to her. Stood in front of her, saying nothing. She'd reach for him. Couldn't touch him. Try to speak. Words wouldn't come. She would wake, feeling a longing that could crush her.

School made her feel the lack of friends, of family. She couldn't concentrate. Didn't hear people when they spoke to her. When she'd get back to Miles's apartment, she'd crawl into bed, stay there. Say nothing to Miles.

He was difficult to understand. Being with people didn't come naturally to him. His eyes would flick toward the door or the window. He'd listen attentively, didn't seem deeply interested. Told her he wasn't much of a student, hadn't gone to college. Didn't tell her much else. She didn't ask. Wasn't sure if she should.

He left town frequently. Sometimes for days. Erica, Shane's wife, would stay with Christina. Erica was an unattractive woman, not particularly outgoing. But, like Miles, attentive and kind. Christina asked her what Miles did for a living. She said, "He's a businessman." Nothing more.

Christina looked through the living room shelves. Miles loved movies. Foreign films, mostly. Names Christina didn't recognize: Kurosawa, Murnau, Truffaut, Varda. The bookshelf was lined with volumes. Hemingway, Faulkner, Woolf, Sontag. Books of poetry, works of philosophy. Nothing on business or marketing.

She snuck into Miles's bedroom. Not much to see. Basic furniture. No decorations. No family photos. All the suits in the closet were black. She sat on his bed, ran her hands over the sheets. It felt like invading Miles's privacy. It didn't stop her. It was exciting.

She wondered if he ever dated. Was there someone in another city? Was that the reason for the out-of-town trips?

She asked him. He told her very little. Bangkok was crowded. London wasn't that rainy. But he never gave her details. Never told her what he did.

They didn't talk about Phoenix. Her head started to clear. Why was Miles in their neighborhood so late? How did he know the men who attacked her family? Who were they? What did they have to do with real estate? She wanted to ask. Wasn't sure he'd answer.

The curiosity mixed with something. Something hard to name. An emotion. Urgent, close to the surface. She couldn't sit still, couldn't concentrate. She kept going back to Miles's room. Looking for something. She didn't know what.

Erica left just after supper. Miles was due back that night. Christina went into Miles's bedroom.

Nothing to see in the main part. No place to hide anything. She tried the closet.

She checked the walls behind Miles's suits. Nothing. There was a filing cabinet in the corner. Unlocked. Nothing interesting in it. He paid his bills on time. Nothing about his business.

What if she moved the filing cabinet? She worried about scratching the floor. To hell with it. She worked it away from the wall, gently. Pushed it to the entrance to the closet.

The wall wasn't any different. Then she caught it. A discoloration, barely noticeable. She knelt down, ran her fingers around it. Rectangular. Could be an error, some kind of patchwork. She traced the bottom, where it met the hardwood floor. Something came loose. A slat in the floor. She worked it free. She plunged her hand in.

She came out with a small metal box. The kind her father kept precious documents in. There was a small lock. No key. But the lock looked flimsy. She twisted it. No luck. She tried again. A little give. She took a breath. The emotion welled up. She tried again, pushing hard. The lock snapped. She tossed it aside. She'd worry about it later.

She opened the box. There were slips of paper. She paged through them. Each had a name, a dollar amount, a location, another name. The names meant nothing to her. Until she found a slip near the bottom. It read:

Michael Santana

Phoenix

Robert Stewart

Christina leaned against the wall. Who was Michael Santana? What did he have to do with her father? Who were any of these people? What did they have to do with Miles?

She ran to her room. She clutched the papers. Got on the computer. Looked up the names. Their professions. Drug dealers, mobsters, gun runners, gang leaders, dictators, military strongmen. Everyone on the list: dead. She sat back in her chair. A voice behind her.

"You found it, huh?"

She spun around. The papers fell to the floor. Miles stood in the doorway. His arms were folded. He leaned against the doorframe. His voice was calm.

"I guess we should talk," he said.

***

"The key to playing a vampire," Lars says, waving his cigarette holder (which contains no cigarette), "is to uncover the many layers involved. On the surface is the quest for blood. Move a layer down from that, and it's a quest for survival. The next layer down is the quest for eternal life. It's driven by the desire to feel the pleasures of this realm: sex, food, drink, freedom. The vampire is, at their core, the libertine eternal. Is this clear?"

The actress, a thin, blue-eyed brunette in her late twenties, clutches the pages of the script. "Sure."

"Great," Lars says. "Then let's discuss the nudity."

Everyone at the table—except Lars—hangs their heads. This includes me, Fabio, Frankie, and Kyra. (Although in Fabio's case, he might be asleep.) The actress stands in the middle of the dance studio we're using for auditions. She lowers the script pages.

"I'm sorry, what?" she says. The confidence in her acting voice replaced by uncertainty.

"Nudity," Lars says, as if it should be obvious. "Once you've removed the various layers—psychological, emotional, strategic—the bra is clearly next."

The actress's eyes move from Lars to the rest of us, wondering if she's supposed to take the babblings of this madman seriously. (To be fair, it's a question we've been asking ourselves all along.)

"I don't remember anything about nudity in the ad," she says

Lars spreads his arms wide, the tip of his cigarette holder nearly hitting Frankie in the face. "Once you've introduced the concept of a vampire movie, the nudity goes without saying. So, we didn't say it."

The actress backs toward the door. "I appreciate your time and everything. But I don't think I'm right for this."

She tosses the pages on a chair and scurries from the room, unconsciously drawing her white sweater over her chest as she goes. Lars examines her resume.

"I like her," he says. "Put her on the callback list."

I sit back in my metal folding chair (inasmuch as one *can* sit back in these things) and look to the plain white ceiling. It's all I can do not to throw my pencil across the room or better yet, stick it in Lars's ear. Here, Augsburg University (a liberal private school near the west bank of the University of Minnesota campus) was nice enough to let us use their facilities for the auditions, and all these actors have been nice enough to show up and audition for our film. And what are we treating them to? Orson Welles, if he just suffered massive head trauma. Frankie leans past Lars and speaks to Kyra.

"Do we have many more to go?" Frankie asks.

Kyra, her mouth tightened to the point of implosion, hands over the audition list. Frankie cringes. She offers it to Fabio, but he's staring at the far wall and doesn't notice. She hands it to me. It's not encouraging. We're only halfway through. It already feels like we've been here for three days. Lars flings a long hand out, requesting the list. I hand it over.

"A few interesting actors here," Lars says. "But I think we've got everybody we need."

The group is thunderstruck (and not in a cool AC/DC way). I ask, "We do?"

"Indeed," Lars says. "We got all the principle actors from the people I've been negotiating with. All this today is just in the interest of casting the net wide."

I take it back. I'd rather stick the pencil in his eye. "May I ask why you didn't mention this before? To us or *any* of the actors?" I say.

Lars lets out a melodramatic sigh; the pain of dealing with less-gifted intellects. "I can't let you in on everything. There must be a certain mystery to the director's process. He needs to keep people guessing, wondering what's going on in his mind."

"I'm there already," I say.

As per usual, Lars ignores me (or misses the sarcasm entirely). He slips a sheet of paper from a leather folder and grandly flips it onto the table. The rest of us peer at it.

"This is the cast," Lars says. "I think you'll agree they are the best choices."

Looking over the list, I think we can agree they are choices for each role. *Best* is pushing it. In fact, I would say every choice Lars has made is diametrically opposed to the choices I would make. Kyra pushes the list back toward Lars.

"This cast completely sucks," she says.

Lars looks amused but not offended. "Sucks in what sense?"

"In the sense they're terrible," Kyra says. "You've got the wrong choice for every single role. Tom Linroy playing the lead? According to the script, the kid is supposed to be in his middle twenties and hard to pick out of a crowd. Tom Linroy is six and a half feet tall and bald. He looks like a fat lumberjack. How is he good for the lead role?"

Our director gives that a serene wave of his hand. "I see qualities in Tom. It's not the exterior that counts, Miss Kyra. It's the inner quality. The soul that shines through the eyes. Believe me, the camera loves Tom."

"I'm glad the camera loves him," Kyra says, "because nobody else does. Am I right?"

Fabio stares at the wall. I study my script. Frankie looks torn. She bites her lip and holds up Lars's proposed cast list.

"I agree with Kyra," she says. "This cast blows goats."

Lars's head snaps back. He regains his air of self-confidence. "Et tu, Francine?"

I'm tempted to remind him the next words in that quotation are, *Then fall Caesar*. Sadly, our Caesar shows no signs of falling. He sits back, steepling his fingers in front of him.

"I still have the majority of the production staff behind my choices," he says. "Fabio's silence and complete indifference indicates he's on my side. And Kyra, I'm sorry, but you are contractually obligated to agree with me."

Kyra snaps a look toward Lars. "Where does it say that in my contact? Come to think of it, where the hell is my contract?"

"All that aside," Lars says, "I am the director. The final say in these matters is mine. The cast you have in front of you is the one we will go with. Now, why don't we take five minutes to cool down before we see more hopeless actors?"

Lars gets up and walks toward the door. Kyra follows him, still agitating to find out what's become of her contract. Frankie slams her hands against the table and leaves as well. Kyra gives up on Lars and buttonholes Frankie as they step into the hallway. I try not to beat my head against the table. Fabio's voice floats in.

"What's going on?" he asks.

I bring my head up. "You didn't hear any of that?"

"Any of what?"

"We were talking about the cast that will eventually doom this project, cost us the money that's been invested, and bring shame and disgrace on us all for generations to come."

"Cool. Then we're on a break?"

"We are."

I head for the door, wondering if the vending machines have vodka. Fabio grabs my arm, stopping me. He clears his throat, trying to be casual (though the ship has sailed there).

"I...I was just...You...you're tight with Carol, right?"

"We're friends."

"Cool. Cool, cool, cool. I don't suppose she ever mentions me?"

Hmm...what to do here? Be honest and tell him Carol *has* mentioned him but only in the context of never wanting to see him again? Or lie and say Carol has been pining for him lo' these many weeks and will never find satisfaction with another man? One way is compassionate, and the other might drive him deeper into despair. Which would be even more irritating. But if I lie and Carol finds out, irritation might be the least of my problems. Decisions, decisions....

"She might have," I say. "We talk about a lot of things. I'm sure you must have come up."

Fabio takes a deep breath, gathering strength. "Just let her know I'm thinking about her. And I miss her."

"Will do," I say.

"Thanks, man."

Fabio mopes out. I follow, trying to keep my distance. The campus at Augsburg isn't large. You can drive the length of Riverside Avenue from Cedar Avenue to Highway 94 and barely realize it's there. The hallways in this particular building reflect the smallness. They're thin and, at the moment, crowded with actors. On the bright side, the brickwork and the pictures of past theatre productions give the place a little personality. I've just found a space in the hallway when my cell phone buzzes. I give it a look and move quickly to answer.

"Thank you for calling the Department of Health and Human Services, now a subsidiary of the Disney Corporation," I say. "This is Walt speaking. How may I help you?"

Lisa's voice is light. "I wish that was more wrong than it is."

"Ripped from today's headlines."

Lisa Cleary is an ace investigative reporter for Taylor Metro Communications, a multimedia syndicate that somehow maintains a bit of journalistic integrity, even in the current climate. But I knew her back in the day, when she was the star reporter for our high school newspaper. And my girlfriend. We came back into each other's lives a few months ago when I helped her with what is now the biggest story of her career. We've stayed in touch since, something for which I'm exceedingly grateful.

"How's the weather there?" she asks.

"Cold. As usual in February. What's it like in New York?"

"Snow and rain. As usual in February."

"You should find an excuse to get out of the office. There must be some sort of malfeasance going on in Oahu."

"I'm sure there is. I'll get to it later." She switches to a more businesslike tone. "Did I catch you at a bad time?"

"No, you caught me at the exact right time. Did you find anything out?"

"Not a lot. Just some basic stuff. You still want it?"

"Couldn't hurt."

I faintly hear papers shuffling. I have no difficulty picturing Lisa's office. Her desk is messy, covered with notes and discarded food containers. The ubiquitous coffee mug rests precariously next to the keyboard. Unlike me, Lisa does *not* need an orderly space to write. I've never been in her office, but I know her well enough to bring it to my mind's eye.

I gave Lisa the name *Grace Jelinski* to see what she could find. Yes, I gave that information to Street, but I don't trust he'll share anything worthwhile. At least, not with me

Lisa comes back on the line. "Grace Jelinski. Forty-one years old. Lives in Brooklyn Point. Here's the address."

I scribble it down on the title page of my script. (Great. If someone doesn't know any better, they'll think Grace Jelinski is, in fact, The Whore of the Vampire.) The information is interesting. Deirdre was killed up in Brooklyn Point. The gunman who came to my apartment claimed he killed Deirdre *and* he was looking for Grace Jelinski. Safe to assume Deirdre was looking for her as well. Now, there's just the small matter of figuring out who the hell is Grace Jelinski and why are so many dangerous people interested in her. Lisa has more info.

"Grace works at Wilryan Realty in Brooklyn Point," she says. "She's been there for about ten years. Not a lot of other information. Graduated from Brooklyn Point High School. Bachelor's Degree in Communications from UMD.

That's it." A slight creak in the background. She's sitting back in her chair. "You mind telling me why you're interested in this woman?"

"Someone I used to know was killed. This woman might know something about it."

Lisa sounds surprised. "Grace is a murderer?"

"I don't think so. Actually, the woman who was killed was a murderer."

"The irony is thick. Care to tell me about it?"

"It's a long story. But I *will* tell it to you sometime."

Her voice grows warm. "I'd like that."

Something in her tone sends an ache through my chest. "I appreciate the info. Meanwhile, one of us has a real job to get back to."

"I suppose I should."

"Any plans to come to the Cities?"

"I'd like to. Longson's lawyers keep stalling, so who knows when he'll go on trial."

We went through hell a few months ago, even if it did turn out to be the story of Lisa's career. We were investigating the disappearance of a friend from high school, a friend who had been working for Senator Bill Longson's re-election campaign. I won't go into details, but let's just say it *really* didn't work out well for Longson. (Or our friend, sadly.)

"Maybe they'll hold out until there's decent weather," I say.

"I can only hope." Her voice softens. "You keep safe."

"I'll do my best."

"After all," she says, "I don't want anything to happen to the kitties."

That tracks. While she was visiting, Lisa bonded with my goofy cats. I think they stirred up some latent mothering instinct in her. For them, they appreciate anyone willing to give them food and affection. (They're cute and lovable and utterly without morals. Though they showed good judgment when it came to Lisa.)

"I'm sure they'll be fine," I say. "If there's one thing they're good at, it's looking out for themselves."

We ring off. I drop the phone into my pocket and think about Lisa, trying to sort out what those thoughts are. I'm interrupted by Lars, who leans against the wall next to me. He's put away the cigarette holder, and his haughty pose is undone by the sagging of his shoulders.

"I'm worried about this Chuck situation," he says.

After a morning of dealing with him at his most arrogant, I'm tempted to instruct him on the fine art of pissing up a rope. But he seems more like my friend here, so I'll play ball. "What about it?" I ask.

"We got into an argument. Over his engagement."

Oh boy. "I assume you didn't take the high road?"

Lars holds his hands out. "How could I? My business partner is about to throw everything away on this pig in a poke of a marriage. I can't stand idly by, can I?"

On the one hand, that's *exactly* what Lars should do. On the other hand, both standing and idleness have never been his strong suits. (Assuming he *has* strong suits. I've known him eight years and have yet to spot any.)

"What did you say to him?" I ask.

"The truth. Inasmuch as any of us can know the truth. It's a nebulous concept at best. But I shared my own with Chuck. I told him he was making a mistake, he was rushing into this thing, and he hadn't considered the full impact this would have on his life. I then invited him to rebut me with any learned argument he could muster."

"And what was the rebuttal?"

"He told me to go fuck myself. There was no reasoning with him after that."

"Understandable."

Lars runs a hand through his quasi-pompadour. "We're not going to get anywhere. Once Chuck believes a certain path is best, there's nothing in heaven and earth that will change his mind. And if nookie is added into the mix, well…"

I pinch the bridge of my nose. "Let me ask you: have you even met this woman?"

"Do I need to? I can read the situation. Chuck is too much a free spirit to be chained to marriage. He'll never be truly happy. And what about my business interests?"

"Still, out of simple fairness, shouldn't you meet the woman before you make judgments?"

That, shockingly, gets through to him. "You may have a point there, brother. I can't talk Chuck out of this thing without a goodly amount of evidence. His mind is too logical. If I meet the woman and can quote her deficiencies chapter and verse, I'll have a much better argument."

"That really wasn't what I—"

Lars slaps me on the back. "Thank you, my friend. Once again, you have crystallized my thoughts and shown me the way."

He strolls off, leaving me to wonder what fresh hell I've unleashed on a woman I've never met and a dude I've never cared for. I can only hope the resulting damage will be confined to a three or four county area.

My work here is done...

***

It seems like a good time to take another trip to Brooklyn Point. According to the information Lisa gave me, Grace Jelinski has a house and a job up there. I'm hoping to find her at one or the other. Just to be on the safe side, I bring Mike along. His skills (breaking-and entering, advanced bullshittery) may come in handy. Speaking of shady actions, there's the little matter of Mike's recent activities.

"You sent Carol a copy of Webster's Dictionary?" I say. "I would have thought it would be the other way around."

"Cute," he says. And that's all he says.

"You're not going to tell me what's going on, are you?"

"I am not."

My hopes weren't high. According to Carol, Mike didn't have any interest in picking up the book. He said Carol could toss it. She didn't, of course. Like me, Carol has an abhorrence of throwing out any book, even an outdated one that, for all we know, still contains various ethnic slurs. Unlike me, though, she's content to wash her hands of whatever Mike and my college buddies are up to. I don't press Mike on the subject, but that doesn't mean I'm giving up. This is just a strategic retreat.

"Where we going first?" Mike asks.

"Grace Jelinski's place," I say. "Lisa gave me the address."

"You think she's actually there?"

"I guess we'll find out."

The address is on the west side of Brooklyn Point, tucked into a neighborhood beyond the railroad tracks. The house is an undistinguished gray rambler on a street of similarly undistinguished ramblers. A waist-high chain link fence surrounds the yard. Everything inside the fence is covered in snow. If there is a front walk—and the gate and the cement front steps indicate there is—it hasn't been shoveled in a while.

"What do you want to do?" Mike asks.

"Doesn't look like anyone's home. We may need to get creative."

"A B&E? *That's* why you brought me along?"

"Sure as hell wasn't to discuss Descartes."

"Don't pretend you've read Descartes."

"Don't pretend you know who he is."

We get out of the car and go up the front walk. The temps are a bit warmer, but that comes at the cost of snow falling. I ring the doorbell and wait. No answer. I try knocking. That doesn't get me anywhere. I look at Mike. We tried doing this the honest way. Mike studies the front door. He's unperturbed. (This is about the only time you'll see him unperturbed.)

"Shouldn't be too hard," he says. He goes to work. A few seconds later, the door pops open. "I was right."

We step inside. I wipe my feet on the mat, which is more than you can say for Mike. There isn't much to the place. The living room is to our right and the dining room to our left. Beyond the dining room is a small kitchen. Beyond the living room is a short hallway, presumably leading to the bedrooms and the bathroom. Mike closes the front door.

"What are we looking for?" he asks.

"Whatever Deirdre was been looking for, I guess."

"That clears it right up."

We go to work. Mike checks out the living room while I take the dining room. The house is clean and has a minimum of decoration. No pictures or mementos. A few prints on the wall, a couple knick-knacks. A desk is propped in one corner of the dining room. There's mail on it. The usual suspects: gas bill, cable bill, internet bill. All the dates prior to a couple weeks ago. There's a sticky note on the desk with the initials *O.P.* scrawled on it. Since it's the only communication that's not official, I pocket it, though I have no earthly idea what *O.P.* is supposed to mean. I walk back to the front and peek in the mailbox. It's empty. I step inside. Mike returns from the back hallway.

"Find anything?" I ask.

"Nothing interesting. She keeps a pretty clean house."

"That makes one of you." I look around. "Why don't you check out the basement?"

He gets a serious case of *Who Farted* face. "Why don't *you* check out the basement?"

"Because I don't like basements. The Boogey Man and I are not on speaking terms."

"Pussy."

"I think that goes without saying."

He disappears down the basement stairs. I decide to check out the kitchen. I don't get much. Grace must have an affection for Hispanic cuisine. Plenty of seasonings, cans of refried beans and tomato sauce, a big bag of rice. I go through the refrigerator. There isn't much. I open the milk. It's expired. Ditto the cottage cheese. A couple of the other dairy products have passed their expiration dates as well.

I step over to the backdoor. A small diamond-shaped window affords me a view of the backyard. A small parking space sits just off the alley. It's covered with snow, as is the walk to the backdoor. I open the door and discover the steps haven't been shoveled.

I walk back to the dining room. I lean against the front door. Things aren't adding up. Did Grace leave the house in a hurry? The expired food in the fridge would tell me yes. That leaving wasn't the plan. But there's no mail in the mailbox. Who abandons their house at the drop of hat but stops at the post office to make sure their mail doesn't pile up? Did somebody grab Grace and take her away? Then why stop the mail? To throw off suspicion? None of it makes sense.

The house itself doesn't add up, either. There's no personal touch here. I don't go out of my way to decorate my apartment, but there's at least a picture of my parents on one table and a college yearbook on one of the bookshelves. Some photos of my nieces and nephew scattered about. The travelling trophy from our fantasy football league on the dresser in my bedroom. Stuff that at least tells you *something* about me. I don't see any of that here. The prints could have come from Target, the knick-knacks from any antique store. Maybe that isn't so weird. But maybe it is.

Mike comes up from the basement. He's looking down at his phone. "Think I found something."

He thrusts the phone toward me. Only now do I realize this isn't Mike's phone. I take it from him.

"This was in the basement?" I ask.

"Yep. Tossed behind a box. They didn't exactly go out of their way to hide it."

"She left the house without this. Was it charging?"

"Nope. It was turned off. Still has some charge in it."

I go through the phone, which doesn't have a lock screen. Like the house, there isn't a lot of personal information. No call history. No apps, save those that came with the phone. And exactly one text message, from *Harry Brighton*. It reads *For you, there is only the desert.*

"Interesting," I say.

Mike takes the phone from me. "This stuff mean anything to you?"

"It does." Weird. Maybe any other time of the year, it wouldn't have occurred to me. But I watch *Lawrence of Arabia* every winter (when you're in the middle of a deep freeze, there's something comforting about a movie that takes place almost entirely in the desert). "Harry Brighton is a character in *Lawrence of Arabia*. And that quote is from the movie as well."

"So...what? Steven Spielberg is involved in all this?"

"At least someone who's a David Lean fan. I'll compliment them on their good taste."

"Which tells you what?"

I throw my head back, triumphant, and say, "I have absolutely no fucking idea."

I click on the contact info for Harry Brighton and put the phone to my ear. Mike steps toward me.

"What are you up to?" he asks.

"Going to give this guy a call."

There is an answer. An automated voice informs me the user has a voicemail box that has not been set up. I ring off.

"Nothing on the other end," I say.

"Five will get you ten it's a burner phone."

"Looks like it. Safe to assume the other end is a burner phone as well."

I affix the *O.P.* sticky note to the phone and put them both in my pocket. I'm about to suggest getting out of here when a car door slams outside. Mike and I exchange a look. Maybe it's one of the neighbors. But we never have that kind of luck. Mike goes to the front room window and eases back the curtains. His shoulders sag.

"Someone's coming up the front walk," he says.

"Son of a bitch."

"One of these days we really should do a proper B-and-E."

I run for the backdoor. Mike is quick to follow. It's a short run through the backyard and to the alley. It doesn't involve someone shouting *Hey you* at us. So, we've got that going for us. Which is nice. We make our way through the alley to the next cross street. I assume most of the neighbors are at work or school. We round onto the cross street and walk down the block. My car is still parked in front of Grace's house. But so is a blue Mustang. I stop.

"Best approach?" I ask.

"Wait him out. When he leaves, we leave."

"And in the meantime?"

"Try to be inconspicuous."

Standing on a lonely street in the middle of a tight-ass suburb? That should be easy-peasy. "Did you get a good look at this person?" I ask.

"Afraid not. They're wearing a big ass parka and one of those flap-eared caps that Lars likes to wear. Could be Sasquatch under there, for all I know."

Mike and I stroll up the block, away from the house. This way, we can keep things in sight without appearing to loiter. We're on the far end of the block when I dimly see someone coming out of Grace's house. I'm too far away to get a good look at them. They appear to be wearing the parka and flap-eared cap Mike described. I start to run, wanting to get a closer look. Mike grabs me by the arm, stopping me.

"You don't want to draw attention to yourself," he says. "Not from that guy, and not from the neighbors."

He's right. We have half-a-chance to get out of this thing scot-free. I should probably take it. Just seeing this person indicates someone is keeping an eye on Grace Jelinski's place. Now I just have to figure out who this person is.

One step forward, two steps back.

CHAPTER FIVE

Miles took the papers from Christina. Locked them in the box again. They went into living room. He sat her down on the couch. He tossed his black suit coat over a chair, poured himself a scotch. He stood in the corner, facing her. Rain clacked against the windows.

"What do you do?" she asked.

"I'm a businessman."

"What kind of business?"

Miles kept his voice even. "What do you think I do?"

Christina didn't answer. She tucked her legs under her. "Everybody on those papers is dead. Including my father." Her voice was tentative. Walking on eggshells. "Did you kill him?"

"No."

"But you knew the men who did. You said it that night. How do you know them?"

"You'd be better off not knowing."

"Or what? Something bad will happen?" Her voice got tight. A tear rolled down her cheek. She wiped it away. "Don't lie to me."

"I haven't been lying. I just haven't told you everything. I'm a businessman. My business is…eliminating people when requested. And when the money is right."

Christina closed her eyes, tried to calm her breathing. "You're a murderer?"

"I'm a businessman. A murderer kills people because they like it. Or they're insane. I do it because I get paid."

"How does money make it okay?"

"Money gives you options. I choose my clients. I choose who gets eliminated. You saw that list. You think the world's worse off without any of those people?"

Something in Miles's voice always struck Christina. It never had a cynical edge. It was matter of fact. The tone her father used after a day at the office.

"Were you supposed to kill my dad?" she asked.

Miles drained the rest of his glass. "I was hired to do it. But I didn't."

"Why not?"

"Because I saw your family." Miles paused. "You guys seemed happy. You had something I never did. I couldn't take that away."

He poured himself another drink. Christina's hands were in her hair. Miles flipped on the stereo. David Bowie's "The Man Who Sold the World."

"What were you going to do?" Christina asked.

"I hadn't thought that far ahead. Then Santana's guys came and…here we are."

Christina's breathing was shallow. Her voice remained calm. "Who is Santana?"

"Michael Santana. He's a drug dealer. Works for a large and rather nasty cartel."

"How did my dad know him?"

"Your dad did the books for him. One of Santana's front companies. He figured out what was going on. He was going to the feds. I was hired to…stop him."

Miles couldn't keep eye contact. Son of a bitch. He could use an olive fork to kill a third world dictator. Couldn't face a sixteen-year-old girl in light blue pajamas.

"Would you have killed my father?" Christina asked. "If you hadn't watched us?"

"Probably."

"Fuck you!"

She came off the couch fast. Darted around the coffee table. Miles set the drink aside. He could handle her. But she deserved to let it out. She clenched a fist. Didn't throw the punch. She turned and stalked down the hallway. Slammed her bedroom shut.

Miles picked up the scotch.

***

Things were quiet. Christina got herself up for school. Made her own breakfast. Left before Miles was out of bed. She went straight to her room after school. Made her own dinner. Did her own laundry.

Miles didn't react much. A sad look her direction. A shrug after some moment of cold truculence. Christina didn't care. She didn't like Miles. You couldn't get to him anyway. How do you give the silent treatment to someone who prefers solitude?

She had trouble sleeping. Her emotions were strong but jumbled. She lay awake.

She couldn't concentrate in school. Struggled to stay seated. Struggled to stand still. She'd draw in a notebook. Ignore the teacher. After school, she'd walk around the neighborhood.

The dreams changed. Now she didn't run. She stood in the living room, saw her family gunned down. It was Miles's fault. No. It was her fault. She'd wake up angry. Wanting to destroy everything in sight.

A thought occurred one night. Ridiculous. But it calmed her. Let her get back to sleep. This time, without the dreams.

Another night, she lay in bed, staring at the ceiling. Miles was in the living room, watching a boring foreign movie. Christina threw aside the covers. She walked into the living room. Waited for him to acknowledge her. He paused the movie, turned her direction.

"Something on your mind?"

She rested one foot on the other. Something she hadn't done in a while.

"I want to do what you do," she said. "I want you to teach me."

***

With the little disaster at Grace Jelinski's house out of the way, our next stop is Wilryan Realty, Grace's apparent place of work. It's at the end of a strip mall on the more prosperous east side of Brooklyn Point. I find a parking space near the front door and start to get out. My partner in crime, however, is not moving.

"Problem, Potsie?" I ask.

"I hate real estate offices," he says.

I can't believe I forgot. In my defense, it's been almost two years since Mike was canned from his once lucrative real estate job because he was caught sleeping with the boss's daughter. (It was as sordid as it sounds.) He hasn't worked in real estate since. I assume he's on some blacklist.

"You think you can suck it up?" I ask.

He lets a breath out through his nose. "All right. But you do the talking. I'm going to sit there and try not to puke."

"Words to live by."

We go inside. A little receptionist's desk at the front welcomes visitors. A handful of desks crowd the middle of the floor, and there are offices at the back. A medium-sized conference room is off to the side. Brochures and business cards line the reception desk, bearing a studio photo of someone named Keith Wilryan. They mention something about specializing in lakefront property. (Since I can't afford property of any kind, I take minimal interest.) There's no one at the receptionist's desk, but a sharp-eyed employee approaches us.

"How can I help you?" she asks.

The employee is a pleasant looking woman with red hair, green eyes, and a perky voice. She wears a green sweater and a plaid skirt under her dark suitcoat. There's a smile on her round face. She wears a gold nametag bearing the name "Tracy." (See, this helps, but it's among the reasons I have a pathological hatred of name tags. Introducing yourself should be a person's prerogative and not the work of a stupid little piece of metal. Don't get me started.)

"I'm looking for Grace Jelinski," I say.

She gets a concerned look in her eyes. "I'm sorry, Grace doesn't work here anymore. Are you with the police?"

"No. We're friends of Grace's family." Sometimes, honesty is simply not the best policy.

"I didn't even know Grace had family," Tracy says. "I mean, she must. But she never talked about them."

"Oh, she has family," I say. "And they have friends. And we, of course, are two of them."

Mike nods. "Of course."

"Of course," I add.

Tracy offers me a handshake. "My name is Tracy," she says, forgetting that the nametag has already done the work for her. "I'm one of the realtors here. I was friends with Grace. At least, I thought I was." Her face clouds, then forcefully brightens. "And who are you?"

"My name's Joe Davis. This is my friend Mike Griffin."

Tracy's eyes get wide. "Joe Davis? As in *Cup of Joe? The Daily Bugle?* That Joe Davis?"

I give her my faux-modest smile, the one that never fails to annoy my friends. I can't see Mike rolling his eyes, but I know he's doing it.

"That's me," I say.

"I am a huge fan," Tracy says. "I love your column. I never miss one. That one you wrote about the Presidential Royal Rumble? That was hilarious. I read it to everyone in the office."

"Thank you."

"I can't believe Grace didn't mention you being a friend of the family. She knew what a fan I am."

I scratch the back of my head. "That's the thing. I…"

I look to Mike, hoping he'll bail me out of this. He gives me a bemused look, as if he's enjoying my suffering. Thankfully, he comes to the aid of the party.

"We *are* friends of the family," he says. "But the family doesn't get along all that well. There's a few factions that fight with each other. We're friends with one faction. Grace is part of another. But the family is still concerned."

I jump in. "Very concerned. That's why they sent us, of course."

Mike nods. "Of course."

"Of course," I add. "What happened with Grace?"

Tracy drops into the empty chair at the reception desk. "She just disappeared one day. Didn't come into work, didn't call, nothing. It really wasn't like her. I got concerned, so I went over to her house to do a wellness check. I have Grace's spare keys. The house was okay and everything. But she wasn't there. She hasn't been back to work since."

"When did this happen?" I ask.

"A few weeks ago.

"And no one has heard from her?"

"Nobody here, at least." She lets out a sigh. "If something is going on with her, I'd like to think she would talk to me about it. She seemed really happy here."

"Grace sold real estate?" I ask.

"No. She worked in the office. Did a little bit of everything: reception, filing, organizing, calling clients, things like that. It was a lot of work, but like I said, she seemed to enjoy it. I just don't know what could have happened."

"Did she ever mention someone named Deirdre?" I ask.

"Deirdre?" Tracy asks, slowly. "I don't remember that name. Is she part of the family?"

"Yes," I say. "She is. Indeed. And I am a friend of hers. Hence, my being here. On behalf of the family. One of which is Deirdre. Of course."

Mike nods. "Of course."

"Of course," I add.

Tracy takes this in stride. "I'm sorry, Grace didn't mention anyone named Deirdre. Like I said, she didn't talk much about her family."

"What *did* she talk about?" I ask.

"Work stuff, mostly. And she liked to cook, especially Mexican food. She watched cooking shows. We'd talk about movies and TV and stuff like that. Y'know, chitchat."

"Was Grace seeing anybody?" Tracy gives me a look. I add, "I'm just trying to get all the information I can. The family hasn't heard from her, and they're upset, of course."

Mike nods. "Of course."

"Of course," I add.

Tracy leans forward, as if drawing Mike and me into a huddle. It works. Before she can dish, though, a harsh voice cuts through the office.

"Tracy, I'm going out to Emily Lake. I—"

The possessor of the voice emerges from one of the back offices. He's a tall guy with a buzzcut and a gut he's doing yeoman's work to suck in. He wears a white shirt, gray slacks, and a striped tie. I would bet my mother's life it's a clip-on.

111

(Relax, Mom. I wouldn't really bet your life. Probably.) He stops when he sees us talking to Tracy. One suspicious look later, he's striding across the office with a gait he might have gotten from the military. (Or he's seen *Full Metal Jacket* too many times.)

"Are these people interested in buying a house?" he asks.

Tracy spins away from us. "Keith, this is Joe Davis. You remember him? He wrote the column about—"

"Did he write a column about moving to Brooklyn Point?" Keith asks. "Because that's all I'm interested in."

Tracy maintains a pleasant demeanor. "He was asking about Grace."

Keith goes from stink-eyed to bug-eyed. "You a friend of Grace's?"

"Not exactly," I say. "I'm a friend of the family."

He sucks on his upper lip. "Grace never talked about her family."

"It's a long and ugly story," I say. "But I am a friend of Grace's family. And that is why I am asking about her. Of course."

Mike nods. "Of course."

"Of course," I add.

Keith's eyes flick between me and Mike. He taps a knuckle on the counter. "Grace doesn't work here anymore.

She stopped showing up. Even if she comes back, she doesn't have a job here. Tracy, on the other hand, *does* still have a job. Why don't you two quit bothering her and let her do it?"

Tracy's eyes drop to the desktop. "They weren't bothering me."

Her boss ignores her. "I'm going to ask you to leave. Unless you're interested in buying a home in Brooklyn Point."

There would be worse fates than living in Brooklyn Point. But frankly, I'd rather buy a cardboard box from the local unhoused gentleman than a beautiful home from this asswipe. I turn to Tracy.

"Thank you for your time," I say.

I move toward the door. Mike, though, puts both his hands on the counter and faces Keith. He takes a deep breath.

"God, I admire you," Mike says. "And your fly's open."

Keith looks down. He discovers said fly is secure. Mike is tickled by this.

"You have a good day, needle dick," he says.

We step back into the cold, leaving Keith to bluster incoherently. That could have gone better. It's becoming the story of my trip to Brooklyn Point.

***

Since we've done yeoman's work pissing off the whole of this suburb, Mike and I decide to make one more stop. I need to see the place Deirdre was killed. We head over to Eli's

Arcade. I'm not sure what, if anything, I'm going to find, but I don't want to leave any stones unturned. (Besides, I may not be welcomed back in Brooklyn Point.)

The artist formerly known as Eli's is in an industrial park on the west side of Brooklyn Point. It's tucked into the far corner of the park's square outline. A stencil outline remains where the sign used to be. I'm about to park in front when Mike taps the dash.

"Go around back," he says. "This place is abandoned. I'm guessing the other places aren't. Someone sees a car parked out front and two guys breaking into the place..."

"I get it."

I pull the car around, calculating which backdoor is Eli's. Mike leads the way to the backdoor and goes to work. I keep my head on a swivel.

"You think we need to worry about an alarm?" I ask.

"Hell of a time to bring that up."

The door pops open. We wait a few seconds but don't hear anything. Mike steps back, letting me know I can go first. Rat bastard. I flip on the light and lead the way inside.

If there was ever much to Eli's, there certainly isn't now. It's a big warehouse space with high ceilings, cement floors, and metal crossbeams. It's surprisingly clean. There's a window-enclosed office in the nearest corner, and the front door is visible in the distance. The front counter is still standing. There's a single old video game in one corner. Beyond that, it's empty. But at least it's heated (just enough to keep the pipes from freezing). I'm getting a world class case of the heebie-jeebies, knowing I'm in the place Deirdre was killed.

"Deirdre was here for a reason," I say. "Maybe she was looking for something. Maybe this is a hideout. But if there *is* something here, it's not going to be in plain sight."

"How do you know that?"

"Because one of the things she was really good at was keeping secrets. Came with the job. And the police didn't know anything about her. They're going to find the body, give a quick look around for any evidence, and move on."

"Jeez, sleep with a contract killer one time, and suddenly, you're an expert." Mike looks around. "We've come this far. Might was well go the full monty. I'm using that right, aren't I?"

"Let's imagine you are."

We start looking. I take one side. Mike takes the other. I poke around the walls, trying to find a secret panel or a cubby hole. I do one entire wall but come up empty. The floor is solid concrete. I doubt anything is hidden underneath. Mike is checking the one video game. It's already plugged it into the wall. I make a beeline his direction.

"What the hell are you doing?" I ask.

"Are you kidding me? This is Splatter Troopers. It's a classic. You realize how much money I blew on this game back in the day?"

"Probably the same amount your parents wasted on giving you a college education."

He's too entranced by the game to mind me. "God, just looking at the start up brings back memories. You got any quarters on you?"

"No. Who the hell carries cash anymore?"

"It's been a real pisser for the homeless, hasn't it?" He eyeballs the game. "Apparently, Warren Newson spent his share of quarters here."

The startup screen features a list of high scores. All of them belong to *Warren Newson*.

"Does it strike you weird that this is the only game still here?" I ask. "Every other game—everything other *thing*—has been cleared out, but this game is still standing."

"Because it's awesome."

I tap the screen. "Warren Newson. I'm going to remember that."

"Swell. Now, you're sure you don't have any quarters?"

"Positive. Besides, we're not here play video games, Biff."

"Yes, mother," he says, slouching away.

We go back to looking. We don't find anything along the walls. We meet near the front. Only the office is left. I don't see any furniture in there. I'm guessing there isn't much to find. I can't help feeling deflated. If Deirdre was here, she was looking for something. But there's nothing to find. Maybe she realized that just before…well, it must have been a dead end in more ways than one.

"I suppose we should take a look in the office," I say.

"After you."

As always. I don't find anything surprising. The room is small. You can see the outlines of furniture past. A few cords dangle here and there. We take the same approach we used in the main room. Each of us takes a wall and looks for some kind of crack or inconsistency. My hopes aren't high.

Which is why I'm surprised to hear Mike say, "I think I've got something."

He's working out a piece of the wall. When it comes free, a small storage space, not much larger than a cardboard box is revealed. I can gauge it because there's a cardboard box sitting in the space. I pull it out. Mike sets the piece of wall aside.

"What do we have here?" he asks.

"I don't know. Maybe this is what Deirdre was looking for."

The box is held closed by packing tape, so we only need a set of car keys to break the seal. If I was hoping for the Ark of the Covenant or the Black Pearl of the Borgias, I'm sorely disappointed. It just contains books and old movies. Mike picks up a copy of *Anna Karenina*.

"It's like somebody raided your storage unit," he says.

"I've never read Tolstoy."

"Wait, don't you have an English degree?"

"Yeah. You have a business degree, and you're working at FedEx right now. Part time."

I go through the books and movies in the box. It's a nice selection. Great works of literature. Works of philosophy. A bevy of classic movies and foreign films. I recognize most of the titles. What I can't figure out is why they're here. It's like somebody hit a garage sale then hid their find in an abandoned arcade.

"Anything interesting?" Mike asks.

"It's cool stuff. Nothing that tells me why it's here." I check inside one of the books. A name is scrawled on it. *Warren Newson*. "Although, there's this."

I hand Mike the book. "Warren Newson," he says. "The champion of Splatter Troopers."

"A true renaissance man."

We pull out more of the books and find the same name scribbled in many of them. Warren Newson. The video game belongs to him. Everything in the box belongs to him. Does Eli's Arcade belong to him? And does he have anything to do with Deirdre? Decent questions. I just wish I had answers. I toss the books back into the box.

"We'll take this with us," I say.

"You sure? It might be evidence."

"If it is, I'll give it to the cops. Until then, I want to find out who Warren Newson is."

"Fine. I don't suppose we can take the video game."

"If you feel like carrying it back to St. Paul, go right ahead."

Mike frowns. His attitude is not improved when I give him the box to carry. We make our way back to the car. Nobody stops us or shouts in our general direction. Mike tosses the box in the backseat. We're quiet until we pull onto the street.

"This might be the first time we've done a B-and-E and gotten out cleanly," Mike says.

"Son of a bitch, you're right. We're on a winning streak."

"One in a row."

Hey, a winning streak has to start somewhere, right?

***

We stop at a convenience store for some sodas. When we get back to the car, Mike insists on taking the wheel for the

119

drive home. He worries I'll be thinking about the case and will be distracted while driving. I let him have his way. Maybe I *would* be too distracted.

Warren Newson. That name is strangely familiar, though I have no idea why. I try not to give it too much thought. I don't want to agonize over it only to remember it's similar to the name of a kid in my second-grade class. I'll give it to Lisa and see if she can find anything.

These thoughts are interrupted by murmuring from Mike. "That's interesting."

"What's going on?"

"Someone is following us."

I look back. A blue Mustang is a half-block behind us. "You sure it's following us?"

"Been a half-block back since we left the convenience store. And he doesn't seem to notice I've done the last four blocks in a complete circle."

"*I* didn't notice you did a circle."

"See why I was the better choice to drive?"

Nuts. I've always objected to Mike's insistence that he's the better driver. And here I go, proving him right. I'm going to have a serious talk with myself later, and I don't think I'm going to enjoy it. Meantime, there's the matter of the guy following us.

"Is that the blue Mustang we saw outside of Grace Jelinski's place?" I ask.

"Be a hell of a coincidence if it wasn't."

"What are you going to do?"

"Lose him."

Mike swings a sudden left at the next intersection. He accelerates (inasmuch as my Saturn Ion will cooperate) down the street. The Mustang attempts to follow but is delayed by an oncoming car with the right of way. It gives Mike time to take a left at the next block. The Mustang, though, is still in pursuit.

Halfway down the block, Mike spots an alley. He spins the car right. We fishtail slightly. Mike's hands glide over the steering wheel, trying to right us. We skid toward a large snowbank at the mouth of the alley. The Saturn, though, finds purchase before we hit it. We straighten out and charge down the alley.

"Nice work, Mr. Bond," I say.

"I'll be expecting a martini when this shit's over."

The Mustang makes an effort to follow us. However, it hits the same patch of ice. Unlike Mike, the driver of the Mustang can't adjust. It crashes into the snowbank.

"Ah, that's a shame," Mike says, flicking his eyes toward the rearview mirror.

The Mustang, though, isn't through with us. The snowbank doesn't detain it. A few moments later, it's again in pursuit. I look to the front again, wondering what Mike's going to do next. (A question I've been asking myself nearly my entire adult life.) An unwelcome notion occurs.

"You think this might be someone from the cartel?"

For a moment, it looks like Mike swallowed a golf ball. "Couldn't be. If they were with the cartel, they would've shot us and called it a day. Or they'd be shooting now."

We come out of the alley and take another left. A few seconds later, the Mustang leaves the alley. I'm wondering how long this thing will go on. And if Mike has an exit plan.

He slams on the gas, breaking the local speed limit by at least twenty miles per hour. The Mustang matches speed. It probably has the power to overtake us. But it doesn't. It's content to stay a half-block back.

"Not sure what he's up to," Mike says, glancing in the rearview mirror. "Doesn't look like he wants to catch us."

"Then what does he want?"

"Maybe we should find out."

Without warning, Mike slams on the brakes. The Mustang halts as well. It stays a half-block back. For a few seconds, nothing happens.

"Okay, go ask him what he wants," Mike says.

"Are you out of your mind? What if he's armed?"

"Again, he would have shot us by now. Besides, you think he's going to do anything with this much potential for pain in the ass witnesses?"

"Good point."

"Exactly. Go to it."

Dick. Or should I say *Richard.* If there's an afterlife, I'm coming back to haunt Mike at all the most embarrassing and inconvenient times.

I get out of the car and start toward the Mustang. I'm tempted to put my hands up or fly a white handkerchief (if I owned a white handkerchief). The front window of the Mustang is tinted slightly, preventing me from getting a look at the driver. I'm halfway to the Mustang when it begins backing down the street. It does a J turn, assisted by the ice on the road, and takes off in the other direction. I run back to the Saturn, wanting to hop in and order Mike to follow. But I wind up stumbling and nearly going down (assisted by the ice on the road). By the time I get my balance again, the Mustang has disappeared around the corner. No idea where it's going or how we can catch up to it. Nuts. I drop back into the Saturn.

"Guess he didn't feel talking," I say. "Luckily, he didn't feel like shooting me, either."

"Where to now?"

"Home, Jeeves."

We navigate our way out of this neighborhood, thanks to some help from the GPS. Once we're safely back on the highway, Mike drops one hand over the steering wheel.

"If we're being followed," he says, "maybe we didn't get away with that break-in."

"Maybe we shouldn't have expected to."

"But you would think *just once...*"

Then again, if we thought *just once,* maybe we wouldn't do the break-ins.

CHAPTER SIX

Miles refused. He turned back to his movie. A black-and-white Japanese thing with subtitles. Christina crossed her arms.

"Why not?" she asked.

"Better question: why would you want me to do it?"

"You seem to be doing okay."

He turned up the volume, despite the subtitles. Christina wondered how much Japanese he knew.

"That can change at any time," he said.

"Yeah, I wonder what that would be like." She sat on the arm of the sofa. "I don't want to feel weak or scared."

"They've got self-defense classes at the Y."

"I'm not talking about kicking someone in the balls if they try taking my purse. I mean, real protection."

Miles didn't look at her. "It doesn't solve anything. Doesn't make you feel strong or in control. My old man wasn't a font of wisdom, but he would say one thing that made sense: you can think you're the toughest son of a bitch in the world, but if you pick enough fights, you're going to find someone who's tougher. I spend my time looking over my

125

shoulder, wondering if someone is coming after me. Wondering if the guy who hired me is setting me up. That the kind of life you want?"

"I have it already."

Miles paused the movie. "You want me to train you to kill people? Make you my padawan?"

"You saw Star Wars?"

"I've seen a lot of things. I'm a man of many and varied tastes."

She sensed he was trying to change the subject. "Yes, I want you to train me."

"And you'll do what?"

"I'll decide that later." She swung her feet onto the sofa. "Someone trained you, right?"

"The army trained me. And some other wonderfully charitable government types. A lot of it I picked up myself."

"You could teach me. If you wanted to."

"Go to college. Create a life for yourself."

Christina stood up from the sofa. "I didn't ask for what happened to me. I didn't ask you to bring me here. When do I get to decide what I want?"

Miles said nothing. Christina walked back to her room. She slammed the door behind her. Miles started the movie again.

***

Miles met with Graham Cheng met in a teahouse in Hong Kong. Cheng owned the place, used it to launder money. Miles had done a job for him. It was time to settle up.

Cheng was half-British, half-Chinese. A bigwig in one of the Triads. Miles had taken out Ananada Tularak, a gun runner who didn't want to share his business proceeds with Cheng. Miles gunned Tularak down on a side street in Bangkok.

It hadn't gone smoothly. Miles rode a motorcycle, his face covered by the helmet. He wanted to gun down Tularak in his car. But the driver spotted Miles. There was a chase. The car barrel-rolled. Tularak stumbled out. Miles shot him through the head. Rode off.

Miles wanted the money wired to him. Cheng would only deal in cash. Miles's business had dropped off since Phoenix. He had to play this Cheng's way.

The teahouse was cramped but clean. Like everything in Hong Kong. Black tables and chairs dotted the tile floors. Booths rimmed the edges. Red and black decorations attached to the support pillars.

Cheng looked more British than Chinese. The eyes had a hint of Asian influence. His black hair hung in bangs. He wore a tan suit with a black shirt and a gold tie. He had a slappable face.

Various goons, all in black, dotted the room. Two at the door. Two flanking Cheng. Two at a corner table. Maybe one in the kitchen. The goons at the door didn't frisk Miles. A good thing. He wanted this to go smoothly.

Cheng sat at a small table, middle of the room. A cup of tea in front of him. Hands clasped under the table. Miles walked over, waited for permission to sit. Cheng sipped his tea, making Miles wait. A power play. Cheng *dabbed his lips with a cloth napkin. Miles sat across from him. Cheng looked up from the tea.*

"*I hear Tularak is gone,*" *he said. Flawless English. A slight British accent.*

"*That is the case.*"

"*Well done.*"

"*Thank you.*"

Cheng snapped his fingers. A goon from the corner table brought over a metal briefcase. He set it on the table between Miles and Cheng. Took out bundles of bills, about half of what was in the case. Snapped the case shut and stepped back. Miles leafed through a bundle.

"*I might be miscounting,*" *he said,* "*but this is about half of what we agreed to.*"

"*It's what I'm paying,*" *Cheng said.* "*I appreciate the work, but this is what you're walking out of here with.*"

"*That's not how I do business.*"

"*It's how I do business. You cocked up the hit. I don't pay top dollar for that.*"

"*Last I checked, Tularak is still dead. I expect payment in full.*"

Cheng picked up his tea. Miles didn't move, didn't flinch. Some goons moved their hands into their coats. Cheng narrowed his eyes.

"*I pay top dollar for the best,*" *he said,* "*You used to be the best. Word around the campfire is you let the cartel down. You don't have it anymore.*"

"*So much for a deal is a deal, huh?*"

"Whatever. Take your money and get the fuck out of here."

Miles gathered the bundles, put them in a satchel he'd brought. He closed his eyes and took a breath. Cheng sipped his tea. The goon removed the briefcase from the table.

"Too bad, man," Cheng said, "You used to be the best. Wish I could have met you then."

Miles's eyes dropped. His foot came up suddenly. The table flew up with it. The teacup was driven into Cheng's face. He fell off the chair, holding his bleeding mouth.

Miles got a knife from his boot. Drove it into the closest goon's throat. He slipped the Berretta from his shoulder holster. Shot the goon on the other side of the table. Blood and brains hit the decorations.

Miles dropped to one knee. He shot the goons guarding the door. Head shots. One crashed through the door. The other went facedown on the floor.

The goons at the corner table opened fire. Uzis. Miles rolled out of the line of fire. The goons closed in. Miles grabbed an ashtray, flung it like a Frisbee. It hit one of the goons in the face. Miles followed up with bullets through the neck and chest.

The other goon ducked behind a table. Resumed firing. Miles slipped behind a pillar. Bullets ripped the wall, the tables, the decorations. The goon started moving.

Miles took out a second Berretta, from the holster at the small of his back. He stepped out from the pillar. Opened up with both guns. The goon dropped behind the table. Cheng was still on the floor. Still bleeding.

Cheng fumbled for his gun. Miles clubbed him with the butt of the Berretta. He dropped the second Berretta, grabbed Cheng by the back of his suitcoat, yanked him to his feet. He jammed the barrel of the gun into Cheng's jaw.

"You're going to put the gun down," Miles said. Matter of fact. Cold. The goon took aim. "Put it down," Miles said.

Cheng spoke through bleeding lips. "He doesn't speak English."

"Then you translate."

Cheng spoke to the goon in Cantonese. The gun remained steady.

"He doesn't want to do it," Cheng said. "He thinks he can take you before you get the shot off."

"Convince him he's wrong." Cheng repeated himself, more insistent. The goon lowered the weapon. "Tell him to put the gun on the floor," Miles said. "Then I let you two walk out."

Cheng repeated the order. The goon's face tightened. He did as he was told. Then Miles shot the goon in the face.

Cheng screamed and dropped to the floor. He cried into his hands. Miles kicked the Uzi across the room. He opened the briefcase, emptied the contents into his satchel. Stood over Cheng.

"Nice meeting you," Miles said.

He slipped on his shades. Left Cheng on the floor, weeping.

***

Christina was becoming a problem. Skipping classes. Being disruptive when she did show up. Falling behind on her schoolwork. She threw a student over a table during lunch. Miles had to go to the school, talk to the principal. The principal lectured Miles. Miles fantasized about sticking a letter opener through the guy's eye. He'd never killed anyone recreationally. He was beginning to see the appeal. Another generous donation smoothed things over.

Miles called Shane, asked to meet for a beer. McKenzie's was the place. Strictly blue collar. Dirty floors, gouged tables, decades of dust. But everyone minded their own fucking business. Miles was at a table near the back, halfway through a pitcher. Shane grabbed a bowl of peanuts off the bar, easing his bulk into a chair.

"Tying one on?" Shane asked.

"You see don't see any shots in front of me. That is when I'm tying one on." He killed the beer, poured himself another. Poured one for Shane. "How's our friend in Hong Kong?"

"He's got to do some restaffing. We may get blowback there."

"Let him try."

"Look, I know Cheng might be an arrogant dipshit, but he didn't get where he is by being weak. He's not going to forget about you. Or anyone who knows you."

"Let's steer clear of Southeast Asia for a while," Miles said. "Make him come to me. Assuming he's got the guts."

Shane hesitated. He took a healthy drink, wiped the foam from his mustache, dug into the bowl of peanuts.

"What's going on with the kid?" he asked.

"Fucking up in school. Behavioral stuff."

"What do you think's causing that?"

Miles hesitated. The only thing more ridiculous than carrying the thought in his head was saying it out loud. "She wants me to train her. And I won't do it."

"Train her...?"

"To do what I do. You believe that?"

Shane sipped his beer. Ran his finger through the wet circle under it. Miles stopped drinking.

"You do *believe it?" Miles asked.*

"It makes a little sense," *Shane said,* "Her family got killed. She's got...what is it? Survivor's guilt."

"I survived a lot of shit. I didn't take it out on other people."

"That's because you got a...what do you call it? An outlet."

"You're an outlet."

Shane set the beer aside. "Look at it her way. No family. No friends. Living in a strange place. With you. You gotta admit you're not exactly Mr. Warmth."

"I'm not trying to be her family."

"This girl's fucked up. She needs something. I know you weren't thinking long-term when you got her out of there. But she's here now. She needs more than clothes and food and a place to sleep. She needs something from you."

Miles finished his beer, poured another. Shane didn't push him. An old Dion song—"Daddy Rollin' in Your Arms"—played on the jukebox.

"I hate that you're right," *Miles said.*

132

"Nice part is it doesn't happen all that often."

They clinked their mugs. Then ordered some shots.

***

Miles weaved down the hallway. Put his hand on the doorknob to Christina's room, took a breath. Opened the door.

She was lying on her side, turned away. A glimpse of bare shoulder. Miles wondered if she slept in the nude. He shook it off. Christina stirred. Didn't look at him.

"You want to do what I do?" he asked.

She half-turned. "Yes."

"We start tomorrow." Christina sat up on her elbows. Both shoulders were bare. Miles looked away. "Get some sleep," he said. "Reveille is at five."

Miles closed the door.

***

"Shoot!" Freddie screams, his voice likely registering on the Richter scale. "Shoot the fucking ball!" He turns to no one in particular, one eye still on the TV screen. "They fuck around with it for thirty seconds, then just throw it at the basket. Nobody on this fucking team can create a shot?"

And no one in the bar is interested in responding. That's for the best, since Freddie isn't in the mood to carry on a two-way conversation. Sporting events bring that out in him. He's a three-hundred-pound Samoan gentleman who currently serves as a bouncer and a barback at The Tav. Rumor has it he was once a neighborhood menace but straightened up his act after The Tav put him on the payroll (largely to keep out the rest of the neighborhood riffraff). He's at the bar, staring at one of the TVs overheard, and urging the Gopher basketball team onto greater effort. I'm at a nearby high-top, trying to enjoy a glass of Grand Brewing Maibock.

My laptop is open on the table. Normally, if I take my writing on the road, I do it at Glacier's. But this task indicates beer would be better. I'm working on rewrites for the script, perusing notes given to me by my beloved director, whose death is now occupying a number of my daydreams. I'm tempted to chuck the laptop across the bar, but I resist (largely because I can't afford a new one).

I'm alone at The Tav but also not. From where I'm sitting, the restaurant is visible. On one end, Lars is on a double date with Chuck and Chuck's fiancée. Chuck is a solidly built guy with dirty blonde hair and a permanently malevolent look, one his fiancée has done nothing to soften. The fiancée herself is a redhead with bright eyes. She seems to be carrying the conversation. Lars leans back in his chair, aloof. His date for the evening is Rose McElhenny, known as Big Rosie to her friends and people who talk behind her back. She's a buxom redhead in her own right, with green eyes and a permanent scowl. She and Lars hook up from time to time, whenever one or the other needs a date or to get laid. Big Rosie fiddles with a pasta dish and ignores her dinner companions (particularly the female one).

And in the other corner (wearing the white trunks) are Carol and her boyfriend, Jeff. Carol, as always, is dressed to impress, wearing a low-cut green dress that provides a little peek of Cleveland. Jeff is a clean-cut gent with dark hair and good grooming. He looks like he hits the gym a lot. The two lean close to each other. Things are going well. It's a study in contrasts between the two tables. I try to be bemused, but I'm not feeling it.

I go back to my work (and make no mistake, this is work). I'm trying to both decipher Lars's notes and turn them into something palatable for the general public (or even a portion of the lunatic fringe). My cell phone rings. It's Lisa. I answer it tout suite.

"Frozen Tundra," I say. "Vince Lombardi speaking. What the hell is going on out here?"

A cool chuckle on the other end. "I take it that's a sports reference?"

"I thought you liked football.'

"For about ten minutes when I had to take pictures for the school newspaper."

"Like ships passing in the night."

"Exactly," Lisa says. "Big sweaty ships in tight pants." Her voice switches from playful to business-like. "You got a minute?"

It's the first time in the last few hours I've felt a lightness in my chest. "For you? Always."

There's a shuffling of papers on the other end as Lisa gets her notes together. "I did some looking into Warren Newson, like you asked. It's a bit of a mixed bag."

"I love a mixed bag. When it involves cheese popcorn. What have got?"

"Warren Newson. Born and raised in Brooklyn Point. Graduated from high school there. Joined the army. Re-upped a few years later. And that's mostly it."

"*Mostly* it?"

"That's where the mixed bag comes in. See, there's no record of Warren Newson being discharged from the army or currently serving. There's no employment record outside the army. There's almost nothing about him after he re-upped."

"Apparently, he hangs out at Eli's Arcade. Or at least he once did." I tell Lisa about what we found, both the video game and the box of stuff. "Did you find out anything else?"

"Sophie Walker is his aunt on his mother's side. She still lives in Brooklyn Point. I couldn't find other family. Both parents are dead. No siblings. No other aunts and uncles. No cousins."

"Parents dead? Is that a Bruce Wayne type situation?"

"No. The father died of a heart attack. The mother had pancreatic cancer. Both died after Warren went into the army."

"Maybe I'll talk to the aunt. See if she knows anything." I finish off my beer. "Thank you for your help."

There's a small thump as her notepad likely hits the desk. "Anytime. It's what I do." Her chair creaks as she leans back. "Do you want to tell me what you're involved in? I'm picking up pieces here and there, but you haven't told me everything."

Oof. That's a tough one. I'm so used to my friends telling me to stay out of something, I'm hesitant to share details with Lisa. Especially when investigation is *her* specialty. I decide to kick that can down the road.

"It might be nothing," I say. "If it turns into something, you'll be the first person I call." Assuming I'm still alive to do so.

Lisa's voice softens. "Keep safe, all right?"

"I'll do my best."

We ring off. There's something about Lisa's concern that gets to me. Other people—my friends, officers of the law, anyone with common sense, what have you—can tell me to stay out of something, and I have no difficulty ignoring them. With Lisa, it's another matter. It's like I can't let her down. I shake it off and get back to work. (Oh joy.)

After a few minutes, I discover Lars standing in front of my table. He's resplendent in his white Nehru jacket, black slacks and gold chain. I resist the urge to throw my drink at him. (I don't want to waste the brew.) He lays a heavy hand on the table.

"This double date is not going well," he says.

I see exactly what he means. Chuck's fiancée is hugging his arm in much the same way her polka dot dress hugs her healthy upper body. (She gives Big Rosie a run for her money in that area; something Rosie is likely aware of and hates.) Chuck ignores everything but his steak, which he carves into with more gusto than I care for. Big Rosie swigs her red wine and tries to position herself so that her blue dress shows off more cleavage.

"It's looking like a bit of a minefield over there," I say.

Lars sighs. "I went into this with an open mind. And I must admit my faith has been rewarded. Laura, Chuck's fiancée, is a delightful woman. Entirely worthy of Chuck."

Someone who can be described as delightful probably exceeds *worthy* of Chuck, but I keep that thought to myself. "What's the problem?"

"The problem is *my* date. Big Rosie is in what you might call one of her off moods."

"I didn't realize she had *on* moods."

"Oh, she does. Usually when it involves sex. And by that, I mean the six seconds before and the six seconds after. The rest of the time she can be rather...unpleasant. Particularly around someone as delightful as Laura."

That tracks, though I know Big Rosie more by reputation than experience. So far, no fisticuffs have broken out. That's on the plus side. Lars glances toward the other corner of the restaurant area.

"Carol looks like she's having a good time," he says.

"She does at that."

"I'd be lying if I said I wasn't a tad jealous."

"Maybe you're a tad jealous of Chuck as well?"

"No, it's not that. I'm only concerned about the business end of things. Romance is a distraction. I made my choice a long time ago. Casual sex or no sex at all. Though, preferably casual sex. For now, I need to get through the rest of the evening, go back to Big Rosie's place, give her the best sex she's ever had, and sleep on this whole problem. If I can get sleep. Big Rosie's a bit insatiable."

Okay, more information than I needed, but that's what I get for being in this conversation. I wish Lars luck. He continues on to the restroom. I try to go back to my work, but my concentration is shattered, and my enthusiasm is waning. I close the laptop. I've just taken a sip of my beer when someone else appears next to me at the table.

"Is that Carol's date?"

Fabio is standing to my right. His white shirt is untucked, and his black pants are wrinkled. His appearance, though, isn't my big concern. It's his demeanor. Up to now, I've only seen two expressions on his face: calm (if clueless) confidence and forlorn distraction. We can now add a third: heart-rending disturbance. His eyes bug out, his breathing is heavy, and his hands clench and unclench. He's either two minutes from a nervous breakdown or he had it two minutes ago. I clear my throat, not quite sure how to handle this situation.

"Um, it looks that way, yes," I say.

Fabio lets out a cross between a sob and a moan. (Soan? Mob? I'll work on it.) He looks close to tears. He drops a hand on my table, steadying himself. "How could she do that to me? She didn't even let the body get cold."

"Everything is cold in this weather."

He hangs his head. "We really had something. I don't know what went wrong."

The answer is obvious. But Fabio doesn't want to hear *She regarded you as a simple piece of man candy and once the flavor ran out, she disposed of you.*

"I know it sucks," I say, "but these things happen."

"Not to me they don't."

"And it just…wait a minute, you've never had a girl break up with you?"

"Never," Fabio says. "Does it always hurt this bad?"

I don't know what bothers me more, that he's never had a girl break up with him or that he automatically assumes I have (and that he's accurate). Still, it's not right to kick someone when they're down. (At least that's what my parents told me. Personally, I've always thought, *Why not? They're just that much closer to your foot.*)

"The good news," I say, forcing out the words, "is that it gets better over time."

"How long?"

"It depends on the relationship."

"What about the love of your life?"

That's a bit of a conundrum. I occasionally chat with the love of my life. It's been seventeen years, and I'm not prepared to say I'm over her. At the same time, I'm not prepared to put Fabio's fling with Carol in the same category.

"It may take a couple of months," I say.

There. That's vague enough, right? However, Fabio's face nearly melts in despair. "A couple of months?" he says. "I can't wait that long."

"Maybe it'll be sooner."

"How soon? I want it to stop *now*."

Hoo boy. My nephew Ty used to throw similar tantrums (and in the same tone of voice). Ty is twelve now and even he has grown out of the tantrum phase.

"It *does* get a little better every day," I say.

"I don't want it to get better. That would mean Carol isn't in my heart anymore. I don't want to live like that. I've got to get her back."

"I don't think that's the healthiest approach," I say.

"To hell with healthy," Fabio says, bouncing on the balls of his feet. "My therapist used to talk about healthy. It didn't get me anywhere. Maybe because I fired him. I don't know. But healthy isn't going to get back the woman I love."

Fabio takes off for Carol's table. She doesn't see him approach. Lars does, though, and he quickly makes eye contact with me. Before either of us can do anything, Fabio goes down on one knee before Carol.

"I love you," he says. "I don't think I ever told you that, but I do. And that means you can't be with this guy here." He turns to Jeff. "With all due respect, you're going to want to get the hell out of here."

Carol and Jeff exchange a few words. They're too far away for me to hear. Based on their physical interactions, she's explaining who the hell this moron is. Jeff leans toward Fabio. He keeps his voice down. He seems to be informing Fabio his presence is not welcome. Fabio hops to his feet.

"Fuck you, man!" Fabio says, in a voice loud enough for the restaurant, the bar, and perhaps Guam to hear. "I'm not leaving. You take your…your*self* and hit the bricks, jack!"

Jeff gets to his feet and steps around the table. He's a little taller than Fabio and a hell of a lot more confident. For a moment, Fabio looks like he'll back down. But he stands his ground. (There's a lesson for you, kids: when confronted by someone bigger, never stand your ground.) Carol tries to get between them. Lars, realizing one of our angels is in serious danger of getting his clock cleaned, starts toward the table. Big Rosie, Chuck, and Laura follow. Jeff goes nose to nose (well, nose to forehead) with Fabio, who looks as if he regrets this action but is too far out on a limb.

"So…you get what I'm saying?" Fabio tells him.

Jeff glares at Fabio. "I get it."

"Good. Good. Glad we cleared that up. So…you gonna get lost? Like I asked?"

"I'm not going anywhere?"

"You're gonna regret it."

"I don't think so."

Lars hovers nearby, dithering about what to do. Big Rosie, on the other hand, has no such hesitation.

"Knock him on his ass!" she shouts.

Fabio turns toward the arrivals. "Who were you saying that to?"

Big Rosie uses her wine glass to gesture to the combatants. "I don't care. I just wanna see some action. Don't stand there waving your dicks at each other. Throw hands if you're gonna!"

Fabio turns back to Jeff. Laura steps past Chuck and over to Big Rosie.

"Don't tell them to do that," Laura says. "Someone might get hurt."

"That's what I want to see," Big Rosie says, as if the answer is obvious. "Besides, do these two look like they can hurt each other? Let 'em fight. It'll be comedy gold."

Laura is repulsed. "That's sick."

That, unfortunately, gets Big Rosie's goat. She uses the wine glass to gesture at Laura. "Who the hell are you to talk to me like that, you simpering, empty-headed little bitch!"

Laura recoils. (But I've got to give Big Rosie credit. You don't hear many people use *simpering* in conversation. I'm glad she's keeping it in circulation.) Chuck looms behind his fiancée and directs his attention to Lars.

"Lars, control your woman," he says.

"She's not really my woman," Lars says. "And that's a little sexist, Chuck."

"Fuck you."

"And that's downright rude."

Laura upbraids Big Rosie for her lack of manners and her bloodthirsty nature. Big Rosie counters by noting what a dimwit Laura is and how Rosie wouldn't be here if Lars didn't need a date. Laura refuses to back down. Chuck again implores Lars to control Big Rosie. Lars again refuses, creating another argument. Fabio and Jeff get back to their own personal set-to.

"I'm only going to tell you this one more time," Fabio says. "Get lost, okay?"

"Why would I do that? I'm having a good time with a beautiful and charming woman, and I'm not going to leave because some little dipshit tells me to."

"Dipshit? Dipshit this!"

Fabio shoves Jeff. At least, that was the intention. He puts both hands on Jeff's chest and applies force. Jeff goes nowhere. Fabio, on the other hand, moves back a few feet. He squares up again, as if that's how he intended it to go.

"Had enough?" he asks.

Before Jeff can reply, Carol steps into the fray. "Fabio, *I'm* telling you: get out of here."

Fabio stamps his foot. "I won't! We love each other. I need you to see that!"

"I won't see it because it's not true!" Carol says. "Now get out!"

"No! Not until I kick this guy's ass!"

145

Carol is beyond the use of words. Instead, she gives Fabio a shove. He crashes into Big Rosie. The impact causes Rosie to spill the contents of her wine glass onto Laura, who recoils, staring at the ruins of her dress. Big Rosie is more upset by the loss of her wine. Chuck stalks back to the table, grabs his coat, and returns to Laura, putting it over her. He guides her toward the front door.

"I'm putting this on you, Lars," he says. "You and me? We're through."

Chuck and Laura storm out. Big Rosie looks forlornly at her wine glass. Carol and Jeff grab their coats and head for the exit, stopping at the front to pay the check. Fabio looks around, confused. Freddie makes his way over to Fabio and informs him he will be leaving now. Fabio allows Freddie to escort him out. (Not that he has much choice in the matter.) Big Rosie grabs her coat.

"I'll be waiting in the car," she tells Lars.

She stalks out, ignoring me as she passes. Lars wanders over. I prop an elbow on the table.

"Rough night," I say.

"It's only going to get rougher. When Rosie gets angry, she gets more amorous. Last time, I nearly wound up in the emergency room with friction burns over most of my body."

"Good luck."

"Thanks, old chum. I'm going to need a lot of it. And maybe some Astroglide."

***

I love my apartment, but I confess that heating and cooling the place is problematic. It's not as if it covers several hundred square acres, but I find myself at the height of every summer and the depth of every winter huddled near the source of comfort. In summer, that's the rather confined area next to the air conditioner (propped in one of the arch windows at the front). In winter, it's the radiator below the arch windows.

The temps outside have dipped again. As a result, I've moved the comfy chair in front of the radiator. I've got an Afghan wrapped around my shoulders, and I'm wearing an Adams College hoodie. Lenny and Squiggy are cuddled up next to me. Here we are, literally and figuratively a collection of pussies.

My cell phone rings. I fish it out of the folds of the Afghan, which turns out to be easier said than done. It's Mike. I can't help feeling this effort is wasted. I answer anyway.

"Paisley Park," I say. "This is the Artist Formerly Known as Unpronounceable Symbol speaking. We are gathered here today to get into this thing called life. How can I help you?"

"You finished?"

"I am."

"Good. You own a trench coat?"

Now, there's something you don't get asked every day. Well, I suppose if you're Harry Lime or Harry Palmer and this was more than fifty years ago, you might. But the rest of us are in the clear. At least, I was until today.

"I can probably get one," I tell him. "Why?"

"Can't get into that. But I need you to go to a meeting with Robbie and Lyle Wills."

Oh, good grief. This again? A cup of hot chocolate might be called for. I dislodge myself from the Afghan and the cats, drawing resentment from at least one of them. I get a packet of instant cocoa from the cupboard. (Hey, I like to cook, but you really think I'm going to melt chocolate for a shot of something warm? What do I look like? Emeril Lagasse? Fuhgeddaboudit.)

"What is this meeting about?" I ask.

"Can't tell you that."

"You sure? I'm going to be part of the damn thing. Wouldn't it help for me to know?"

"No, it wouldn't help at all. The less you know, the better this will go. You get it?"

"No. Not at all."

"I thought you wanted to help T.J."

Dammit. If Mike thinks emotional manipulation is going to work on me, he's dead right. "Fine," I say. "When is this thing?"

"We'll let you know. Keep your schedule open."

"Did we just meet? My schedule is always open."

"Remember the trench coat." It sounds like he's about to ring off, then adds: "I don't suppose you own a fedora, do you? Is that too much to ask?"

"Yes. That's the bridge too far."

"It's okay," Mike says. "We can live without it."

"I'll take your word on it. I have to."

Mike rings off. I return to the futon and wrap myself up in the Afghan. Just to distract myself from that nonsense, I go back to thinking about the information I've gathered so far. Deirdre was looking for someone named Grace Jelinski. Grace is from Brooklyn Point. Grace has recently disappeared without an explanation. A gunman is looking for Grace and killed Deirdre in the process. She was killed at Eli's Arcade. The only thing I found at Eli's was a video game and a collection of books and movies belonging to someone named Warren Newson. Warren also disappeared many years ago. How does all this fit together? I don't have a fucking clue.

The phone rings again. Are you kidding me? I dig around the Afghan and again come up with the phone before it goes to voicemail. Jim Street is calling. This never makes me feel good. I answer but skip the cute greeting.

"Thought we should talk," is how Street opens the conversation. "You got a minute?"

"Sure," I say. "When and where?"

"How about right now?"

"You going to come to my place?"

"Why don't you come to mine?" Street says.

That's disconcerting. Street is usually content coming to me. Am I in trouble? Am I walking into a trap? Has being constantly under attack made me paranoid?

"Okay," I say. "Where is your place?"

Street gives me the address and, for a second, I think he's messing with me. The address is in Lowertown, a former cluster of warehouses in downtown St. Paul. It has been undergoing a multi-generational process of gentrification. There's a post office on Kellogg, but beyond that, I don't know of any state or federal buildings in that neighborhood. I repeat the address, just to make sure I'm getting it right. Street confirms.

"You got time to come down now?" he asks.

"Assuming my car starts."

"See ya soon."

Street rings off. I stare at my phone. What does Street want to talk about? Does he know I've been nosing around this case? Is he giving me a come to Jesus talk or is it something worse? I guess I'll get the answers soon.

Assuming I want them.

***

While everything in Lowertown seems to be converted or awaiting conversion, the building to which Jim Street has directed me isn't on that list. It appears either a wrecking ball or a stiff breeze would take it out entirely. It's brown brick and four stories high. A large wooden door with chipped and fading green paint is the only visible way in. Most of the windows are boarded up. I find a parking space out front. I get the feeling I'm going to be either arrested or mugged. Frankly, I don't know which is worse.

I get out of the car and stand in front of the door. The wind is whipping, and the temp is hovering around zero. The door is locked. I pound on it, not wanting the rigmarole of digging in my pocket to get out my phone. After several seconds, I consider getting back in the car and going home. Then the door opens. A guy best resembling Elvis peeks out.

"Joe Davis," he says, as if greeting an old friend. "Come on in. Jim is waiting for you."

He leads me inside. I've met this guy before. He's one of Street's men, though I know him more as Elvis than by his actual name (which I have long since forgotten). He's wearing an all-black ensemble, including leather jacket, dress shirt and slacks. His thick hair is swept back, and he sports a pair of thin sideburns. The place we're entering is lit, but that's about all you can say for it. It's completely empty. The floors are cracked, but the large beams in the ceiling look sturdy. It's barely warmer than the outside. A metal staircase is off to our right. I follow Elvis that direction.

"Were you sitting here waiting for me?" I ask.

"Nope. Saw you on the CCTV."

Elvis leads me up to a metal walkway rimming the upper part of the warehouse. I can't help wondering if we're going to take poles down to a Batcave. Nah. That would be too much to hope for. Elvis stops at what seems to be the door to a meat locker. He pushes back a panel, revealing a keypad. He punches in a code. A moment later, he tugs open the door.

The room I walk into completely contrasts the rest of the warehouse. Yes, it still has the exposed brickwork and the heavy beams overhead. But the rest of it is desks, filing cabinets, and office equipment. A picture window looks out on the Mississippi River. I gape at the setup. A few people are familiar. Elvis, naturally. Also, a guy in a beret, currently stationed at one of the desks. Ric, Street's partner, has a desk in front of an office near the back. He's talking on the phone. Elvis closes the door behind me.

"I'll let Jim know you're here," he says.

Elvis ducks into the back office. Ric hangs up the phone and stands. A moment later, Jim Street emerges, wearing a black shirt, gray slacks and a silver tie. No suitcoat. (What are the odds this guy sleeps in silk pajamas? Pretty good, right?) He walks across the office and offers me a handshake.

"Thanks for coming in," he says. "Wanted to get your opinion on something."

What the wha…? "My opinion? On what?"

"Follow me."

We go to a small conference room to the left of his office. Ric follows us in and closes the door. We sit at a round table.

"What is this place?" I ask. "You can't tell me the BCA is headquartered here."

"I've got my own detail," Street says. "Gives me a little freedom. No bureaucrats. Better for everybody."

If there's one thing I can understand, it's a nonconformist who prefers to work on their own. "What can I help you with?" I ask.

Ric slips something out of a folder and puts it on the table in front of me. Street taps it with his forefinger.

"This guy look familiar?" he asks.

It's a sketch of a guy with slicked back hair, a mustache, big eyes, and a craggy face. In other words, the absolute spitting image of the gunman who broke into my apartment.

"This is the guy who came after me," I say. "Where did you get this?"

"Gave the information to a sketch artist," Ric says. "He does pretty good work."

"Damn good work," I say. "Any idea who this guy is?"

Ric sets a paper in front of me. It's from a criminal file. A mugshot sits near the top. The hair is a little shorter, but there's no mistaking the rest of him. This is definitely the guy who broke into my apartment.

"He is the ironically named Angel Sastre," Ric says. "Works for the cartel. A higher up in Victor Merced's organization."

There's a buzzing in my head. "Cartel? Like a drug cartel?"

"No," Ric says. "More like a bouncy house cartel."

Street speaks out of the corner of his mouth. "Enrique."

"Sorry," Ric says. "Yes, a drug cartel. A big one. Marijuana, meth, cocaine. You got the gelt, they got the melt. Until recently, the cartel was run by a guy named Amado Guzman. He's currently taking a dirt nap."

"Adios, scumbag," Street says.

I'm trying to stay calm, but my breath is in short supply. "This cartel operates in Minnesota?"

"That's the interesting part, Slick," Street says. "They run the whole damn southwest, but we have no evidence they do anything in Minnesota."

"Then what are they doing here?" I ask.

"Don't know that," Street says.

"What did Deirdre have to do with them?"

"Don't know that, either."

"And Grace Jelinski?"

"Going to refer you back to my first two answers."

Great. If I opened a window and shouted *Anyone know anything about a murderous drug cartel?* I'd know exactly as much as I do right now. "Did you find out *anything* about Grace Jelinski?" I ask.

Ric stops chewing his gum. Street avoids eye contact, making a show of deep regret and frustration. "Not a damn thing," Street says. "The woman is a complete mystery. Don't know what to tell you."

The truth would be a nice start. If Lisa could find some rudimentary background info on Grace, it's hard to believe a guy with connections to every law enforcement database in the country came up empty. I had the sneaking suspicion Street would lie to me to keep me off the trail. I guess he doesn't know about Lisa. I give him my own regretful headshake.

"That sucks," I say. "But I appreciate you looking."

155

"You gotta have a little patience, Slick. Guys like this don't leave notes saying *I'm in the Ambassador Suites, room 212. Feel free to stop by.*"

"That wouldn't be sporting, wouldn't it?" I say.

"Not at all." Street's smirk disappears. He leans toward me. "Talked to the chief of police up in Brooklyn Point."

Swell. "Hank ratted me out?"

"She's a smart cop. Too smart for Jerkwater, USA, but that's her business. She said you positively ID'ed Deirdre and asked a bunch of questions about the case."

"I'm a concerned citizen," I say.

"You're also a pain in the ass. You find anything in Brooklyn Point worth sharing?"

As long as he's buttered me up, why wouldn't I swap info? It's not like Street is holding out on me, right? I'm also aware any info I give them will disappear down the rabbit hole.

"Nothing yet," I say. "Just what I've given you."

Street's eyes bore into me. "You sure about that?"

"I am."

There is no way Street believes me. But beyond breaking out the rubber hoses or the waterboarding implements, he has no way of dragging the information (such as it is) out of me. He sits back.

"If that's how you want it," he says.

"That's just how it is."

Street gets up from the table while Ric opens the door. Street leads the way out. A few people look up as we cross the office but quickly pretend they've got better things to do. Street opens the main door and steps out. He closes it behind me, leaving Ric behind.

"I would greatly appreciate it if you left this to the professionals," he says. "If these guys could get to Deirdre, what do you think they'll do to you?"

I try not to let him see the shiver that runs through me. Deirdre was far closer to indestructible than me, and the cartel still got to her. But then, I didn't ask for this, did I? I look around the warehouse.

"Please tell me you have Batpoles you can slide down," I say.

"Sorry. Can't take a chance on messing up the suit."

He disappears back into his office. I leave here certain of two things: 1, I'm not going to give up this case; and 2, Batman would never give a shit about his suit.

CHAPTER SEVEN

It started with a ten-mile run. Nothing about soccer prepared Christina for it. She stopped three times to vomit. Miles was nursing a Category Five hangover. He didn't vomit once. He expected Christina to give up. She made the whole run. She tried to go up the steps, back to the apartment. Miles grabbed the back of her sweat-soaked shirt, guided her toward the back of the building.

"You're going to give me some jumping jacks," he said.

"Are you crazy?"

"I don't know. Passed all my psych evals. I might have a dissociative thing, so maybe the evals aren't reliable. But I feel okay."

Two hundred jumping jacks. One hundred pushups. Christina got through the jumping jacks. Her form on the pushups was for-shit after the first ten. Miles wanted to scream at her, like his old DI. (Miles still prayed—or the closest he came to praying—that the guy would run afoul of the wrong people, and they'd hire Miles to kill him). He didn't want to draw attention from the other tenants. He squatted down, whispered a series of insults about Christina's resilience. Tears streamed from her eyes.

Snot rolled out of her nose. Drool hung from her lips. She didn't quit. She finished. Miles let her lie in the grass.

"Go take a shower," Miles said. "Get ready for school."

"Are you serious?"

"Yes. I don't want to hear anything about mouthing off to teachers, skipping classes, or knocking around other kids. If I've got to talk to that dipshit principal again, this whole thing is over. You got me?"

She tried to get up. Didn't make it. "You expect me to get through school like this?"

"Yes. But very poorly. Tomorrow won't be great, either. It'll get better. Just not soon."

"When do we get to the other stuff?"

"When I say so."

Miles walked back into the building. Christina struggled to get off the ground.

***

Miles thought Christina would see the error of her ways. Get back whatever common sense she might have had. This ridiculous ambition would be beaten out of her.

But she didn't quit. The weather didn't matter. Rain. Snow. Mud. Ice. She kept going. She mastered ten miles, so he upped it to twelve. Two hundred jumping jacks became four hundred. One hundred pushups became two hundred. They got up at four instead of five. She didn't quit. His amazement gave way to admiration. He didn't let her see that.

It was May. Rain coming down in sheets. Christina's face in the mud with every pushup. Soaked to the skin. Miles paced around her. A rain slicker covered his black workout gear. Christina hit two hundred, rolled to the side, away from the puddle.

"Get cleaned up," he said. "Go to school."

Christina sat up, released her wet hair from her ponytail. She wasn't breathing hard. "This is bullshit."

Miles turned around. "What was that?"

"You heard me. I could've gotten more than this from the Y."

"You're welcomed to go there."

"Fuck this." She got to her feet, more easily than Miles expected. "You're supposed to teach me to do what you do."

"This was what I did first. And I wasn't much older than you."

She let it go. They got back to the apartment. Miles laid a few towels down. Christina glared at him.

"Let me guess," she said, "we're going to keep doing this for another year, then you kick me out after graduation."

"You're making a hell of a case for it." Miles held up a hand, stopping her protest. "We'll talk about it when you get home from school."

Christina stalked off to her room to change.

Miles thought about it. He watched a few movies. Read some Bukowski. Went for a walk once the rain let up. Christina came home. Miles was in his favorite chair, sipping a latte. She leaned against the front door, holding her books. Miles set his latte on the end table.

"Next phase starts tonight," he said. "You ready?"

A tremor crossed her face. Nothing else. "What do we do?"

"Put on your workout gear."

Shane dropped them off at a warehouse. Drove off without saying anything. Miles had a key. He led Christina through a maze, boxes stacked high. He stopped at a blank stretch of wall. Ran his fingers along the base. Pulled the wall up like a garage door. Flipped on a light.

It was a workout room. Only the center was lit. Shadows hung on the edges. A large mat on the floor. A heavy bag and a speedbag in one corner. Kendo sticks, nunchucks, and the like scattered about. No decoration. A musty smell.

"This is yours?" Christina asked.

"The whole building. It hides this place. The boxes out there are empty. Except for the one with the Ark of the Covenant." Christina looked at him, "I'm kidding," he said.

Miles slipped off his shoes and socks, padded to the center of the mat. Turned toward Christina. She stayed near the door.

"What now?" she asked.

"Now?" Miles said. "Now we go to work."

They worked on defense. Miles preferred Aikido. He incorporated some Muay Thai, judo, jeet kun do, jiu-jitsu. He was patient and exacting. Merciless in sparring. He didn't break bones or dislocate joints. The one bloody nose he gave her was an accident. Beyond that, he beat the living shit of her. Her body was a mass of bruises and welts. She learned to ignore them during morning exercise. In bed, she sometimes held a pillow over her face and cried. She didn't quit.

She got smoother with every discipline. Rarely made the same mistake twice. Miles found himself rooting for her. Against his will

Fall came. Miles took his first job in a while. Berlin. Shane's wife Erica looked in on Christina. She stuck to the routine.

They worked with sticks and nunchucks. He taught her to assemble and disassemble a piece. He didn't let her fire it. He taught her to use a knife. Didn't give her an actual knife. She didn't protest.

They worked through the winter. Miles brought her to the shooting range, also concealed in the warehouse. She was a better shot than Miles expected. She learned to relax. Think of the gun as an extension of her arm. She was a natural.

School was uneventful. Christina attended every day. Did all her homework. No incidents. Teachers let Miles know she was a joy to have in class. Miles didn't respond.

***

Miles sat on the couch, a movie on the TV. Christina plunked down next to him. They kept their eyes on the screen.

"Homework done?" *Miles asked.*

"Before we went to the gym."

Christina studied Miles's face. The lighting was low. Miles liked it that way. He was aware of her proximity.

"What movie is this?" *she asked.*

"Dr. Zhivago. David Lean."

Christina nodded, as if she understood this. For all she knew, David Lean was the guy behind the counter at the convenience store. Miles knew this. The scene was on a streetcar.

"Is it a good movie?" she asked.

"Not one of Lean's best. But it's always worth a watch."

"What's it about?"

"Hard to say in twenty-five words or less. It's a love story between a poet and the woman who inspires him."

"That wasn't so hard."

"Well, you could describe Hamlet as 'Depressed guy can't sack up and kill his uncle,' but it doesn't give you the flavor of the thing."

She waved toward a handsome, swarthy guy with a mustache. "Is that Zhivago?"

"It is. The blonde at the front of the frame is Lara. He's going to fall in love with her."

"They aren't in love now?"

"Not yet." On screen, Zhivago and Lara brushed against each other. The image cut to the trolley pole bumping the electrical line, creating a spark. "But they will be."

They watched the movie in silence.

***

Shane asked Miles to meet him at McKenzie's. They found a table near the back.

"You remember Cheng?" Shane asked. "From Hong Kong?"

"Not fondly."

163

"The feeling it's mutual. He's back in business. And looking for you."

A glib reply—Let him*—sprang to Miles's lips. He bit it back. He felt tired. This shit wasn't supposed to be complicated. Somebody hired him, paid him half up front. Miles did the job. They paid the other half. Simple. Only a toad like Cheng could screw that up.*

"Does he know how to get to me?" Miles asked.

"Not yet. But…"

"But?"

Shane scratched his jowls. "Shit can change."

"Meaning?"

"The girl. Sorry. Christina."

Shit. "Cheng knows about Christina?"

"That's what I hear."

"But he doesn't know where I'm at," Miles said.

"No."

"Have we covered our tracks with Christina?"

"Far as I know. You're both off the grid. But if the wrong guy gets the right info, hands it over to Cheng…"

Shane didn't have to finish. He was right. No such thing as completely covering your tracks. Maybe Cheng had a contact. FBI, MI5, CIA, MI6. Things could get interesting.

"I can handle it," Miles said, half-believing it. Shane said nothing. Miles asked him, "You okay?"

Shane set his beer down. "You sure it isn't time to hang it up?"

"Get out of The Life?"

"Yeah." He took a breath. Gathered strength. "You used to be careful. The Discipline. That's what you called it. But you didn't take out that guy in Phoenix. We're still digging out from under that. And you brought home a souvenir."

"Easy there, Kemo Sabe."

Shane held up his hands. "You want to stay in The Life and keep her around? It's a...what do you call it?"

"Achilles's Heel?"

"Yeah. A big one. The second somebody figures it out, they're going to use it against you." He took another sip, gaining some liquid courage. "I don't want to seem ungrateful. I made plenty of money with you. I got a nice place. My kids are going to college. Erica and I have enough to retire on. And you? You got investments. You got off-shore accounts. You got protection, and you got a fuckload of money. You don't need to keep doing this."

Miles didn't say anything. Shane was right. The shit in Phoenix cost him. The shit with Cheng cost him. He did have plenty to retire on. And that tired feeling kept coming over him. Yes, he was good at what he did. No, he didn't know what to do next. Maybe it was healthier to take time and figure out. Maybe he needed to add that to The Discipline. You're indestructible. Until you aren't.

"Maybe I'll think about it," Miles said.

Shane let it go. He downed the rest of his beer, poured himself another.

"Christina's doing well?" Shane asked.

"Real well."

"What happens next? After you're done training her?"

Miles finished his own beer. "That's an excellent question."

He didn't go into it. Shane knew better than to ask. They listened to the jukebox. Drank their beers. Said nothing else.

***

Spring came. Graduation was a few months off. The sessions at the warehouse continued. Christina mastered the forms. Picked up moves Miles didn't teach her. She was good. She had the potential to be better than Miles. If she wanted that.

Evening in the apartment. Miles preparing dinner. He cut up vegetables, placed them on the breakfast bar, a dip alongside them. Christina snacked while Miles worked. Candles were lit. Miles liked to do that every now and again.

"I'm almost done with school," she said, casually dipping a carrot. "What comes next?"

"College. But you don't seem all that interested."

Her brow furrowed. "I thought I was going to work with you."

"I've been training you. Doesn't mean we're Batman and Robin."

"What am I supposed to do?"

"I found my own way into The Life. You'll find your own way."

She was hurt. Miles could sense it. He couldn't tell her the truth. Couldn't tell her she was safer without him. And he was safer without her. She wouldn't want to hear it.

"What a fucking waste," she said. "Why did you bother?"

"You asked me to train you."

"I meant getting me out of Phoenix."

She walked down the hallway. Slammed the bedroom door behind her. Miles set aside the knife. Stared at the empty kitchen.

***

Three nights later, they came for him. Miles was walking home from McKenzie's. He'd had beers with Shane. He was going to stop at a convenience store, get a bottle of iced tea. He spotted them from the corner of his eye. Parked halfway down the block, stuffed into a Lincoln Town Car. Asian, dressed in black. Cold eyes. Staring his direction. Miles appeared to ignore them, went inside the store.

The place was empty. The clerk was in his early twenties. Skinny, long hair, scraggly goatee. He sat on a stool, reading a magazine. Behind a glass partition, thick as a concrete block. A picture window at the front, covered in iron bars. Harsh fluorescent lights. Grit on the black-and-white floors. Stains on the beige walls. Miles moved casually. Grabbed an iced tea from the cooler. Strolled to the counter. The kid looked annoyed. Set aside his magazine. Miles put the bottle on the counter.

"You got a backdoor to this place?" Miles asked.

"Why?"

"I'm going to need it. And you're going to want to get down."

167

The kid thought Miles was joking. "What's going on?"

"In about thirty seconds, some guys are going to come in here. They're going to pretend they're robbing the store. They're actually trying to kill me."

The kid tried smiling. "C'mon…"

Miles slipped the Beretta out of the shoulder holster. "Trust me. Get down."

The kid went white. He fumbled for something behind the counter. "I'll call the cops."

"Probably a good idea. But this will be over by the time they get here." He pointed to a hallway on the other side of the cooler. "Backdoor is that way?" The kid dropped like a pebble in the water.

Miles moved to the hallway. He could run out the backdoor. Maybe they had it covered. He couldn't take a chance.

He knelt near an endcap. He kept an eye on the front. He'd see them come in. They wouldn't see him. He was outgunned. Outnumbered. He'd need to surprise them.

The first one came through the door. Uzi in one hand. Miles shot him through the mouth. He pitched forward. Crashed through a display of salty snacks.

Miles dropped to the floor. His movements felt slow. He closed his eyes, took a deep breath. The others came in. Opened fire. Bullets ripped apart the displays, the cooler.

The bullets stopped. Eye of the storm. Miles snuck a look. Three of them. He moved from the endcap to the cooler. He took out a second Berretta.

Miles popped up. Fired both guns. A gunmen fell. The other two ducked down. Miles slipped behind a shelf of pharmaceuticals. Glanced toward the back hallway.

Two down, two to go. Maybe somebody outside. Miles moved near the front. He stayed low. The gunmen had probably spread out. He couldn't go through the front door. Couldn't get through the backdoor. He'd have to shoot his way out.

A wire display rack nearby. It looked light enough. Miles grabbed it. Chucked it toward the front counter. It clattered on the floor. Sounded like a bomb going off. A gunman fired. Exposed his position. Miles put one through his ear.

The last gunman kept a cooler head. He slid into the opening at the end of the aisle. Had a clear shot. Opened fire. Miles wasn't there.

Miles moved back to the cooler. The gunman had his location. Miles might have one shot. Picture it, he told himself. Picture where he'll be. Get off the first shot. Don't miss.

The gunman came around the corner. Miles got off three shots. All three caught the gunman in the face. He fell back, destroying a magazine rack.

Miles passed the cooler. Stepped over the gunman's body. Disappeared down the back hallway. He didn't check on the kid at the counter.

Miles came out the backdoor. He was shot in the right shoulder. He spun around. The Berretta chit the ground. Another shot. Left leg, halfway up the thigh. Miles hit the pavement. His right arm unable to move. His left arm pinned under him. No way to reach the other Berretta.

He took quick breaths. Tried to focus. They were single shots. The guy didn't have an Uzi. Not that it mattered now.

The gunman came into view. T-shirt, jeans, light coat. Had Miles dead to rights. Savoring it. He extended the gun. Aimed.

Three shots. Three splotches of blood on the gunman's shirt. He collapsed to the pavement. His legs folded awkwardly under him.

Miles rolled on his back, looked down the alley. Someone came from the shadows. She lowered her Berretta, rushed to Miles. She knelt beside him. Her eyes flashed with excitement.

"Are you all right?" Christina asked.

"I will be. We've got to get out of here."

She helped him up. He leaned heavily on her. They rushed, as best they could, down the alley. Christina was smiling.

"Still think you don't need a partner?" she asked.

***

"Here's the deal," Robbie says, "you sit there and say nothing. I do the talking. The trench coat looks good."

This is what I get for working a dream job and not being busy during the day. I'd rather be out in Brooklyn Point, seeing what I can find. Instead, I'm here, helping out my idiot friends for God knows what reason.

I'm at a table in the restaurant area at The Tav, wearing a hand-me-down trench coat from my father and feeling like an asshole. For his part, Robbie wears a white shirt, a cheap tie, and tan slacks. The same thing he usually wears at work (save for his name tag). It covers a frame that resembles one of those in-shape/out-of-shape guys you'd see back in the Fifties: powerful arms and chest looming over a beer gut. His hair is close-cropped, making his skull look simian in appearance.

"The guy's going to be here any minute," Robbie says. "You ready to go?"

"Sure," I say. "What is the meeting about?"

"Can't tell you that."

Oh, for garden seed… "Robbie, I'm going to be *in* the meeting. You sure you don't want to tell me what it's about?"

"No. Orders from Mike. I'm supposed to play this…ah, what's the word for it? When you can't really tell somebody something?"

"Close to the vest?"

"You sure? Sounds a little fruity."

"Trust me," I say, knowing Robbie will not, in fact, trust me.

Lyle Wills walks in a few minutes later. He wears a rumpled gray suit and a black overcoat. He runs a hand through his soon-to-be nonexistent hair. Robbie rises to meet him, giving me a subtle hand gesture telling me to remain

171

seated. Wills sits across from me, keeping his coat on. He's sniffling, his face is red, and his eyes are glassy. I assume he's suffering from a cold (or an advanced cocaine habit). I fix a glare on him. (It seems like what I'm supposed to do here).

Robbie tilts his head toward me. "This is Carson. He's with the bureau."

Wills's eyes get wide. "*The* bureau?"

"Is there another?" Robbie asks.

"So, this *is* serious."

"Bet your ass," Robbie says. "We been after this guy for months. You up for helping us?"

Wills wipes sweat from his brow. "Yeah, I am."

"Good to know."

"How are we going to do this?"

"Simple," Robbie says. "You set up a meeting with Griffin. Tell him you're going to bring The Method. We'll work with you. Take Griffin down. Simple as that."

Wills looks at me. "And the bureau will back us up?"

"We will," Robbie says, turning to me. "Right, Mr. Carson?"

For a moment, I'm panicked. I haven't been briefed on an answer. Robbie tilts his chin down, giving me the slightest of nods. I give Wills my best cop face (which isn't much).

"We'll back you to the hilt," I tell him.

His body practically folds in on itself with relief. "That's good to know. You guys are going to nail that bastard."

"Absolutely," Robbie says. "Carson and the boys at Langley are good to go."

Wills's face clouds. I pretend to scratch my nose, hiding the lower half of my face. I speak out of the corner of my mouth.

"Quantico," I say. I stretch my arms, ducking my mouth behind my left one. "The FBI is in Quantico. The CIA is in Langley." I drop my arms. "Sometimes, there's cooperation between agencies. We keep the boys at Langley in the loop."

Wills buys it. "Any idea when the bust is going to happen?"

"We'll let you know," Robbie says.

A server finally comes around to take our order. Wills orders a double scotch. Robbie is content with a beer. I'd love to order a martini, but I should stay in character. I ask for a club soda with a slice of lime. (I don't even like club soda. Come to think of it, I don't like lime.) We've just settled in when a voice rumbles across the restaurant.

"Hey Joe!" Freddie says. "I need to talk to you!"

Freddie is waddling with purpose toward the restaurant area. Robbie tries to remain calm (though he *does* bite through his lower lip, drawing some blood). Wills's eyes narrow.

"Joe?" he asks.

"Joe Carson," I say. "Did you think my first name was *Agent?*"

Wills raises a hand, backing off. I get up from the table and cut Freddie off. I'm hoping to keep this conversation private. (Though, given the boom in Freddie's voice, what exactly constitutes *private?*)

"Who's this asshole bothering Carol?" Freddie asks.

Freddie has always been protective of Carol. It's an open secret (at least among my friends) that he's got a crush on her and simply doesn't have the courage to act on it. It's endearing in a way. Freddie is a one-man wrecking crew, but his greatest fear is a skinny woman, barely more than five-and-a-half feet tall. This unrequited attraction takes the form of Freddie acting as a big brother to Carol, whether she likes it or not. (Though I get the feeling Carol kind of likes it.)

"You're going to have to narrow that down a little, Freddie," I say. "A lot of assholes bother Carol."

"The guy bothering her on her date. That shit ain't gonna fly."

No, but Fabio's carcass might, if Freddie has his way. "It's just a guy she was seeing. He's a little obsessed, but he's harmless."

"She shouldn't have to deal with that. It ain't right. I see that guy in here again, it's his ass. You know what I'm saying?"

"Absolutely. Don't worry. This thing will blow over." Or it will just blow. Could go either way.

Freddie eyeballs me, then makes his way back into the bar area. I return to the table. Wills seems curious.

"What was going on there?" he asks.

I look to Robbie, who has nothing to suggest. "Just dealing with an informant," I say.

"The big guy with the cornrows?" Wills asks. "He's an informant?"

"I've said too much already," I tell him.

"But I—"

"Or do you want this to get ugly?"

Robbie scowls at Wills. That and Freddie's general appearance is enough to back Wills off. He mumbles his apologies and finishes his scotch. He thanks us and departs (leaving us to pay the check). Once he's disappeared from view, Robbie claps a hand on my shoulder.

"Quick thinking," he says. "You should be proud of yourself."

"I'd be prouder if you told me what was going on."

"Can't do it. Just trust that you did good."

Robbie gets up from the table, wishes me a good day, and takes off. He gives me no new information. However, he *does* leave me with the check.

Same old, same old.

***

I decide to go up to Brooklyn Point and, hopefully, chat with Warren Newson's aunt. The smart thing would be to call ahead and make sure she's home. But I don't want to take a chance on her putting me off. If I show up at her house, there's more likelihood she'll talk to me. At least, that's the plan. (My plans tend to go awry.)

It feels weird to be doing this alone. I'm used to relying on Mike and his endless fountain of bullshit. (You don't need to thank me for that image. The work is its own reward.) My Saturn Ion protests this whole idea. But it agrees to go along, condemned to a life of servitude.

Sophie Walker lives in a nice neighborhood on the west side of the city. It's a little rambler on a street of little ramblers; all probably built during the post-WWII boom. It's gray with white trim. There's a maple tree out front and an attached garage on the side. I park on the street and stroll up to the front door. There's a light breeze, but in this weather, it's enough to send a chill down my back. Thankfully, Sophie Walker answers the door promptly.

On a guess, she's in her late sixties, maybe early seventies. She's a plump woman with a crown of auburn hair. She wears a light sweater over an orange blouse and a flannel skirt. She scrutinizes me, probably hoping I'm not a Jehovah's Witness. Let's hope my intro goes well.

"Hi, you don't know me, but—"

"You're Joe Davis, aren't you?" she says, her face lighting up. "*Cup o' Joe*? I read your column all the time." This would be a lot more fun if Carol were here to roll her eyes. But I'll take whatever opening this gives me. "I'm so sorry. Please come in. Would you like a cup of coffee?"

"If you have some made."

"I do. Have a seat."

The house is nice and cozy. There's a little dining nook, just off the living room. Said living room dominates the place. There's a fireplace on one wall and a piano on another. A couple of bedrooms are visible beyond. A picture window looks out on the street. The floors are hardwood, various prints cover the walls, and a few houseplants sit atop the piano. The furniture is clean but worn. Everything looks as if it's been here a while. Sophie directs me to a small table in the dining nook and bustles into the kitchen.

"Not that I'm not happy to meet you," she calls to me, "but what brings you by?"

"I'm looking into something."

"For a column?"

"Maybe. It depends on what I find."

Sophie returns with two mugs of coffee. Mine is a tan-and-brown mug with the silhouette of a moose. Hers is a checkerboard sort of arrangement. My mom once had a tablecloth resembling that pattern. Sophie sits across from me.

"How is it I can help you?" she asks.

"I'm curious about your nephew. Warren Newson."

Sophie's hands freeze on the coffee mug. Something—maybe shock, maybe sadness, maybe panic—flashes in her eyes. "Why do you want to know about Warren?" she asks.

"His name came up in connection with a murder."

"That's not possible."

"I don't mean as a suspect," I say.

I give her the broad strokes. A woman was killed at an abandoned arcade. I had reason to check into the murder. (I leave out the part about the gunman.) While doing that, I stumbled across Warren's name in an arcade game.

"I had a friend look into Warren's background," I say. "She came across your name. And that's why I'm here."

"This woman who was killed. Is she a friend of yours?"

I consider that. "No. But I want to know what happened to her. Is it okay to discuss Warren?"

"Of course. Nobody's asked about him for so long." She walks over to a bookshelf built into the wall. "Warren was my sister's son. They only lived a few blocks away. I saw Warren a lot. I was a second mother to him." She murmurs just loud enough for me to hear. "Maybe a better mother to him." She picks out a photo album and comes back to the table. "He was a good boy. Smart. Liked books and movies. He wasn't much of a student, but I think that's because he was restless."

She sets the book in front of me and points at a photo. A skinny teenage kid with a blue striped shirt and a bad haircut. His face is round, and his eyes distracted. His awkward phase has extended deep into his teen years. He's a geek like so many other geeks I knew in high school. Myself included. He stands next to a sandy haired kid flashing a peace sign.

"Nice looking kid," I say. "Who's his friend?"

"Simon. Warren's best friend." Sophie's eyes linger on the photo. She closes the album and sits down. "Warren went into the army after high school. We stayed in touch as best we could. But he went into military intelligence or something like that. He'd never tell me where he was or what he was doing. Eventually, we lost touch. I don't know where he is." She gazes out the window. "I do miss him, though."

"You haven't heard from him at all? Has anyone?"

"I don't think so. If Simon had, I think he would have said something."

"Simon still lives around here?"

"Yes. I see him at the grocery store every now and again. He's a good kid. Well, I guess he isn't a kid anymore."

"There's no one else Warren would be in touch with?"

"Not that I know of. All his other friends have moved away. He didn't really have any girlfriends. His parents are gone. Just Simon and me."

This is starting to feel like a dead end. (There might be a pun in there. Pardon me if there is.) Sophie folds her hands on the table. I get the feeling this brings up old memories. Maybe old regrets. I take another sip of coffee. It's of the Folger's/Maxwell House variety—anathema to a coffee snob like me—but on a cold day, it's not half-bad.

"There's a woman named Grace Jelinski," I say. "She worked at a real estate agency around here. Wilryan Realty."

"I've heard of them."

"Grace disappeared a few weeks ago."

Sophie's brow knits. "Is she the woman who was killed?"

"No. That was…someone else. I don't suppose you've heard of Grace."

"No, I haven't."

"She wouldn't have any connection to Warren?"

"Not that I know of."

Nuts. I'm chasing a ghost here. Warren Newson goes into the army and disappears, save for a box of his stuff at Eli's

Arcade and his name in a videogame he'd apparently mastered. Okay, try the Hail Mary.

"Did Warren ever mention someone named Deirdre?" I ask. "This was the woman who was killed."

"I've never heard that name. How would Warren know her?"

She's being honest and not accusatory. I'm not a hundred percent certain how to answer that question. Partly because I don't want to explain my relationship (such as it was) with Deirdre. Partly because I'm not sure how Warren fits into it. I flip a hand.

"I don't know," I say. "I found Warren's name at Eli's Arcade. That's where she was killed."

"Eli's Arcade. Oh my goodness, I haven't heard about that place in years. Warren and Simon spent so much time there. And so much money. No matter how many times I told them it was a waste."

"And Warren stayed in touch with Simon after he went into the army?" I ask.

"Yes. Warren came home on leave a few times. He'd stop in to see me, and he mentioned spending time with Simon. They would be hit some of their old places. They liked to go to their old elementary school. Brooklyn Heights."

"Really?"

"It's been closed for years. The city doesn't know what to do with it. I'm not sure how the boys got in there. And I didn't ask."

"Does Simon live close by?" I ask.

"About six or seven blocks away. Over on Clark Street. I'm not sure I have the address."

"I can look it up. What's his last name?"

"Gray. Like the color of my house. Simon Gray."

I make a mental note (though it's not difficult to remember a name like *Simon Gray*). For now, I've got all the information I can get. We chat about the weather and my column while I finish my coffee. Before I leave, a thought occurs to me.

"When I checked out Eli's Arcade," I tell her, "I found a box of stuff belonging to Warren."

Sophie's eyes light up. "To Warren?"

"Yes. It was a collection of books and movies. The books had his name inside. I took them with me. I probably shouldn't have. They're out in the car. Would like them?"

Sophie looks down. Her voice cracks a little. "Oh my. Yes, I would like that very much."

I waste no time going out to the car and collecting the box. Per Sophie's direction, I bring it into one of the bedrooms at the back. (A guest room that probably functions as her office.) She tells me she'll go through it later and thanks me for bringing it.

"I hope you find who killed that girl," she says.

"I hope so, too. I'm sorry if bringing up Warren's name is painful."

"It's alright. You had to ask." She looks back toward the box. "And I think you made it up to me. Don't you?"

I'll let others decide that. I thank Sophie for her time and head out. For her sake, suddenly, I want to find out what happened to Deirdre. And to Warren. Maybe she would appreciate it. Maybe there would be some kind of justice.

That would be nice, wouldn't it?

CHAPTER EIGHT

Miles recovered from the wounds. A less-than-honest doctor did the work. He was paid well. Miles stopped taking jobs. Decided to draw on his retirement funds. He took Christina as his partner.

"What does being a partner mean?" she asked. They were sitting in Miles's apartment, three nights after graduation.

Miles was on the couch, trying to find a comfortable position. "You do the work. I'm your handler."

"You're going to be my Shane? You think you can do that?"

"Who do you think taught Shane?"

She felt something almost foreign. Something she hadn't felt since Phoenix. A lightness. An optimism. It felt like something she'd learned to live without. Happiness.

"What happens to Shane?" she asked.

"We'll deal with that. Right now, we need to get out of Brooklyn."

Miles looked toward the whiskey cabinet. He was shit out of luck. Wouldn't mix with the meds. Cheng was going to pay for that, too.

Cheng would lie low for a while. He had to re-staff. He'd be scared shitless. Thinking Miles was coming from him. He was half-right.

Miles sat up. The pain rolled through him. He grimaced. Christina touched him on the shoulder. Miles looked away.

"A thing you need to understand," he said. "You don't get caught. Rule number one. Get rid of anything that might compromise you. Freedom is survival. That's The Discipline. You understand?"

"I do."

"You might get tested. Not passing that test? Not an option. The mistakes you make in this business aren't the kind you learn from."

"I get it."

"Good. Get some sleep. More training tomorrow.."

Christina stood up. "Are you going to be okay?"

"Been worse than this."

"Good," she said. "I don't want to cart you to that doctor again."

Christina walked to her room. She unzipped her sweat jacket. She looked back at Miles. The jacket slid off her shoulder. She stepped into her room. Miles held the look.

***

Shane met Miles at the warehouse. They had to sell it, get Miles out of his apartment lease. Shane walked into the gym. Miles was in a metal folding chair, parked in the middle of the floor. An empty chair across from him. The rest of the room was dark. Shane took a seat.

"No training tonight?" Shane asked.

"Gave Christina the night off."

Shane took a nervous breath. There was a weird vibe. "Got any beer around here?"

"No."

Miles's face was stern. No trace of glib. Sweat soaked Shane's armpits and neckline.

"How should we—" Shane said.

"I know it was you."

Shane ran a dry tongue over dry lips. "What do you—?"

"Cheng's guys knew where to find me. They hadn't been following me. They didn't just happen to hit a moving target. We were having beers at McKenzie's. They knew where to find me. You told them."

"C'mon, Miles, I—"

"Don't. Don't make it worse." Miles leaned toward him. "You got scared. You wanted out. You thought they could do it for you." Miles's shoulder twinged. "You were almost right."

Shane looked around. No way out. No way past Miles.

"I tried telling you," he said. "You got sloppy. I had to think about Erica and the kids. I didn't have a choice."

"Actually, you did. You could have come to me and asked out. I would've set you up. You'd be out of it. Safe. But you didn't do that."

"What are you going to do?"

"Erica and the kids will be fine. I guarantee that. And my word counts."

"And me?"

The silence hung in the air. "I won't kill you, Shane. You kept me safe. And you've been a friend."

"You're not going—"

The bullet went through Shane's left eye. He toppled to the floor. Landed at Miles's feet. Christina walked out of the shadows. Her clothes matched the darkness. The Berretta was at her side. She looked down at Shane.

"Too bad," she said. "I liked him."

"I did, too." Miles stood up. "You passed the test."

"Good."

"We need to take care of the body. Think you can handle it?"

"Yeah."

"Good. There's a rubber tub down the hall. We'll start there. We've got to move him."

"That's not going to be easy."

"It won't." Miles walked to the door. "I'd help you. But with the shoulder and the leg..."

"Or maybe you're just an asshole."

"Maybe."

***

"Once upon a time, I thought two men fighting over me would be romantic and exciting," Carol says, stirring sugar into her mug of dark roast. "Turns out it's not all it's cracked up to be."

Sure, it's a cold day (as they all are at the moment). But some hot goss helps. We're at Glacier's, sitting at a table near the back. (It's best to get as far away from the front door as possible.) Carol is on break from work. I lean back in my chair and prop a foot on one knee.

"It might still be romantic," I say. "You just need Chris Pine and Idris Elba fighting over you instead of Frick and Frack."

Carol squares me with a look. "I wouldn't say Jeff is Frick or Frack. And he's not the problem. Fabio is."

I thought as much. I've seen a lot of Fabio lately (to my great consternation) and the only time he shows a sign of life is when he's obsessing over Carol and her new boyfriend. I have to imagine that's trying not only for Carol but for this Jeff guy as well.

"Any new developments?" I ask.

"Oh, yes," Carol says. She sips her latte and dabs her lips. "He's started sending me little gifts, as if that's going to turn my head. Seriously, does he think he's going to win me back with something that shallow?"

"I'll remind you of two things. First, shallow is what Fabio does best. Second, the whole basis of your relationship with him was knocking boots with an attractive piece of man-candy. It doesn't exactly give you the high ground, does it?"

"Still, I've made it clear I'm moving on. Does he expect me to say, 'Oh, since you've bought me a really pretty necklace, that changes everything'?"

My eyebrows go up. "A necklace? Fancy."

"Maybe. But I didn't want anything to do with it. Any of that stuff. The necklace, the flowers, the cashmere scarf. I either destroyed them or I sent them back to Fabio."

I point to her scarf. "Isn't that cashmere?"

"Okay, fine. When in the hell am I going to be able to afford a cashmere scarf?"

"Your integrity inspires us all."

Carol runs a hand through her hair. "It's getting difficult. Jeff *really* wants to beat the hell out of Fabio. I don't know how much longer I can stop him. Especially if Fabio keeps showing up on our dates."

My coffee cup stops shy of my lips. "He's showing up on your dates?"

"We were at the Stone Mill. Jeff gives me an innocent peck. Suddenly, Fabio's at the picture window, screaming that he loves me. Then he starts crying and slides down the window. Everyone in the restaurant was looking at us. I had to hold Jeff back. He wanted to kick Fabio's ass."

"End of story?"

"Not exactly," she says. "Fabio was still in the street when we left. He ran after us, asking me to give him another chance. He said Jeff wasn't right for me. That he and I were meant to be together. Jeff grabbed Fabio's jacket. He wanted to kick his ass. But Fabio had gotten the attention of the whole restaurant. Everyone could see us through the windows. Jeff couldn't do anything in front of witnesses. He gave Fabio a warning and let him go."

"That's a good thing."

"For Fabio maybe. When Jeff and I got back to my place, I wanted to get…active. But he was so pissed off, all he could do was rant and rave about Fabio. I couldn't get him to…"

"Activate?"

"Yeah. When we were having breakfast this morning, he kept asking me where Fabio lives. He was pissed when I wouldn't tell him. He wouldn't kiss me when we left for work."

"He'll get over it. My concern is Fabio. The behavior is kind of creepy."

"If it was anyone else, it might be creepy. With him, it's just pathetic."

There isn't a whole lot to add. Carol will handle Fabio in her own way. Hopefully, he'll still be in one piece when it's all over. Carol has to get back to the office, so we decide to be on our way. She slips on her black coat and joins me in moping toward the front door.

"How's the investigation going?" she asks.

Not as good as I would hope is the simple answer. I wanted to talk to Warren Newson's friend Simon the other night after leaving Sophie's, but he wasn't home. I *did* chat with a neighbor and got an idea when he'll be there.

"I'm going back out to Brooklyn Point tonight," I say. "There's a guy I need to talk to."

I give her the rundown on finding Warren Newson's name, getting some information from Lisa, and chatting with Warren's aunt Sophie. We stop near the door, mainly to avoid going back into the cold. Carol twists her mouth to one side as she thinks.

"Is there any connection between this Warren Newson guy and Deirdre? Or Grace Jelinski?"

"Not that I can find. I'll talk to Simon. See what he knows."

"Good luck to you."

Good luck with this case. Wouldn't that be a nice change of pace?

***

As Sophie mentioned, Simon Gray lives only a few blocks from her. Like her, he lives in a little rambler. He's home this time. Most of the lights are on. The house is surrounded by a chain-link fence in the tiny front yard. The front walk hasn't been shoveled, but there's a trodden path to the side door. The sun is waning (a month ago, it would have been dark by now). I huddle into my coat, walk to the side door, and knock. A moment later, the curtain covering the little window is pulled back. A suspicious face appears. He looks me over, then opens the door.

"Hi," I say, hoping these introductions will be brief. "My name's Joe Davis. I'm a writer. I was hoping we could talk."

"About what?" Simon asks, in a voice that's surprisingly gentle.

"Warren Newson."

He stands there, looking mildly concerned. He's a middle-aged guy with brown hair and a scraggly beard, both flecked with gray. He has a thin mouth and glassy eyes. What I assume are his work clothes—an untucked blue dress shirt and black slacks—hang off his thin frame. After a few seconds, he realizes the cold is filtering in. He steps back.

"Come in," he says, as if being forced into it.

The kitchen is small and lit by fluorescent overhead lights. The linoleum floor could use a sweep and a mop. The small counters are dotted with crumbs and stains. (If you think this bothers me, please remember I've been Mike's friend for twenty years. Filth only bothers me in *my* place.) Simon picks up a whiskey and moves to the faux wood table, as if he has to consider every move. He doesn't offer me a drink. That's a shame. He huddles around his glass.

"You're a writer?" he asks.

"I have a column with *The Daily Bugle*. Have you heard of us?"

"Can't say I have. Sorry."

On the one hand, that's a bummer for *The Bugle*. They probably want to create more inroads in the suburbs. On the other hand, Simon's lack of knowledge regarding exactly what I do for a living gives me a free hand.

"I'm doing some investigation," I say, failing to mention that writing dick jokes is my main function at *The Bugle*. "There was a murder in Brooklyn Point recently."

"I heard about that."

"There might be a connection between the victim and Warren Newson. I'm trying to get some background information on Warren."

Simon knocks back some of the whiskey and pours himself another. "Not sure what I can tell you. I haven't seen Warren in years."

"I talked to his aunt. She said the same thing."

"Sophie's a sweetie. I always liked her." He scratches his beard. "Warren and I were best friends. We graduated and he went into the army. That was that."

"You lost touch?"

"Not right away. We'd do phone calls. He'd come home every now and again. It stayed that way for a few years."

"Then he joined military intelligence?"

"I guess so. He couldn't talk about it. Not long after, I didn't hear from him at all. I didn't know how to get ahold of him. It's too bad. He was a good guy."

"Tell me about him."

Simon sits back in the chair, a slight smile crossing his face. He reminisces about Warren Newson. It's an interesting picture. Warren was a bright and funny, if awkward, kid with an undertone of seriousness. The seriousness came from his upbringing. Simon doesn't go into detail, but he gives me the impression it was a lonely existence. As a result, Warren carried a lot of anger. Sometimes it came out as humor. Sometimes not. He could have gone to college but chose the army instead. Simon wasn't sure about it. Neither was Warren's family.

"The good part was, it didn't change him," he says. "I knew some guys who went into the army and came back complete assholes. But Warren was pretty much the same guy. Like the army didn't affect him at all. He just had shorter hair."

"And he never told you what he was up to?"

"He said it was better if I didn't know."

I've at least got a clearer picture of who Warren Newson was. It still doesn't tell me how he might be connected to all this. I shift in the little chair, which creaks in response.

"Did Warren ever mention somebody named Grace Jelinski?" I ask.

194

Simon snaps me a look. "Not that I remember. Who is she?"

"A person of interest. I don't suppose he ever mentioned someone named Deirdre?"

"Nope. Hate to break this to you, but Warren wasn't much of a ladies' man. At least, not when I knew him. Maybe it changed later." He sips his whiskey. "I honestly couldn't tell you if he's alive or dead. Sophie would know if anybody would, and if she doesn't..." He focuses his bleary eyes on me. "How do *you* know about Warren?"

"I found his name at Eli's Arcade."

"Eli's? Boy, that brings back memories. I'm guessing his name was in the Splatter Troopers game?"

"That was the case. It was the only game left in there."

"I'm not surprised. It was the most popular game back in the day." He sits back. "That all you found there?"

"No. I found a box of books and movies that belonged to Warren. I gave them to Sophie."

"That was good of you."

"Any idea how they might have gotten there?"

Simon takes a moment to think. (I'm guessing it's an effort.) "Nope. That was the thing about Warren. You'd think you knew him. But there was always a part of himself he kept away from people. Wouldn't tell you what he was up to."

He goes to the freezer, tosses fresh ice cubes into his glass, and pours himself a refill. Still no offer to share.

"You have any mementos of Warren?" I ask.

"I might."

He wanders out of the kitchen, weaving slightly. I pick up the bottle and fight temptation. (C'mon, one sip. He'd never know.) Simon comes back into the kitchen, holding a yearbook. He hands it to me, then drops into his chair.

"This is all I kept. It's from our senior year."

I page through it. There isn't much here. Warren appears in his senior photo only. Ditto Simon. There aren't many signatures. I'm guessing Warren and Simon had a fairly exclusive social circle. In fact, there's only one dedication of any length. It's signed by John Tuttle. But there's no photo of this guy in the book.

"Who's John Tuttle?" I ask.

"Warren. It was a name he used. If he was in trouble and someone needed a name, he'd give them John Tuttle. I think he got it off a TV show."

"*M*A*S*H*."

"I'll take your word on it."

I set the book aside. "Sophie said you and Warren used to visit your old elementary school."

"Brooklyn Heights. We'd hang out on the playground if the weather was decent. When it wasn't, Warren knew a way to get into the gym. We'd shoot baskets and talk. Maybe drink a little. Hell, no one else was using the school. Might as well make ourselves at home."

I tap my fingers on the table. "Any other places you guys used to hang out?"

"The Iron Gate Mall."

"Is that in Brooklyn Point?"

"Yeah. Stretching things to call it a mall. It was just a little square with a pizza joint, a movie theatre, and a drug store. Great place to grab a slice and hang out. Maybe go to a movie. Warren liked movie magazines. The drug store had a pretty good selection. There's not much to Brooklyn Point. We found our kicks where we could."

"I grew up in a small town. You don't have to explain it to me." I try to be casual. "Is the Iron Gate Mall still there?"

"In name only. It shut down years ago. One of those off-brand churches built a space in the parking lot. The mall itself is still there. Just sitting empty."

That isn't much to go on. But Warren Newson's name has a tendency to turn up in abandoned places. (Hey, one in a row, right?) Besides, I probably shouldn't leave any particular stone unturned. It may be worth a look. Not that I have to share that with Simon.

"What do you think happened to Warren?" I ask.

"I don't know. Something tells me he's dead. He would have at least stayed in touch with Sophie. That's the only explanation I can think of."

The drawback to all this nonsense I've been investigating the last few years is that I start to sense when somebody's not telling me everything. I get that same vibe from Simon. But you can't ask follow up questions about a vibe. And he's been willing to answer the questions I *have* asked. I thank him for his time. He stands and steadies himself.

"You think they'll find out who killed that woman?" he asks.

Funny, I already know who killed her. It's more a matter of why and what she was up to. And what the likes of Warren Newson and Grace Jelinski have to do with it. But I don't need to share any of that with Simon. (Hey, *I'm* allowed to not tell people everything, right?)

"We can always hope," I say.

I bid Simon good night. When I get to the car, I catch a glimpse of him in the window, his drink still in his hand. At least he gets to hang out in a nice warm house tonight. Me? I've got one more errand to run before my night is over.

CHAPTER NINE

Graham Cheng had two years to live. He didn't know it at the time. Miles sent Christina on other jobs. Waiting until she was ready.

They moved to south Florida. A place criminals could move among criminals without being noticed. They settled in Jupiter, a glorified suburb of West Palm Beach. Easy access to Miami. They found neighboring one-bedroom condos. Small but with everything they needed.

There was a movie on at Miles's place. Fellini's 8 ½. Christina couldn't follow it. Miles enjoyed it. She liked hearing him discuss it. Miles refilled his whiskey.

"I've got to book the flight to Hong Kong," he said, "You can use the Kara name again. When Cheng goes, it's going to draw attention. We've got to make sure you're covered."

He dropped back onto the sofa. Christina studied him. He was still lean and athletic. No ill effects from the bullet wounds. But he was different. He'd lost the tension in his face. The old placid look had been a shield, covering a current running through him. Now, it was genuine.

Miles reached for the remote. Christina snatched it first. She curled up in her corner of the sofa.

"Is Miles your real name?" she asked.

"No."

"I'm guessing Slayne isn't your real last name?"

"It's not. But it is somebody's real last name. Guy I knew in the army. He's dead, so I figured he wouldn't need it."

"What is your real name?"

Miles held his drink in front of him. "Warren. My real name is Warren."

A corner of Christina's mouth rose. "That's a nice name."

"Never cared for it."

"Where did you come up with Miles?"

"I always liked that name. I don't even think of myself as Warren anymore. Miles is the name I created. That's who I am."

"Interesting." She leaned toward him. "What's the last name?"

"Newson."

"Ah." Christina offered her hand. "Pleased to finally meet you, Warren Newson."

"Keep it between us. I don't want to have to kill you."

"Like you could." Miles's face darkened. She put a hand on his leg. "I'm kidding."

"It's not that."

He drained the whiskey, went to the kitchen for a refill. Christina followed, tossing aside the remote.

"What is it?" she asked.

"Hong Kong won't be easy. Cheng's got guys around him. He'll be hard to get to."

"You told me that."

"It's just...different."

Miles walked around the breakfast bar. Christina stepped into his path.

"You're worried," she said.

"Maybe."

"You don't think I can do it?"

"I think you can. But there's always the unexpected. Keeps me up at night. I don't..."

He looked at the floor. Christina cupped his chin.

"You don't want anything to happen to me," she said. "Because..."

He pulled away. "Because I've had too much to drink."

Christina grabbed Miles's shoulders. "Don't do that. You don't want anything to happen to me because..."

Miles held her eyes. "Because I care about you."

"Because you love me?"

"Because I care about you."

She decided this was good enough. "Kiss me."

He did. When they parted, she laid her forehead against his. Her fingers traced his arms. She looked toward the bedroom.

"Let's go in there," she said.

Miles set the glass down. He led her to the bedroom, ignoring the movie.

***

Christina wasn't experienced. She didn't lack enthusiasm. For Miles, it was strange. He had learned to cultivate distance. He could lock away a part of himself. Even during an intimate act. This time, he couldn't. He held her, stroked her hair, looked into her eyes. Afterwards, they lay together, tangled in each other.

"Are you okay?" he asked.

Her eyes were bright in the darkness. "I'm perfect."

He kissed the top of her head. "This feels weird. I never figured out what we're supposed to be."

"You don't want to feel incestuous?"

"That would be nice. Takes the edge off, you understand."

"I do."

Miles closed his eyes. Christina rested her chin on his chest.

"Have you ever been in love, Miles?" she asked.

"Does lusting after Salma Hayek count?"

"That's a crush, not love. There's no risk."

Miles's heart rate picked up. He hoped she couldn't sense it.

"I shouldn't have let you read those romance novels," he said.

She swatted his chest. "You know it's true, don't you?"

"Yeah, I do," he said. "I remember one time, I was on a date with this woman. We went back to my place, had a good time."

"You're telling me this while we're in bed? Read the room, darling."

Miles ignored her. "Middle of the night, I got up and went to the bathroom. I looked at myself in the mirror. All night with this woman, I'd been joking, smiling, having a good time. That wasn't the guy in the mirror. I started wondering: is this the real me and the other guy is a mask? Or is the other guy real and this *is the mask?"*

"What was the answer?"

"I'll let you know when I figure it out."

They lay in silence. Neither of them dozed.

"I want you to call me Warren from now on," he said.

"I thought you hated that name."

"I do. But Miles isn't real. I invented him. Warren is who I really am."

"You want people to call you Warren?"

"No. I want you *to call me Warren. Everyone else can call me Miles."*

Christina accepted that. "I need a new name, too. For a new life. I think I figured one out."

"What is it?"

She laid her arm across his chest. "Deirdre."

***

After leaving Simon's, I pull over and do some thinking while the car warms up (not fast enough for my taste). I don't want to drive back to St. Paul right away. Deirdre was checking out Eli's Arcade when she was killed. If Warren Newson is connected to this, she might have been checking out his old haunts. It's just a matter of selecting which one. I drive past Brooklyn Heights Elementary, but there's a cop car patrolling the neighborhood. I try the Iron Gate Mall instead.

The mall is on the east side of Brooklyn Point. It shares a parking lot with The Church of The New Hope, a squat building that could pass for a post office. The mall is made of cement blocks with wooden trim. There are (or were) four stores built around a little square gathering area in the middle. The entrances to all the stores are boarded up. I'm not sure how I'm going to get inside. I wish Mike was here. (And how often do I say that?)

I circle the mall. Snow is piled high on the edges of the lot, the ghost of snowstorms past. Everything appears to be deserted. I park and sit for a while. No one comes or goes. The night is getting colder. I might as well take a chance. I'm not able to pick the locks, so this will require brute force. (And how often do I say that?) I take a tire iron from the trunk.

The pizza joint is the first stop. I tap the tire iron on the door. The glass shatters, made brittle by the cold. A layer of plywood lies behind it. I kick it a couple times. It gives slightly.

Batter up.

I line up the tire iron and try to swing like my dad taught me: elbow up, nice and level, step into it. The plywood gives way slightly. Vibrations from the impact run up my arm. Thank goodness I'm wearing gloves. I try another swing. The plywood mostly gives way. One more. It gives way entirely.

I switch on the flashlight on my phone and step inside. The restaurant isn't large. A host station stands to the right of the entrance. A few tables are stacked against the wall. The heat isn't on. (Apparently, the pipes have permission to freeze.). I try the light switch. Nothing.

The kitchen is halfway across the restaurant, along the right wall. I push through the stainless-steel double doors. A large pizza oven sits on the far side. Most of the other equipment is gone, save for a rusting sink. Grit covers the floors. There are stains on the walls. I walk around but don't see anything. I even open the door to the pizza oven, just in case. Nothing. I step back into the main room.

Someone stands in the doorway to the restaurant. I jump the second I see them. There's a silhouette of a guy with a ponytail. That might be a gun in his hand. He steps forward. He has a slight limp. It's Angel, the gunman who broke into my apartment.

"Hi," I say. I have to open the conversation somehow. He doesn't answer right away. "How did you find me?"

"Followed you. Been following you." He raises the gun toward my face. "Grace Jelinski."

I try to take a breath. Nothing there. "I don't know where she is. I can't help you."

"Then you aren't any good to me."

I dive to the floor just as he fires. It sounds like a cannon blast in the quiet of the restaurant. I'm covered in dust but otherwise unpunctured. Angel fires again. The bullet pings off the floor near me. Everything in my line of sight is shaking, like a Michael Bay film (only worse, if that's possible). I get up on all fours and crawl, looking for something. A weapon? An exit? My body is moving faster than my brain.

Another shot. This one clips my peacoat, but not my person. I have to do something. I can't outrun a bullet. I do the only thing I can think of: I chuck my phone at Angel.

I don't have a good arm under the best of circumstances, but providence is with me here. The phone hits Angel in the cheek. He shouts a word in Spanish. (Going to guess it's NSFW. At least most people's W.) He brings a hand up to his face. He still has the gun, but it's pointing at the floor. A second later, I'm on my feet and covering ground. I lower a shoulder and crash into Angel's midsection.

We hit the floor. The gun slips out of his hand. I roll off him and look for it. Angel grabs me by the collar and throws me backwards. I slide a few feet. He searches for the gun, moving well for a guy with a bad wheel.

I crawl toward the front door. My hand comes down on something. The tire iron I used to break in here. I get to my feet. Angel stalks toward me. I swing the tire iron. He puts his hands up, instinctively. The tire iron crashes into his wrist. He lets out a scream, spitting out another less-than-family-friendly word in Spanish. He bends at the waist, clutching his hand.

Angel's foot lashes out. It kicks me in the right knee. An electric shock of pain rolls up my leg. I hit the floor again. (Hello, dust mites, my old friends…) I clutch my knee.

Angel stands over me. He has the gun in his left hand. Not sure if he's a good shot with his left, but at this range, he doesn't need to be. I've got no place to go.

I close my eyes. Two shots ring out. I flinch, waiting for the pain. But I feel nothing. Something hits the floor next to me. I open my eyes. Angel is looking at me, surprised. There's a bullet hole between his eyes.

I slide away and get into a sitting position, trying to catch my breath. There's another figure in the doorway. It starts toward me. Boot heels click on the floor, resonating in the still air. The figure moves into the thin light. I recognize the honey-colored hair. The cool blues eyes settle on me. A slight smile twists her mouth.

"Hello, darling."

PART TWO

A COLD AND A BROKEN HALLELUJAH

CHAPTER TEN

Deirdre returned from Hong Kong. She was in perfect condition. Which was more than you could say for Graham Cheng's organization. Cheng was dead. So were his top lieutenants, most of his foot soldiers. Smalltime operators moved in like scavenger birds to pick the bones. Calls for Deirdre's services increased. So did her asking price.

Miles and Deirdre maintained separate residences. Sometimes, they spent days in each other's company. The outside world didn't exist. Then they'd go back to business.

Miles tried to give Deirdre the college education she was lacking. He gave her books on English poetry, U.S. history. He talked philosophy and religion. She liked listening to him, trying to please him. Returning the gift he'd given her.

He kept an office in Jupiter. A tiny, windowless number in an undistinguished office building. Deirdre stopped by to give him a book report. A Theodore Roosevelt biography he'd assigned her. She found him with his feet up, a whiskey in his hand. He stared at the wall. Deirdre leaned on the doorframe.

"You okay?" she asked.

He told her to close the door. She lounged in the seat across from him. He dropped his feet to the floor, set aside his whiskey. Flicked a notecard over to her.

"Got another job," he said. "If you want it."

Deirdre picked up the card. A name and address. Jeffrey Alban, Albuquerque, New Mexico. "What's the story?"

"He's a lawyer. Setting up shell companies to cover assets. He's gotten nervous lately. The feds are getting close. He might help them. Sell out his friends."

"And who are these friends?"

"The cartel."

Deirdre didn't move. Her eyes held Miles's.

"Santana?" she asked.

"Different guy. Omar Fuentes. He used to run Texas and the Gulf Coast. He got New Mexico after the cartel took it away from Santana. Punishment for…Phoenix."

Deirdre looked down at the card. "I'll take it."

"You don't have to. You've got status. You can turn down work."

"I'll take it."

"Fine. I'll make the arrangements. You fly out tomorrow or the next day."

"Good."

Deirdre walked to the door. So much for the book report. Miles's voice followed her.

"Be careful," he said.

Be careful. *It was as close to affection as Miles came. He expressed love for Hemingway, Truffaut, The Beatles, M*A*S*H. Never an actual person.*

"I will," Deirdre said.

She walked out of the office. Miles was alone with his whiskey and his thoughts.

***

Albuquerque was beautiful. Deirdre wasn't there for the scenery.

She started tailing Jeffrey Alban the first day. He was paunchy, fussy about his comb-over. He lived in a middle-class neighborhood. Had a pretty blonde wife, two handsome children (a boy and a girl, both teenagers). He drove a Crown Royal that had seen better days. Clearly, he was good at hiding money.

Deirdre kept an eye on Alban's place. She settled into a house across the street. It was for sale, unoccupied at night.

She wanted to dislike Jeffrey Alban. Wanted him to be selfish, neglectful, possibly abusive. He wasn't any of those. He spent time with his wife. Helped the kids with homework. Shot baskets with them in the driveway. Drove the kids to school in the morning. Didn't stay out late, didn't neglect the family. Said good night to the kids at bedtime.

Miles called the third night. "You still in Albuquerque?"

"Still."

"What are you doing?"

"Casing the house. Waiting for a chance."

"Fuentes is getting antsy."

"Sure."

Silence on the line. "Albans has a family," Miles said.

"He does."

"You've been watching them. Wondering what that life is like."

"I don't have to wonder."

Another silence. "You going to be able to do this?"

Deirdre closed her eyes and took a deep breath. "Yes."

"Let me know when it's done."

"Will do."

They hung up.

***

The opportunity came the following night. Alban went back to the office after dinner. It was in the corner of a strip mall, on the outskirts of Albuquerque. Deirdre circled behind the place. The back of it faced a freeway, Protected by a soundwall, a high embankment. She approached the backdoor. Picked the lock, stepped into the darkened hallway, carefully closed the door.

She stuck to the wall. A cheap wooden door opened to the reception area. The door to the main office on the far side. Deirdre drew the Berretta. Pushed open the office door.

Alban was at his desk, feet kicked up, reading a file. Deirdre came through the door. Albans jumped. Dropped the file, slid his feet off the desk. Gave the gun a bug-eyed look. Raised his hands.

"Fuentes?" Albans asked. His voice high and tight.

"Yes."

"I—"

Deirdre shot him through the right eye. He crashed onto the desk, slid to the floor. She added two more shots. Walked out of the office, out of the building. She touched nothing. Nothing touched her.

***

Deirdre stood in the living room. Watched the Albans' house across the street. The children were in bed. The mother was in her room, maybe reading. Wondering where her husband was.

She'd fly back to Jupiter. Go straight to Miles's house, Make love with him. He would hold her, know there was something on her mind. But he wouldn't ask. She turned away from the window, dialed her phone. Miles answered. She spoke before he could.

"It's done."

***

The first thing Deirdre does is yank me to my feet, none too gently. My ears hum from the gunfire. This can't be a dream or some vision of the afterlife. But it sure as hell feels like it. Deirdre moves toward the door, still holding the gun. She looks back at the restaurant floor.

"Get the tire iron and your cell phone," she says. "Don't leave a trace of being here."

I look at Angel's body. "What about him?"

"Let the police worry about that. Let us worry about the police."

I collect the cell phone and the tire iron. I'm moving on autopilot. Deirdre leads us outside. The cold slaps me in the face.

"There's a rest stop on the highway, a few miles south," she says. "I'll meet you there."

"How will I find you?"

"I'll find you."

I stick close to the wall. When I look back, Deirdre has disappeared. Typical.

I don't run across anyone else on my way out of Brooklyn Point. The rest stop is where Deirdre said it would be, the last one before you hit the Twin Cities. The place is empty. No sign of Deirdre. I park the Saturn and wait. After a minute, I decide to go inside. The rest stop itself is a squat cement building. I'm about to go through the door when I hear a voice off to my right.

"Over here, darling."

Deirdre is barely visible in the shadows. I'd rather get out of the cold, but I'm not calling the shots. I walk toward the corner. A little path leads around the building, toward the picnic tables. Deirdre stops along the wall.

We stand there, not saying anything. She looks the same as last time. She's nearly my height and has large blue eyes, and honey-colored hair. She's dressed all in black and is doing yeoman's work to appear unaffected by the cold. I tuck my gloved hands into my coat pockets.

"I'll start with the cheesy line," I say. "You look pretty good for a dead woman."

"Surprise."

"I saw you lying on a slab in the morgue. Who was I actually looking at?"

Her face falls. "You never met Emily, did you?"

"Your assistant?"

"Yes. That was her you saw." She shivers. "Is this state *ever* warm?"

"Just not when you're here, apparently." I let out a breath. "What the hell is going on?"

Deirdre is losing her fight against the cold. "Let's go sit in your car."

Hearty Minnesotan or not, that idea sounds good to me. When we get the car, I crank the heater up. Deirdre curls into the passenger seat. I speak without looking at her.

"Is Emily your twin sister?"

"No. My…I don't have siblings. Emily looked a lot like me when we met. We made certain…adjustments to make the resemblance a little stronger."

"Plastic surgery?"

"If that's what you want to call it."

"The DNA identified you."

"It was Emily's DNA, assigned to me. It was best if I stayed off the grid."

"Lucky break for one of you."

Deirdre ignores my snark and lets out a breath through her nose. "Emily wasn't supposed to be there. I told her not to do anything. She always had a headstrong streak."

"What *was* she doing there?"

"Looking for Grace Jelinski. Just like you."

I pinch the bridge of my nose. "Probably worth asking: who the hell is Grace Jelinski?"

"I don't know.

"Ah. Well, that clears it right the fuck up."

"I know it's confusing. I wish I could tell you more, but I can't."

I drum my fingers on the steering wheel. Okay, Joe, take it easy. You'll get answers eventually. Right?

"Can you tell me what *is* going on?" I ask.

Deirdre taps a knuckle on the window. "The cartel wants me dead."

"Why?"

"It's a long story. I don't want to get into it. But I had a peace agreement with them. Now I don't. And they're coming after me."

"And they want Grace dead, too?"

"So it seems. Grace is dangerous to them. That's all I know."

"Dangerous? Until a few weeks ago, the woman worked in a real estate agency. Did the cartel forget to file paperwork on a hideout?"

"I don't know the details."

"How do you even know Grace is dangerous to them?" I ask.

"Somebody told me. A long time ago."

"Can we get ahold of this person?"

Deirdre frowns. "No. He's gone."

It hits me. Why the hell it didn't hit me sooner, I don't know. Maybe I've been distracted. Maybe I've been trying to block out everything I know about Deirdre. Maybe I'm an idiot. But I've just put two-and-two together.

"Warren," I say. "You once told me your mentor was a guy named Warren. Is there any chance his name was Warren Newson?"

Deirdre's eyes dip. "That was his real name, yes. His working name was Miles Slayne."

217

"Miles Slayne? Seriously?"

In my opinion, you might as well call yourself Dude Eliminator Johnson as to give yourself an alias like that. But one look from Deirdre tells me I should keep that opinion to myself.

"Did he tell you why Grace was dangerous to the cartel?" I ask.

"No. He just told me to find Grace if I ever needed protection. He didn't give me details. He...there was no time."

I raise my fingers from the steering wheel. "Grace is from Brooklyn Point. So was Warren. Did—"

"I'd prefer if you called him Miles."

She's glaring at me. Her eyes are cold, but her nostrils are flared. It's a look that tells me not to mess with her.

"Grace is from Brooklyn Point," I say. "And so was... Miles. Did they know each other?"

"I don't know. The name only came up once."

Swell. Deirdre's back from the dead and unable to tell me much more than I already know. I drop my hand off the steering wheel, trying not to get frustrated or petulant.

"The cartel operates out of the southwest," I say. "Grace was born and raised in Minnesota. How would they even come across each other?"

"I wish I could tell you."

"How did you find *me*? Not I'm ungrateful."

A corner of her mouth rises. "I've been keeping an eye on you. When the peace with the cartel was broken, Emily and I closed up shop and went into hiding. I went to Seattle. Emily must have come here. When she missed a check-in, I knew something was wrong. I tracked her here and found out…what happened. She must have been looking for Grace. I knew you'd look into it. I started following you."

"Thank you for that. Where do we go from here?"

"We find Grace Jelinski. Together."

Lucky me. As long as I'm hanging out with Deirdre, there's a great chance I'm going to wind up like Angel. I prepare to put the car in gear. Deirdre makes no move.

"Don't you have a car?" I ask.

"Nothing I want to hold on to. Is my old apartment still available?"

"It wasn't really *your* apartment. But I think it's empty again. The old tenant always got a creepy feeling. Saw blood running down the walls, twins appearing out of nowhere. Voices saying *Redrum*. Stuff like that."

"You're not funny."

"I have many, many readers who would disagree with that statement." I back out of the parking space. "This time I won't supply toiletries or bedding."

"That's not like you, darling."

I pause. "You're right. It's not. I'll give you everything you need."

"That's more like it."

On the one hand, my mom would have been appalled by my initial lack of hospitality. But she'd be mollified if I told her my truculence was directed at a contract killer. Then she'd want to know why I'm hanging out with contract killers. Trust me, Mom, you're better off not knowing.

***

Somehow, I sleep past ten. Not that my dreams were particularly restful. I pull on a blue bathrobe and stumble out to the kitchen. The hardwood floor is cold. (I don't know how the cats put up with it.) My eyes and mouth are gritty. This despite not drinking after I got home (only through heroic self-denial). I get some kibble for Lenny and Squiggy, then start the coffee. I plunk down at the breakfast bar. This is where I have to remind myself *No, that really did happen last night. Deirdre is still alive. She saved you from a cartel guy who tried to kill you. That was real. That part where Emily Watson wanted to throw over John Krasinski for you? That was a dream.* I can't win.

The front door flies open. I dive toward the butcher block and grab my sharpest chef's knife. The intruder comes to a halt and puts his hands up. It's Lars. No need for the knife. (Although, let's not be hasty.)

"Problem, brother?" he asks.

I lower the knife. "Sorry. Guess I'm a little jumpy."

"Understandable. What with…our friend downstairs."

We're back to the euphemism *our friend*. I return the knife to the butcher block. Lars closes the front door and glides to the breakfast bar. He pats his hands on the counter. Something is bothering him.

"Everything okay?" I ask, pouring us some coffee.

"Developments with Chuck and Laura have taken a turn," he says, scooping up the mug I put in front of him.

"What's going on?"

"I took your advice and decided to get to know Laura better. I called her up and asked her to meet for coffee. She was more than agreeable. We met at Glacier's."

"And how did that go?"

"Surprisingly well. Laura is an intelligent and charming woman. We had an enthralling conversation. We spoke of philosophy, ethics, politics, the arts. She's more than a perfect match for Chuck. As far as I can tell, her only flaw was her willingness to sleep with me."

I nearly do a spit-take. "Her what to what?"

"Willingness. To sleep. With me. I was surprised myself. But given the bonding of the previous few hours, it seemed entirely natural. She was tender, enthusiastic, receptive. And that was *before* we broke out the massage oil."

I'm not sure if there's such a thing as an anti-erection, but I might have one right now. "You slept with Chuck's fiancée?"

"I have a lot of regrets about that. In theory."

"How does Laura feel?"

"She also has regrets. Not enough to stop her wanting more of the good wood from me. But regrets, certainly."

This is a disaster. As irritated as I've been with Lars over the movie, he's still my friend. I don't want to see his life ended prematurely. Which will almost certainly happen if Chuck finds out he and Laura have been making the beast with two backs.

"You're not going to see Laura again, are you?" I ask.

"I don't know," Lars says. "I don't want to hurt Chuck. But Laura has requested that I again fuck her silly. That's a direct quote. I'm not sure which direction etiquette lies."

"It lies with you not getting laid. Particularly with Chuck's fiancée."

"I get it, I get it. I need to put aside my own need to taste the sweet, sweet nectar that is Laura and consider Chuck's well-being. I hate to say I told you so, but she is not worthy of him. She's proven as much."

"By doinking you."

"Please. Let's not get mired in trivial details. The bottom line is Chuck cannot marry this woman. Unfortunately, my proof positive is her infidelity with me. And I can hardly bring that up to Chuck."

"I might up to Chuck."

"There has to be another way to get Chuck out of this mess. I just have to think of it." Lars glides to the front door (taking my coffee cup with him). He stops. "Hate to ask, brother, but how long do you think our friend will need the space down there?"

"I'm not sure. Hopefully, we can clear this whole thing up soon, and she can be on her way. That's the best-case scenario." I omit my lack of faith in best-case scenarios.

"Understood, Mon Ami," he says. "We're in this together. Hopefully our friend will—" He whips open the door and comes to a sudden halt. "Be stopping by soon."

Deirdre steps into the apartment, wearing the same black sweater and slacks she wore last night. (Or she's got a duffel bag full of the same clothes stashed some place. It could go either way.) Lars scurries out. Deirdre looks around my apartment.

"It hasn't changed," she says.

"Why break up a good thing?" I say.

She makes her way over to the breakfast bar and slides easily onto one of the stools. The cats keep their distance. It's true. Cats do have good instincts.

"Something smells good," she says. "You must have coffee on."

"I do. Would you care to mooch a cup?"

"I would. Thank you, darling."

I bristle a little at the *darling*. Once upon a time, I might have considered it cute. Those days are long over. Still, one has duties as a host. I fetch the purple Adams College mug out of the cupboard and pour a cup for my guest. She looks over my get up.

"Just starting the day?" she asks.

"This is my usual wake up time. How about you?"

"I've been up for hours. It's a habit I learned. Back in the day."

I'll admit being curious about that. But I've learned to curb my interest in Deirdre. The more I know about her, the more dangerous I am to her. I join her at the breakfast bar and look toward the arch windows. "Do you think the cartel is keeping an eye on the place?"

"I doubt it. They're not *case the joint* types. They're *storm the building and shoot everyone in sight* types."

"That's…comforting."

"Welcome to my world." She keeps an eye on me (and I doubt those eyes miss too terribly much). "I'll be honest, sweets, I'm not feeling the love."

"Did you expect to?"

"You thought enough of me to investigate why I was dead. I thought you cared a little."

"I was mildly curious. When your friend with the limp came around and threatened to kill me, it became more about self-preservation."

"And that's all it was?"

"Yes." I set my coffee aside. "Last time we left things, you killed an innocent woman."

"She wasn't innocent."

"She didn't do anything worth dying for."

"Don't be cross, darling."

"Don't be cute, Christina."

She grabs my throat and squeezes. It's not enough to choke me out, but it definitely gets in the way of the old air flow. She's got an iron grip.

"Let me be clear about something," she says, her voice even, "I let you get away with that the first time. Christina is dead. I buried her a long time ago. Do you understand?"

"Certainly," I say, dismayed by how weak my voice sounds.

Deirdre lets go. I take a few quick breaths. This is why I dread her appearance. Just when you think she's a civilized human being, she reminds you she is, in fact, a killing machine, nothing more. I rub my neck.

"So much for the beginning of a beautiful friendship." She says nothing to that, so I move on. "Is the cartel still going to come for me?"

"After what you did to Angel? Most definitely."

"After what *I* did to Angel? You shot him."

Deirdre bats her eyes and puts a hand to her chest, feigning shock. "Me? But I'm dead. How could I kill anyone?"

She's got me there. I could tell the cartel the truth, but we're not exactly on speaking terms. I could tell Street what happened, but how do I do that without mentioning Deirdre? And then, who would keep me safe from Deirdre? I might not have wanted her help before, but I need it now.

"I guess this *is* the beginning of…something," I say.

Deirdre holds up her coffee cup in a toast. "Nice to be working with you again, darling."

She'll pardon me if I don't join her in the toast. My eyes are again locked on the arch windows, wondering if someone will throw a grenade through them or if a sniper is lurking.

"May I ask how you managed to piss off an entire cartel?" I say.

"I told you it's a long story. And it's not the entire cartel. It's one member. His name is Victor Merced. Angel worked for him."

"How do you know they're coming after you?"

"Someone in the cartel let me know. It was something Miles set up. Emily and I had a burner phone. He called. I don't even know his name. He just had a code name."

"What was it?"

"Peter Clemenza."

I can't help laughing. "Clemenza? I assume he left the gun and took the cannoli?" Deirdre seems confused. "Peter Clemenza is the name of a character in *The Godfather*."

"You're sure?"

"It's my all-time favorite movie."

Deirdre mumbles, "God, you and Miles *would* have gotten along." She sips her coffee. "In any event, we had a peace agreement. Don Pedro ran the cartel. He kept his end. He died recently. It let Victor finally come after me. Emily decided to look for Grace Jelinski. Have *you* found anything?"

"Nothing more than what I told you. I *did* find a box of stuff belonging to Warren Newson. At Eli's Arcade. Probably explains why Emily was looking there."

She props her elbows on the breakfast bar. "I was the one who made up the box. After he died. He said that in the event of his death, he wanted it sent to this address in Brooklyn Point. I just dropped it in the mail."

"Fitzgerald Investments owns Eli's Arcade. That must be a shell company. Something Miles used to...protect his funds."

"Yes. He built a lot of those. I could never keep track. I handed the whole thing over to Emily. She tracked down most every place Miles had money stored."

"He didn't share any of that with you?"

"No. He had a tendency to keep things close to the vest." Her voice gets quiet. "Even with me." She brushes away whatever emotion might be there. "It's what he did with Grace Jelinski. That's why I hoped you could find her. I know you talked to two people up in Brooklyn Point. Who were they?"

I wonder how long and how closely Deirdre has been shadowing me. I'd object to the invasion of my privacy, but it resulted in her saving my ass.

"One was Miles's aunt Sophie," I say. "As far as I can tell, she's the only family he has left. The other is a guy named Simon. A friend of his from high school."

"Did they know anything about Grace?"

"No. They both told pretty much the same story. They kept in touch with Miles for a few years after he graduated high school and went into the army. Then he just disappeared. I'm guessing that's when he..."

"Entered The Life. Yes."

"Neither of them knew anything about Grace Jelinski. They hadn't heard the name, even though Grace apparently grew up in Brooklyn Point and was living there until she disappeared."

"Do you think they're telling the truth?"

I bob my head. "Sophie, probably. Simon seemed like he was hiding something. Or maybe I'm reading into it."

"Maybe. Any idea where to go from here?"

"Try to find out more about what Miles might have been up to. What Emily might have been looking for. I assume Miles might have hidden something in one of his old haunts."

"It wouldn't surprise me," Deirdre says. "Miles was good at hiding things."

"He and his friend Simon liked to hang out at their old elementary school. I was thinking of checking that out."

"Then I guess that's where we go next."

Swell. Don't get me wrong. I'm not one of these lone wolf types. I don't mind dragging my friends into this nonsense (whether they like it or not). But Deirdre is definitely not one of my friends. Still, I'm not going to tell her no, both out of gratitude for her saving my life and the ever-present threat of her ending it at any time.

"We'll need to wait until tonight," I say. "I hope you can pass the time until then."

There's a knock at the front door. That's a little odd. Carol and Mike generally call before coming over, and Lars never bothers to knock. I assume someone let the Jehovah's Witnesses into the building again. Or they found their own way in. (The security door at the front is secure in name only.) I check the peephole.

James Street is there. Hank Maxwell is with him.

The BCA *and* the Brooklyn Point Police Department paying me a visit. This would be a banner morning if a contract killer wasn't hanging out at the breakfast bar. I look toward Deirdre.

"Or you may want to run for the hills," I say.

CHAPTER ELEVEN

Three years later, Miles got a call from Victor Merced. Victor wanted a meeting. Miles couldn't help smiling. Victor had cajónes. *You had to give him that. Miles said he was out of the game. Victor wasn't moved.*

"Heard you got someone working for you," Victor said. "A woman."

"Sometimes, I think I work for her."

"Heard she did good work in New Mexico. I want to hire her."

Miles was glad they were on the phone. Victor couldn't see his amusement. "She's not available."

"There's good money in this."

"I'm sure there is. I'm also sure she's not available." Curiosity got the better of him. "Something you can't trust your own people with?"

"Something where I might want to avoid blowback. Don't want my people involved."

"Aren't your people Santana's people?"

Victor was quiet. "Just keep your ear to the ground."

The line went dead. Miles set the phone down, tried to quell the uneasy feeling.

***

Two weeks later, Michael Santana was gunned down in his bedroom. The same house where Miles had met him. The authorities knew it was a hit. They had no evidence. Nobody in Santana's organization was talking. The FBI didn't make it a priority. Neither did the local cops. The cartel feigned ignorance. They gave Santana's territory to Victor. Life moved on.

A year passed. Victor called again. Miles was out for a walk. An undistinguished neighborhood in Jupiter. Rows of houses all the same, as the song said. He was walking past a tennis court. Answered on the third ring.

"Going to need your girl," Victor said.

"For what?"

Victor's voice had an air of command. The old barbarian's edge was still there, though. He spat out the name.

"Fuentes."

231

"Trouble on the home front."

"He wants a piece of my territory. Thinks I can be taken. Word around the campfire is your girl is pretty good."

"She is," Miles said. "I don't think she's available."

Victor's voice darkened. "Why not?"

"She just isn't. You know how this business goes."

"What's your girl's name again?"

"Deirdre."

"You sure it's not Christina?"

Miles stopped walking. Everything was still. Somewhere, the ocean crashed against the shore. He tried playing the game.

"I don't know what you mean."

"No, I think you do. Cops and the feds might think we killed that girl in Phoenix, but we know better. Couple years later, you're out of the game and you got some chick working for you. Even Michael—God rest his stupid ass soul—put that one together. Now, I could be sending people after you, but I'm not. I'm trying to do business. Your girl don't want my business, that would be a shame. Safer route is working together. You get that?"

"I get it."

"What do you say?"

Miles closed his eyes, took a breath. "I'll put in a good word and get back to you."

"Don't take too long."

Victor rang off. Miles slipped the phone into his pocket, kept walking.

He got back to the apartment. Spent his time pacing. Rerunning the conversation. He looked at himself in the mirror. He was still trim. The rest of it appalled him. When did he start wearing shorts and floral print shirts? He looked old. Complacent. The opposite of what had kept him alive. He didn't recognize this guy. He sure as hell didn't like him.

He walked to the closet, slid the door open. In a corner, gathering dust, were his old black suits.

Victor knew about Deirdre. Deirdre would never take money from Victor. She'd go after him. Be reckless. She'd need help. Guidance.

And not from a guy in a floral print shirt.

***

Weirdly, this situation *is* like dealing with the Jehovah's Witnesses. Once they've seen the peephole darken, they know you're home. Unlike Jehovah's Witnesses, I can't just ignore them and hope they'll go away. Cops are tenacious that way.

Something in my look causes Deirdre to get up from the stool. She mouths "Cops?" I nod. She moves down the hallway without another word. As soon as she's out the backdoor, I greet my visitors.

"Wow, James Street and Hank Maxwell," I say. "It's like looking at the Justice League."

If either is impressed, they hide it magnificently. Street's eyes narrow. "Okay if we come in?" he asks. "We got something to talk to you about."

"Sure, sounds good," I say. As if my objection would have stopped them.

They step inside. Hank avoids eye contact. I've got a better than average idea why they're here. But I still have to play dumb. I return to the breakfast bar. Hank positions herself near the futon. Street follows me.

"Interesting situation up in Brooklyn Point," he says. "Somebody from the Church of the New Hope called the Brooklyn Point PD and said there was an abandoned vehicle in the lot of the Iron Gate Mall. It looked as if one of the stores had been broken into. The police checked it out and..."

Street gives Hank her cue. "We found a dead body in the old pizza joint," she says. "Turns out, it was someone you know. Angel Sastre."

"From the cartel?" I ask. (This is as close to a Benedict Cumberpatch-level performance as I'm likely to come.)

"The very same," Street says. "We know you've been looking into this, even though you were warned not to. Now Angel turns up dead. That seems like an interesting coincidence."

My eyebrows go up. "You think I killed him?"

"Didn't say that," Street tells me. "In fact, that really wouldn't be my first guess."

"But you might know something about it," Hank says. "*That's* fair, isn't it?"

"Normally, yes," I say. "But I don't know anything."

Street gives me the scrutinizing cop face. It's not as deadly as Carol's sodium pentothal glare, but it's intimidating, nonetheless. "Hank says you ID'ed Deirdre's body."

"I did," I say.

"And you're sure it was her?"

"Of course."

Street keeps the look going. He taps the breakfast bar, then paces away, his eyes scanning the room. I hope like hell I haven't left anything incriminating in view "Angel took one in the forehead," he says. "It was good work. The kind a professional might do."

I try to keep from shaking. "You'd know better than I would."

Hank slips her hands in her coat pockets. "But you might know something about *who* put this Angel guy down."

"I don't," I say. "I'm sorry."

Street opens his mouth to say something, then stops. He focuses on the breakfast bar. "You two-fisting it, Slick?"

"Excuse me?"

"Two coffee cups on the breakfast bar. You have a guest?"

Danger, Will Robinson. "My friend Carol stopped by."

Hank steps forward. "You didn't clean her cup right away? That doesn't seem like you."

This thing is going tits up rapidly. Before I can say anything in my defense (or think up what that might be), Street points toward the backdoor.

"I heard a door close before you let us in," he says. "Thought it might be one of the neighbors. Might not be, though. Am I right, Slick?"

I shrug. "I don't know what you heard."

Hank crowds in on me. "*I* thought I heard you talking to somebody."

Easy, Joe. Try not to hyperventilate. "I was chatting with the cats. I do that."

At least, I do when they're anywhere in sight. Uncooperative bastards, never helping with a good alibi. Street and Hank have me hemmed in.

"Who was in here, Slick?" he asks.

"The three of us," I say. "Me, myself, and I."

Defiance is the only way I can stop the bleeding. But it's not doing any good. Too much blood in the water already. Street turns to Hank.

"Take the deck and the stairs," he says. "I'll check out the inside."

Hank immediately moves down the hallway. Street disappears out the front door. I'm not sure what to do. We're on the verge of a hard-target search that might end with them finding Deirdre. I don't like to think what she'll do if they've got her trapped. (Going peacefully is probably not on the table.) I follow Street out the front door.

He stops at the landing outside Lars's (and Deirdre's) apartment. Lars steps out his front door, holding a tray of food. He comes to a halt when he sees Street. He starts to turn back, but Street stops him.

"What are you doing?" he asks.

Lars dillies the dally. "Having breakfast. As you see."

"Why aren't you having it in your apartment?"

"Well, I...I do like to have breakfast on the lanai. From time to time."

"Uh-huh. Where were you actually taking the food?"

Lars has run out of bullshit. The funny thing about him is he's a terrible liar. Sure, there have been a lot of people (and I mean, a *lot* of people) who have felt taken in by Lars. But that doesn't mean he was lying. His being full of shit was more a matter of poor planning and mere force of events. But that doesn't make him a liar. (As opposed to Mike, who lies like it's a bodily function and a rather disgusting one at that).

"I am…it's a…what you see…"

Lars stops before he goes full *Homina, homina, homina.* However, he instinctively looks past Street to the apartment across the hall. Street spins around.

"There?" he asks. "You were going there?"

Lars's jaw is working, but nothing is coming out. Street doesn't press him. (*What's that, girl? Timmy fell down a well?*) There's a faint knock in Lars's apartment, coming from his backdoor. Lars turns and calls through the apartment.

"It's open." Because of course it is.

Hank's voice can be heard in the hallway. "Tracks going down the back steps. Looks like they end at the apartment next door."

"Go around. Someone will let you in." Street turns to Lars. "You're the super here?"

Finally, a question Lars can answer. "I am."

"Then you got the keys to this place."

"I…I do."

"Get 'em. We're checking it out."

Lars turns back, then completes a full turn, facing Street again. "Do you have a warrant?"

"Does anybody live here?" Street asks.

"Perish the thought."

"Then I'm just checking out a vacant apartment. Maybe I'm interested in living here. It's your job to show me, right? Or do you need me to call management?"

I'm not sure if Street intended it, but he's hit on the perfect tactic. Lars lives in fear of the building management, knowing they could fire him at any time, thus forcing him to pay rent and live like an adult. As a result, he prefers to go through life anonymously, letting management assume he's doing a good job (if they only knew).

"I'll find the keys tout suite," Lars says, rushing into his apartment.

Street takes a position outside the door to the vacant apartment. I come down the steps and join him.

"You sure this isn't a waste of your time?" I ask. "Lars told you no one lives there."

"We'll see, won't we, Slick?"

That's what I'm afraid of. Lars returns with the master keys and gives me a brief apologetic look. I nod, letting him know it's okay. His hands were tied. I only hope we get a cell together. (Or do I hope that?)

Lars fumbles with the keys, then opens the door and lets Street lead the way into the apartment. It's a mirror image of my place, with the breakfast bar and the bedroom flipped to the other side. It more accurately parallels Lars, with an additional bedroom off the hallway leading to the backdoor. I

239

hope Deirdre hasn't left much of a footprint, even in her short time here. Of course, if she's here, that would be one hell of a footprint.

The place is largely empty. There's no TV in the living room. No sign of foodstuffs in the kitchen. There *is* an easy chair in one corner.

"What's with the chair?" Street asks.

"That was left by the last tenants," Lars says. "Horrible people. Possible terrorists."

Street chooses to believe my idiot friend (or he simply doesn't have a decent counterargument). There's no sign of Deirdre. Lars and I stand in the doorway and silently pray. (Lars's religious beliefs are…interesting, to say the least.)

Street moves down the hallway. He flips open the backdoor and lets Hank in. He jerks a thumb toward the first bedroom. She slips inside. Street takes the second bedroom. Lars and I peek into the second bedroom. Street stands in the middle of the room. He isn't pleased.

"There's a mattress up against the wall," he says. "The last tenants leave that behind?"

"Absolutely," Lars says. "Filthy, filthy people. Boo on them, I say. Boo."

Street continues to look around. The closet door is closed. Lars and I glance at each other. We've found Deirdre's hiding place. We have to hope Street doesn't.

But he does.

"Hank, I might have something," he calls out.

Hank pushes past Lars and me. Street nods toward the closet door. Hank takes her service revolver from the holster at her hip. Street puts a hand on the doorknob. He flips the door open. Hank brings the revolver up.

And nothing happens.

Hank lowers the weapon. Street steps around the door. His shoulders sag.

"Nothing," he says.

He walks back across the room. Hank follows him. They check out the rest of the apartment, but there isn't much to see, and apparently, even less to find. Lars and I meet them at the front door.

"Listen, Slick, I don't know what's going on," Street says to me, "but you didn't make any friends in the cartel. You want out of this alive, I suggest you talk to us."

He makes a compelling case. But I've got an ace in the hole as far as protection goes. Assuming she doesn't kill me first. I give Street a regretful look.

"I'm sorry," I say. "I don't know what to tell you."

Hank looks at me, faintly betrayed. Street tosses a hand.

"Been nice knowing you, Slick," he says. "You change your mind, you know where to find me."

241

He and Hank disappear down the stairs. Lars and I return to the landing. The cops leave the building. We keep an eye on them. They get into an SUV and pull away. Lars and I run back into the vacant apartment. We go straight to the bedroom and peek in the closet. Nothing.

"Where the hell did she go?" I ask.

"I'm right here," Deirdre says.

It startles the hell out of us. After a second, we realize where it's coming from. Lars and I look up. The ceiling extends about three feet above the door. There, wedged into this little spot, is the lady of the house. We step back, and Deirdre drops to the floor.

"Glad he didn't look up," Deirdre says.

That makes two of us. Apparently, I'm working with Catwoman.

***

"If you want to act on screen," Lars says, waving his hands as if conducting an orchestra, "you need to do less. Don't worry about showing me the feelings or the intentions. Feel them or think them strongly enough, and they'll come through. Give your feelings a name. A shorthand descriptor you bring up from your catalogue of emotions. That way, they're always there, ready for you. Imagine this…" He takes on an air of calm. "You see this? This is a cool, beautiful serenity. I call it *Stairway to Heaven*. But this…" He snaps into a look of wariness. "I call this one *Smoke on the Water*. And this…" He gives us a sense of calm command. "I call this—"

"*Surfin' Bird?*" I say, doodling in my script.

It gets a laugh from everybody at the table. Everybody except Lars, who's having his authority undercut, and Fabio, who's probably too depressed to find anything amusing. Lars draws himself up to his considerable height.

"Comments from the peanut gallery aside," he says, "I call this *The Magnificent Bastard*. You see? I have everything I need at my command. But I keep it all inside. Complete…emotional…and in-tel-lec-tu-al constipation."

There's silence. No one is sure whether to take this idiocy seriously. (Welcome to my world, kids.) Four folding tables have been pushed into a square in the middle of the choir room at Augsburg. Water bottles and coffee cups dot the landscape. Someone was kind enough to bring donuts. (Not the production staff but someone.) Everyone is here for the read-through of *Whore of the Vampire*, the soon-to-be-hit vampire/heist movie coming to an obscure film fest near you. (Or more likely, *not* near you.) I sit at the head table. Lars occupies the center spot. He wears a baseball cap with *Goodfellas* stitched into it and a pair of glasses with one frame blacked out (ala John Ford). Frankie and Kyra are to his left, occasionally conferring. Fabio is to his right, wearing a pair of shades and not moving. He may be asleep. (Or dead.) The actors and production staff are ringed around us. They stare at Lars the way the cast and crew of *Apocalypse Now* must have stared at the sight of Marlon Brando hanging in a tree and throwing coconuts at Francis Ford Coppola. (That's probably not true. People took Brando and Coppola seriously.) Lars gives us a sweeping gesture.

"With that said, let us begin the journey."

We dive into the reading of the script. Kyra reads the action sections in the same tone of voice a teenager uses to describe their parents' latest debacle of decorum. Her glasses keep sliding down her nose, and she keeps using her middle finger to push them back up (generally, while facing Lars). For me, this is my writing, no matter how much feedback and guidance (or direct orders) I've been given by others. Everyone will think these ideas are mine, even the ones I was cajoled (or directly ordered) into writing. My only relief is to scribble down various ideas for killing vampires and imagine Lars as the vampire. Our director sits serenely, making notes of his own. One of the actors, a metrosexual looking dude named Grant, raises his hand.

"I just had an observation about this scene," he says. "It seems pretty..."

"Erotic?" Lars asks.

"Pornographic. There's a lot of sex and most of it is degrading. Do we really need this?"

Lars thrusts a hand toward Grant. "You have to understand. The sex is entirely necessary. It's a metaphor."

"A metaphor?" Grant says. "For what? Fucking?"

Lars takes a deep breath through his nose. "Yes." Before Grant can respond, Lars plows on. "We're here to read the script, not litigate it. I assure you I have gone over it thoroughly and have signed off on every element. If some of those elements have been clumsily rendered, that is the responsibility of the writer. I assure you they will be worked out in the filming. Now, if we can move on?"

Anyone get the number of that bus I was just thrown under? Nevertheless, the reading persists. Lars stops to give exact line readings to many of the actors. He also responds to any concerns from the crew by repeating his policy of working out things during filming. He acts as if Fabio and Frankie aren't there. (And in Fabio's case, he's more or less correct.) Frankie's mouth hangs open, as if to say *What the actual fuck?* When we take a break, he reminds everyone it's a *hard ten*. (Thus, probably inspiring a good number of actors to mutter, "I got your *hard ten* right here.")

Kyra bolts across the room. Her face is red, and her hair is coming out of its ponytail. Frankie tries talking to Fabio but gets no response. She disappears into the hallway. Lars grandly walks to the entrance, remaining aloof from his actors (something for which they're grateful). Fabio finally raises his head. He takes off his sunglasses and looks around, surprised to find the room mostly empty. I trudge out to the hallway—again crowded with students—and look for a bench to sit on. Kyra and Frankie are in conversation. I don't think I'm welcome to join them.

I drop onto a bench, hoping nobody talks to me about the script. My phone rings. Swell. I am *so* in the mood to chat right now. The caller ID tells me it's Lisa. Okay, disregard my previous grumpiness. I'm taking this.

"Thank you for calling our production of *Heaven's Gate: The Next Generation*," I say. "This is Alan Smithee speaking. How may I help you?"

Lisa chuckles. "The movie is going that well?"

"If I could, I'd go back and kick the Lumiere brothers in the nuts."

"I hate to add to your miseries, but there's something I need to tell you."

I have a moment of panic. Lisa's hurt? She's sick? She never wants to talk to me again? Or worse, she's engaged to some dipshit? I try to keep my breathing steady.

"What's going on?" I ask.,

"One of the people you asked me to look into. Grace Jelinski? I think I gave you some wrong information."

My first reaction is to be almost dizzy with relief. This *isn't* something serious. Then I remember Lisa is a journalist and a damn good one. Any form of misinformation, to her, is a sin. I adopt an appropriately serious tone.

"What's going on?" I ask.

"I did a little more looking. It would have been very difficult for Grace Jelinski to have graduated from Brooklyn Point High School. Since she died when she was six months old."

"Excuse me?"

"I found a death certificate for Grace Jelinski. Apparently, she was born with a heart defect. She died during surgery at about six months old."

"Are we sure it's the same Grace Jelinski?"

"Same date of birth, same hospital. What are the odds there are two Grace Jelinskis born in the same hospital on the same date?"

"Slim and/or none."

Lisa shuffles through some notes. "Here's something else I found out: Grace may have graduated from Brooklyn Point High, but there's no record of her attending Brooklyn Point Junior High or any of the elementary schools up there. There's no record of her between her birth and high school graduation."

"Save for her unfortunate death."

"Exactly. Someone was using the identity of Grace Jelinski as a cover. It's not new. You take someone who died young, who has no real footprint in the system, and you graft that onto someone else."

"Begs the question: who the hell have I been looking for?"

"Can't help you there. I can do some more research, but I'm not sure if I'm going to find anything. Have you been making any progress on your end?"

That makes things a bit ticklish. I don't want to lie to Lisa. I haven't done it in the twenty years we've known each other, and I'm not going to start now. But there is self-preservation to consider. You don't go telling a nationally renowned journalist that you're harboring a previously-thought-to-be-dead contract killer. I stay both on and off the topic.

"I haven't found much," I say. "I still wonder why the cartel would have any interest in Grace."

"Can't help you there, either." There's a faint squeak in the background. Lisa sitting back in her chair. "You sure this is something you want to be messing with?"

"I'm in too far to stop."

"Oh? How do you mean?"

I tap my foot, trying to think of something to say. "If I promised to give you the full story later, can we let it go for now?"

"That was designed to make me *not* interested in what's going on?"

"It's the best I can do."

She takes a moment to contemplate the situation. "You're all right, though, aren't you?"

"Hanging in there. I'll leave this movie off my resume, but otherwise, I'm in the clear."

"Maybe you can get a script doctor to come in and take credit for it."

"If he's taking credit for this, he's a script mortician."

She moves into a lilting laugh. There's an ache in my chest. I try to ignore it. Lisa's voice is gentle when she returns to the line.

"Promise me you'll take care of yourself," she says.

"I promise."

We wait a moment, then ring off. The flow of traffic moves back toward the rehearsal room. Ugh. I'm going to have to go back and do this. I fall into line, on my own personal Bataan Death March. I could just quit, I suppose. But a Davis is nothing if not determined. And insane.

CHAPTER TWELVE

The overnight shift at the factory was miserable. It suited Allison's purpose. She stayed out of sight during the day, had only a few co-workers. They weren't interested in her. The owner was co-operative. He sent her paychecks to Allison's aunt. They were in her aunt's name. So was the apartment Allison lived in. She was off the grid. Or as close as she could get.

The apartment wasn't much. One-bedroom, threadbare carpeting, stains on the ceiling, cracks on the walls. Lovely view of a brick wall. Bass thumping and TV noises from the neighbors. Day-sleeping was hard. Ear plugs and exhaustion helped.

She got to the top of the stairs, trudged down the hall. Third door on the right. Bass thumping from next door. It wasn't nine yet.

She opened the door. Spotted the guy on her couch. She jumped. He looked like she remembered him. Dark hair, blue eyes, calm face. Dressed all in black. His arms were stretched across the back of the couch. One foot propped on the other knee. She closed the door, leaned against it.

"Nice to see you, Miles Slayne," she said. "Thanks for calling ahead."

"Ruins the element of surprise. Good to see you, Allison. You're looking…"

"Don't say well. *I know better."*

Miles scrutinized her. Baggy clothes, no makeup, greasy hair. "How about You look good considering?"

"I'll take it." She dropped into the straight-back chair. "Thank you for coming. Sorry. I'm just on edge."

He slid forward, hands dropping into his lap. "I was surprised to hear from you."

"You thought I was dead?"

"Didn't think the odds were in your favor. I'm surprised you kept my card."

"I thought I might need it." She hung her head. "I liked Michael. But I knew what he was. And wasn't."

Miles leaned back. "What can I do for you?"

Her eyes didn't meet his. "I need protection. The cartel will come for me. It's only a matter of time. I can't keep this up."

"I'm not in the protection business."

"That's not what I hear."

Miles kept his eyes on her. "I make exceptions. Michael knew?"

"He guessed."

"Well done." He dropped his feet to the floor. "Victor's after you."

"I'm a loose end. Victor doesn't like loose ends. I was there when Michael was killed."

"Tell me."

She gave him the whole story. Her voice was monotone, pushing the emotion aside. It helped her get through it. Miles listened impassively. Allison knew she had no capital. Nothing he wanted.

"I don't have much money," she said. She slid to the edge of the chair, their knees practically touching. She laid a hand on his thigh. "I could offer you something else."

Miles put his hand on hers. "Don't."

"My God, I can't even do this anymore."

"It's not that. I'm with somebody right now."

"You love her?"

"She is...very. I...She's important." He cleared his throat. "You could go to the police."

"I don't trust the police. They only help you if they can use you." *She withdrew her hand. "I trust you. That's why I called."*

Miles's foot tapped on the hardwood floor. He stood up, buttoned his coat.

"You got anything you want to take with you?" he asked.

"No. Easier to travel light."

"Let's go."

She followed him to the front door. He opened it for her.

"Where are we going?" Allison asked.

Miles smiled. The first time she'd seen him do it.

"Home," he said.

***

I walk into my apartment, greet the kitties, and toss my stuff on the futon. Another day, another disaster on this movie. I should let it go. I'm going to lose my mind if I keep this up. All my troubled thoughts go better with a drink.

I grab the bottle of vodka from the drinks shelf. There's a knock on my front door. It's an odd little rhythm. *Tap-tap. Tap. Tap. Tap.* It's an approximation of the opening riff from "Last Train to Clarksville." I used it as a secret knock about a year ago. I'm impressed my visitor remembers. I step over to the door, still holding the bottle, and carefully open it. Deirdre is on the landing. I make sure no one is around, then usher her into the apartment.

"Home from the movie?" she asks.

Everybody in my life knows about this debacle. "Thank the Lord. Drink?"

"If you insist."

I grab two lowball glasses and pour us each a couple fingers. We do a quick toast. After a sip, Deirdre taps my phone, resting on the breakfast bar.

"Heard any more from your friends in the police?" she asks.

"Not yet. I can't help wondering if they're staking out the place."

"They aren't. I would have seen them."

That's one area where it helps to have a professional around. We settle at the breakfast bar. Deirdre looks around, restless. This makes me nervous. Deirdre is accustomed to action, not hiding. If there's nothing to do, she'll invent something. And that usually creates trouble for me.

"What do we do next?" she asks.

"There's a place I want to check out. Brooklyn Heights Elementary. Miles went there. Apparently, he liked to hang out there. At least, that's what his aunt and his friend told me. It's abandoned now."

Deirdre's face clouds. "You met Miles's aunt?"

"She's a nice lady. I assume you've never met her."

"No."

"Did Miles ever talk about her?"

"He mentioned having an aunt that he liked. That's it."

That's an area where Miles and I *really* differ. Informationally, I'm not at all reticent when I'm dating someone. I have a litany of stories, and a new girlfriend provides a new audience for my best material. I can't imagine being with someone and leaving out key parts of my history. Then again, Miles's work benefits from reticence, and mine benefits from oversharing. To each their own.

Deirdre is ready to move on. "Why is this elementary school worth checking out?"

"Miles had a habit of hiding things in places that were meaningful to him. Maybe there's something there. It's worth checking out."

"Fine. When do we leave?"

"As soon as we finish our drinks," I say.

As if in response, she takes a healthy sip. Larger than she normally does. I tap the counter in front of her.

"You okay?" I ask.

"Never better."

Judging by her tone, we're going to let it go at that. She gently takes the vodka glass out of my hand and carries both hers and mine to the sink. She leans against the counter.

"We'll take off as soon as we sober up a bit," she says.

"I'm not drunk."

"But you're not sharp, either."

That's true. Although, I'm pretty sure alcohol has nothing to do with it.

***

255

Every time I drive by an elementary school, I realize I was spoiled by my own. Cobb-Cook Elementary was named after two guys from my hometown of Porter's Bay, both of whom served in World War I. It had been built in the early twenties when Porter's Bay was awash with iron ore money. The building was made of brick, the stairs were marble, the handrails on the stairways were lacquered wood, and the classrooms were spacious and comfortable. Sure, a crappy addition had been slapped on sometime in the Fifties, but it didn't detract from the grandeur of the place. When I drive by elementary schools these days, they all seem to come from the same cookie-cutter that created the crappy little addition to Cobb-Cook. I pity the generations of students who will never have a school with actual personality.

Sadly, Brooklyn Heights Elementary is one such featureless school. I'm sure it had sentimental value to Miles Slayne, but that doesn't change the lousy aesthetic. It's flat and sandy colored and runs the length of a city block. A section on one side stands taller than the rest of the building. I assume that's the gymnasium. For an abandoned building, though, it looks well-maintained. No graffiti or broken windows. The sign for Brooklyn Heights Elementary School is still intact. If one didn't know any better, they'd assume the place was still in business. Deirdre and I sit in my Saturn across the street, contemplating the situation.

"According to Simon," I say, "he and Miles used to sneak in. I wonder how they did it."

Deirdre points at a door near the gym. "That's a good spot. Less traffic along the back. Coverage from the trees in the boulevard. Entrance is recessed. That's where you'd do it."

"That makes sense."

"Let's go."

We abandon the car and cross the street. Snow is piled high on the boulevard. Thankfully, someone has trod a path through it. We duck into the recessed area, and Deirdre goes to work on the door. A few seconds, it pops open.

"Disco," she says.

Deirdre steps into the darkened room and finds a light switch. The fluorescents are a shock to the eyeballs. We're in a small gym. It has your standard floor with weird lines and circles for various activities. A retractable partition rests against the wall, capable of turning one gym space into two. A small stage with an even smaller backstage area sits on one end. Like the gym, the place has been remarkably well preserved.

"What do we do now?" I ask.

"Search the building. You start at one end, I'll take the other. We meet in the middle."

Assuming The Boogeyman has taken the night off. Deirdre sends me to the far end of the building. I'd feel better if A, this place wasn't so spooky; and B, I had the slightest idea

I'm looking for. It's like searching for a piece of hay in an enormous stack of needles.

I catch a break in that all the classrooms are unlocked. Then again, they're all empty, so why lock up? I poke around the walls and the floor, wondering if there might be some kind of hidden cubby hole. No luck. I move from classroom to classroom but get the same result. Deirdre and I meet in the lobby near the office. The look on her face tells me she hasn't found any more than I have.

"Just two places left," I tell her. "The office and the gym."

"I'll take the office."

Sadly, there doesn't appear to be much to the gym, either. There isn't any equipment left, which is a bummer. Even a tennis ball would help. (For all my pretentions to intellectualism, all I really need to be happy is a tennis ball and a wall to throw it against.) I look around the walls and floors but come up empty. The only thing left to explore is the stage.

I check the stage floor but don't find anything. There are staircases off each end. One leads back to the hallway and the other to a small office. I check out the office first. Back in the day, the janitor must have camped out here. No furniture to be seen now. I feel along the wall, finishing up by running a hand over the vent near the floor. Then the screen comes away.

At first, I think it's just the building falling apart. Then I look into the vent. There's a little cubby hole. I take out my phone and shine the flashlight into it. A cell phone is sitting in there, connected to a charging unit. I disconnect the phone from the charger and turn it on. Fortunately, it doesn't require a passcode or a fingerprint. Probably a burner phone. I look through the contacts. There's just one other number. No name attached. I debate calling it.

"Find something?"

I jump, causing the phone to fly up in the air. I grab it before it hits the floor. Deirdre stands in the doorway.

"Did you float in here like a vampire?" I say. "I didn't hear you coming."

"That's the idea, darling."

I hold up the phone. "Found this hidden in the vent."

"Anything in it?"

"Just one phone number."

"Did you call it?"

"I was about to when the bejeezus was removed from my person. Thank you very much."

She squares me with a look. "You want to get to it?"

Ugh. I don't like talking on the phone under the best of circumstances. But I make the call. No answer. The voicemail box hasn't been set up. I go through the text messages. There's one, sent from this phone to the same number I just called. It just reads: **For you, there is only the desert.**

"Bingo," I say. (And I will not be pulling out a Bingo card, thank you very much.)

"What do you have?" Deirdre asks.

I show her the message. "I found the phone that received this message. It belonged to Grace Jelinski."

"Then who owns *this* phone?"

"Couldn't be Miles, because of...obvious reasons. Emily?"

"I don't think so," Deirdre says. "Emily would have used the phone to find Grace. That message feels like a warning."

"Miles and his friend Simon used to hang out here. I'm guessing Simon sent the message."

"We should talk to him."

I agree, but I'm still hesitant. Do I want Deirdre there? Do I even want to share my hesitation? I (metaphorically) gird my loins (though, doing it literally might not hurt, either).

"We can drop by," I say, "but are you comfortable letting me do the talking? I think this is one of those *catch more flies with honey than vinegar* kind of situations."

"That's fine. Until it's not." She looks around, as if she's trying to picture something. "Besides, I'd like to meet Simon."

"Why?"

Deirdre opens her mouth, then snaps it shut. "Because I do."

I guess we're not going into detail. Quite the partnership we're developing.

***

It doesn't take long to get to Simon's house. I find a parking space between the pools from the streetlights, just out of view from his front window. Deirdre considers the house.

"Clearly, not a success story," she says.

"We can't all be famous, the idol of millions."

"I suppose. Let's go."

We walk toward the house. The temperature is dropping rapidly (and I didn't think it could get much lower.) Simon is visible through the little window on the side door. He's seated at the kitchen table, crawling into his nightly bottle. When I knock, he looks startled, then annoyed. He peeks through the window and yanks the door open.

"What's going on?" he asks.

He notices Deirdre standing next to me. His jaw drops slightly. He doesn't know who this woman is, but she must be trouble. I try to get Simon's attention.

"I want to talk," I say. "I came across some information."

His wary look is firmly in place. "About Warren?"

261

"In a sense."

Simon doesn't seem pleased. He glances over at Deirdre. "Who the hell is this?"

Before I can answer, Deirdre says, "I'm the next person to knock you on your skinny ass if you don't change your tone."

Simon promptly lets us into the kitchen. He retreats to the table and takes a healthy drink of his whiskey. I sit across from him. Deirdre leans against the kitchen counter. Simon's eyes are a little bleary.

"What do you need?" he asks, his voice a croak.

"I found a phone at Brooklyn Heights Elementary," I say. "A burner phone, stashed in a heating vent. I think you might know something about it."

Simon looks away. "Sorry. Can't help you."

"Actually, I think you can," I tell him. "There was a message on it. I know for a fact it was message for Grace Jelinski. And I'm pretty sure you're the one who sent it."

He opens his mouth, then closes it again. He doesn't issue another denial, probably knowing it's a waste of time. With Deirdre looming nearby, not fucking around would be a good policy.

"Yeah, it was me," he says. "It was something Warren set up."

Deirdre and I exchange a look, trying not to let our excitement show. "You know where Grace Jelinski is?"

"No. But I used to."

Deirdre's face tightens. She wants answers. Now. I move quickly before things get…shooty.

"Tell me what's going on," I say.

Simon's eyes grow sad. "Warren turned up here one day. Years ago. Right out of the blue. I come from work, and he's sitting at my kitchen table. We went over to the old elementary school. It was like old times." He sips his whiskey. "He told me he needed a favor. There was some girl he was going to hide here in Brooklyn Point. He needed me to keep an eye on her, make sure everything was okay."

"And that was Grace Jelinski," I say.

"Warren said he was taking care of everything. Got her a house, got her a job, set her up with a little bit of money. He gave me two burner phones. Told me to keep one around here and to stash the other at the school. He said I might get a message on the phone I kept around here. If I did, I was supposed to send the same message from the phone at the school."

"*For you, there is only the desert,*" I say.

Simon nods. "That was a warning to Grace. I never had any idea what it meant. But that was all I did. I met Grace a couple of times. She's a hell of a looker. But she didn't seem too interested in me. That was that."

"Until you sent her the message."

"Got it a few weeks back. Did what I was told. That's all I know."

"And you didn't hear from Warren after that one visit?" I ask.

"No. No idea what happened to him."

Deirdre looks at the floor. I'll let her break the news to Simon, but something tells me it's not going to happen. I stick with the task at hand.

"Do you have any idea where Grace is?" I ask.

"No. Like I said, we didn't really talk. I don't know anything about her." He holds up a finger. "I take that back. I know one thing. She doesn't own a car. She said she couldn't afford one. Her boss, Keith, would give her a ride. She told me that right after she started working at the real estate place." He finishes his whiskey. "And *that* is all I know."

That might make Keith's behavior toward me a little more reasonable (if no less assholish). It also confirms my theory that Grace couldn't have gone far. She didn't own a car. If she's hiding, she's hiding locally. A return trip to Wilryan Realty might be in order. Deirdre steps toward the table, causing Simon to recoil.

"Warren never told you why he wanted to hide Grace?" she asks.

"No, he didn't," he says. "Said it was safer if he didn't get into it. He played things close to the vest, you know?"

Deirdre's eye dip. "I know."

There doesn't seem to be a lot to add. Simon knows only the very little Miles let him know, and he didn't ask questions (which might be why Miles trusted him enough to do this). I get up from the table.

"You may want to be careful," I say. "The guys coming after Grace aren't particularly friendly. If they know you have anything to do with her…"

Fortunately, I don't need to expand on that. Simon drains his whiskey. I turn to go. Deirdre, though, isn't moving.

"You knew Warren in high school?" she asks. "What was he like?"

Simon looks around, as if searching for the answer. "He was a decent guy. Funny. Didn't have many friends. Kept his distance. Even from me sometimes. Loved movies, TV, books." He gazes blearily at Deirdre. "Did you know him?"

Deirdre looks as if she's trying to come up with an answer. Instead, she steps out the kitchen door without a look back. I say an awkward goodbye to Simon and follow her. Neither Deirdre nor I say anything. We get in the car, and I turn the heater on full blast. Deirdre looks out the window while I maneuver the car toward the highway.

"Everything okay?" I ask, figuring that's a benign way to start.

"Fine," she says, out of reflex as much as anything. Then she calms slightly. "Warren liked to play things close to the vest. I understood that. If he had just trusted me with this Grace Jelinski thing, we wouldn't be in this mess. But somehow, he could trust a guy I don't even know."

This puts me in an awkward position. My instinct is to say something comforting (stupid human interactions). But that requires me to guess at the motivations of a guy I'll never meet. I wave a hand, as if I can pull the answer out of the air.

"Maybe he was protecting you," I say. "The less you know, the safer you are."

"I don't need protection. Not anymore."

I'm not sure what that means, but I *am* sure she won't answer me if I ask. I leave Deirdre to her thoughts. I'm not going to get anywhere with her. Nor am I certain I want to.

***

We're silent on the drive home. Once we're back at my building, Deirdre goes directly to the abandoned apartment. I say good night. She says nothing in return. I go up to my place. The snow and ice have, at least, been cleared from my deck.

(Because I do it myself rather than leave it to the superintendent.)

The cats aren't waiting in the hallway. That's never a good sign. It usually means they're hiding. And if they're hiding, they're scared. As far as I know, there are only three things that scare them: small children, vacuum cleaners, and unwanted visitors.

It doesn't take me long to spot my visitor/intruder. He sits in my desk chair, a foot propped on the other leg. He's a solidly built Latino, maybe in his forties. The shaved bald head gleams in the light spilling through the window. I set my keys on the little table, next to the picture of my parents. (Been nice knowing you, Mom and Dad.)

"You're Joe Davis," he says.

"I am. And you are…?"

"Victor Merced. Wanted to see the *puto* who killed Angel. Before you join him."

If I wasn't big on visitors before…

CHAPTER THIRTEEN

Deirdre walked into Miles's apartment. She knew something was wrong. He was pacing. Wearing black. She stood in the doorway. The humidity competed with the air conditioning. Streetlight filtered through the windows. She tossed her keys on the table, walked to the kitchen.

"Need a beer?" she asked, opening the fridge

"Yes," he said. "But I'm not going to have one. Been doing that too much."

Deirdre popped the top. "You look exactly like you did when I first met you. You haven't put on a pound."

"Mentally. Takes the edge off."

"Isn't that the idea?"

Miles ignored her. Deirdre hopped up on the counter, letting her legs dangle.

"What's going on?" she asked.

He turned toward her. His eyes lingered on the beer. "Victor Merced wants to hire you."

"The guy who killed Michael Santana?"

"Michael…and others."

Deirdre set the beer aside. "Like who?"

His shoulders sagged. "Your family…"

She looked at the floor. "It was him." Miles nodded. Deirdre closed her eyes, took a breath. "Why is he still alive?"

"Because nobody hired me to kill him."

"I would have done it for free."

"That's why I never told you."

She slid off the counter, walked over to Miles. Slapped him hard across the face. He made no effort to stop her.

"I'm not going to work for him," she said. "I'm going to kill him."

"Maybe you can do both."

She grabbed the beer off the counter, took a slug. "Why does Victor want to hire me?"

"Because you're the best. And he thinks he's got us over a barrel."

"He knows about Christina."

269

"Victor knows he didn't eliminate you. He figures I got you out of there. He knows you're working for me. He put it together."

"But he doesn't want me dead."

"Not if you can be useful to him."

"Then he's going to be really disappointed."

Miles stood in front of her. "This life is dangerous enough. You keep everything business. Emotions don't get involved. That's The Discipline."

"So, you lied to me instead."

"No. You never asked, I never volunteered information."

Deirdre's face was cold. "You're a real son of a bitch, you know that?"

"I can be. But I had to look out for you."

She closed her eyes. Rolled her head, loosening her neck. "If you're supposed to keep emotion out of it, why did you save me? Why did you train me? Why are we together?"

"Nobody's perfect."

She wanted to know more. She didn't press him. Miles would tell her what he wanted to tell her. Nothing else.

"I work for him, and I kill him," she said. "How do I do that?"

"We kill him," Miles said. "You're not doing this alone."

"I don't need help."

"You think you can take on a cartel by yourself?"

"I'd love to find out."

"You're emotionally compromised," he said. "I'm not going to stop you doing this—"

"Good idea."

"But I'm going to help you. Like it or not."

A corner of her mouth rose. "You're getting back in the game?"

"Just this once."

"Because you love me?" He didn't answer. "Doesn't that make you emotionally compromised?"

Miles picked up the beer bottle from the counter, took a sip. "Nobody's perfect."

***

First thought is this Victor guy looks way too comfortable in my desk chair. It's the one chair in my house in which no one else is allowed to sit (save for Lisa). Of course, this might not be the best time to get territorial. Or too attached to breathing. The apartment is deathly quiet (and yes, that's the appropriate choice of words). Victor's thick frame is encased in black leather, practically bleeding into the darkness. I stand still, letting Victor know he need not fear any sudden moves from me (not that the thought is keeping him up nights). He swivels in the chair.

"Gotta be honest, homes," he says, "you don't look like the kind of guy who could take out Angel."

"To be fair, it was self-defense."

"That *was* one of Angel's problems. He liked to shoot first."

"Ask questions later?"

"No. Angel wasn't all that curious." He jerks a thumb toward my computer. "You're a writer. Some pussy little column on the internet. How you get involved in this kinda shit?"

"It's…a really long story."

"You ain't going to have time to tell it." He rubs his neck tattoo. "I knew Angel a long time. He had that limp, but he was the toughest motherfucker I ever met. That includes that *perra* and her fuckin' boyfriend. And you took him out?"

"Upsets happen. You ever hear about the Vikings losing to Atlanta in the NFC Championship Game? That still hurts."

"You think this shit's funny?"

"Not remotely." I'm just trying to delay the inevitable. Victor doesn't need to know that.

His smirk disappears. "You didn't kill Angel, did you?"

"If I didn't, who did?"

"Deirdre. Angel didn't kill the cunt, did he?"

I hold my hands out. "Far as I know, she's dead. What happened with me and Angel? That was between us."

That's as good as I get for tough guy dialogue. I hope Victor buys it. I'm not going to make his path to Deirdre any easier. He remains still, maybe waiting for me to break down. Then he shrugs.

"Have it your way, homes."

The gun comes out of nowhere. He pulls the trigger. Just before he does, I dive to my left. The shot sounds like a sonic boom. I land on the kitchen floor and slide. I'm still in one piece. For the moment.

I bounce to my feet and search the counter. I need a weapon. Or the next best thing. Victor comes around the corner. I grab the first thing I can find and chuck it at him.

My mom and I both love to cook. For her, it makes gift-giving easy. She can always get me some kitchen tchotchke. Two Christmases ago, she got me a glass bottle with a pour spot for olive oil. It adds a little style to my kitchen. It's also the weapon I'm using to save my ass.

Victor doesn't see it coming. It broadsides him in the cheek. He stumbles backwards, bumping into the wall. The bottle rattles on the floor. It doesn't break. (Now I have a reason to get out of this and go on living.) Victor swears in Spanish. There isn't enough room for me to make a run for it. He pushes off the wall and raises the gun again.

However, the bottle, while still intact, has spilled a goodly amount of olive oil on my floor. I discover this because *Victor* discovers it. He steps into a puddle and slips, toppling sideways. His head smacks against the breakfast bar on the way

273

down. The gun clatters on the floor, winding up at my feet. I grab it.

Victor gets up. He tries to back off but slips in the olive oil again. He crashes backwards into the wall. He flicks his eyes toward the gun in my hand.

"This how it went down with Angel?" he says.

"You don't see him around anymore, do you?" Okay, now I'm just doing tough guy dialogue to flex on him.

"You gonna do anything?"

"Depends. You gonna try anything?"

Victor's mouth tightens. "This ain't over."

"It is for now."

He moves toward the backdoor, keeping it casual, letting me know he's not afraid. The front door flies open. I'm worried it's Deirdre. If Victor spots her, he'll know she's still alive and all hell will break loose (eventually). But it's not Deirdre. It's Old Man Albertson.

Victor throws a look back. He sees a guy of indeterminate advanced age holding a pistol. The look goes from concerned to amused.

"What are you going to do, old man?" he says.

The old man responds by cocking the gun. "Blow your fucking head off."

Something in Mr. Albertson's demeanor must tell Victor he's not fucking around. Victor turns down the hallway.

He's moving at his own pace, the swagger still in place. Nothing to fear. Old Man Albertson is having none of it.

"Move your ass!" he says, in a voice that would make a drill sergeant piss his pants.

Victor runs to the backdoor. He doesn't even try to keep the bravado going. A second later, he's out into the night. Old Man Albertson lowers the pistol.

"Who the hell was that?" he asks.

"A guy from a drug cartel," I say. "You know it goes."

Old Man Albertson cocks an eyebrow. Before he can ask more questions, Deirdre comes through the front door. Her gun is held down by her side. She's dressed normally, save for her not wearing a shirt. (She *is* wearing a bra, so there's a modicum of decorum.) Her face is slightly flushed. She looks from me to Old Man Albertson and back again.

"What the hell is going on?" she asks.

"Just had a visit," I say. "From Victor Merced."

Deirdre speaks under her breath. "Son of a bitch." She steps toward me. "Are you alright?"

"I'm fine."

"Wasn't much to be scared of," Mr. Albertson says.

He hefts the pistol. A corner of Deirdre's mouth goes up.

"You scared him off?" she asks.

"That is the case, little lady."

275

Normally, I would expect anyone calling Deirdre *little lady* to leave the conversation with fewer limbs and more orifices than when they entered it. But she takes no offense.

"Nice work," she says.

He looks down. If I didn't know any better, I'd say he's blushing. Maybe he's like me and can't take a compliment. Or maybe it's been several decades since he last saw a woman in her brassiere. Whatever the case, I feel strangely left out. I point to the mess on the floor.

"The olive oil?" I say. "That was me."

Deirdre glances at that direction. "You were cooking?"

"No, I…" But whatever I say is going to sound lame. "It's a long story."

Deirdre becomes aware she's in a state of undress. She holds her arms across her chest. "I was getting ready for bed. I heard a shot. I wasn't sure that's what it was. I should have reacted sooner." She turns to Old Man Albertson. "Looks like I didn't have anything to worry about." She focuses on the pistol. "H&K VP9?"

He smiles. "Twenty in the clip."

"Nice." She looks toward me. "You going to be okay?"

"I think so," I say. "I'm going to have to buy more olive oil, but I'm okay otherwise."

She steps to the door, still holding her arms over her chest. Old Man Albertson joins her, moving with a bit more spring in his step than normal. He opens the door for Deirdre.

"I'll walk you back to your place," he says. "Which one is it?"

"On the right, one floor down," she says.

"Just move in?"

"You might say that. My name is Deirdre. I'd shake your hand, but…"

"That's all right. I'm Leo Albertson."

My head snaps his direction. "Your first name is Leo?"

"Something wrong with that?"

"No, I just…didn't think of you as a guy with a first name."

The usual disgusted look returns to his face. "Everybody has a first name."

I let it go, safe in the knowledge I'll never call him *Leo*, much the same way I'll never call Mr. Somrock, my high school English teacher, by his first name of *Bill*. Deirdre and Mr. Albertson step through the front door. He closes it behind them.

Great. Old Man Albertson gets the girl, and I get to clean up a puddle of olive oil. Suppose I should count myself lucky to be alive. I just wish I felt lucky.

***

It's a mark of how well the script for *Whore of the Vampire* is coming along that I refuse to work on it in any other place than The Tav. It's late afternoon (Happy Hour, ironically), and I'm parked at a high top near the bar. Nick, the bartender, has seen me toiling away and knows better than to ask me about it. Sadly, not everyone has that attitude.

"Who are you going to thank in the Oscar speech?"

Carol stands in front of my table. I don't remember seeing her come in. Still, it's an excuse to set this garbage aside. I close my laptop.

"Probably the Academy," I say. "And whichever quality director takes over this project after we've fired, killed, and eaten Lars."

Carol cringes. "That movie has been cursed from day one."

Truer words... "Here by yourself?"

"No. Jeff and I have a table in the restaurant."

"Anything else from Fabio?"

"All quiet on the western front. I admit it's creepy. I keep waiting for the other shoe to drop. Is it possible Fabio has finally given up?"

"Anything's possible. But I wouldn't say it's likely."

She leans on the table. I know that look. It's the international signal Carol would like to change the subject. No objections on my end.

"How's the investigation going?" she asks, putting the usual irritating ring around *investigation*. "I see the cartel hasn't gotten to you yet."

"Not for a lack of trying."

I tell her the story of Victor attempting to kill me, and Deirdre and Old Man Albertson spoiling the party. Her jaw drops. When I'm finished, she says exactly what I knew she'd say.

"Old Man Albertson's first name is Leo?" she asks.

"I couldn't believe it, either."

"I'm glad they were able to bail your ass out."

"I would like it noted that I knocked the guy goofy with an olive oil bottle. I was holding my own."

"Keep telling yourself that, tough guy. What are you going to do next?"

"Not sure. Maybe a trip to Wilryan Realty. I'm going to talk it over with...our friend. See what she wants to do."

"From what you told me, the manager wasn't too terribly cooperative the last time you visited. Maybe you should bring...our friend along this time."

"I'll take it up with my staff."

"Your call. Meantime, I should probably get back to Jeff." She lays a hand on my forearm. "Stay safe, okay?"

I assure her I'll be all right. She doesn't buy it but lets it go and returns to her table. I should open the laptop again.

No way I can do that without another beer. I belly up to the bar. Nick saunters my direction.

"What's it going to be next, my friend?" he asks from behind his wealth of beard.

"Another Grand Maibock, sir."

"Got it." Nick pours the beer. "Your friend Carol is in with her new guy. What happened to the old one? The guy with the hair?"

"It didn't work out." Seems like the most diplomatic way to put it.

"That's too bad. He was a good tipper."

"I'm sure you'll see him again."

Turns out I'm more accurate than I thought (or hoped). No sooner has Nick handed me a pint than I turn and practically run into Fabio. He has seen better days. There are dark smudges under his eyes, and he's got a growth of beard (or a reasonable facsimile). His clothes are wrinkled, and his fly is open (but I'm too polite to mention it). Even his mop of curly hair has escaped its gel captors and entered full frazzledom.

"Hey Joe," he says, "what's going on?"

"Just working on the script."

"For what?"

"The...movie." That gets nothing. "The one we're making." Still nothing. "*Whore of the Vampire?*"

It dawns on him. "The thing with the boobs?"

"Uh...I guess that covers it."

"Cool. Good luck with that." He turns toward the restaurant area. "Carol's here." Before I can say anything, he steps past me. "Have a good one."

Nothing good can happen here. I put the beer on the table and follow Fabio. Carol and Jeff are near the window. Fabio comes to a halt. I hear whimpering. He drops into a nearby table. Not before Carol spots him. She turns to Jeff. I wonder what the hell to do.

There's a moment where I think everything will work out. I have no idea where this optimism is coming from, but it's delusional. Fabio stares at Carol and Jeff as they try to carry on a conversation. He starts humming *The Way We Were*. Carol and Jeff try to ignore it. Both Fabio's singing and crying get louder. (I'm amazed he can do both at once. Roy Orbison would have killed for that.) Carol closes her eyes. Jeff gets to his feet and starts to take off his suitcoat. Carol, though, stalks toward the table. Fabio picks up a menu and tries to hide. (It would be more effective if he wasn't holding it upside down.) Carol slaps it away. Fabio pretends to be surprised.

"Carol!" he says. "What are you doing here?"

She speaks through gritted teeth. "You know exactly what I'm doing here. I'm trying to spend time with my boyfriend. You are making that difficult. Again. This needs to stop."

Jeff tries to step around Carol. "Listen, man—"

Carol steps in front of Jeff. "I've had enough of this, Fabio. You need to leave us alone. Do you understand me?"

Fabio tosses the menu aside. He drops to one knee and takes Carol's hands. "Marry me."

This might be romantic if it wasn't so pathetic. Jeff rears back to punch Fabio. I jump between the two of them. I catch Jeff's fist in my hands. It feels like I caught one of my brother Kevin's fastballs. Jeff draws the fist back again. I'm afraid he's going to direct the next one at me. Carol decides to lay into her former boyfriend.

"Listen to me, Fabio," she says, "it is *never* going to work between us. We have no future whatsoever together. I will go my way, and you will go yours. Do you understand?"

Fabio looks stunned (but at least he's stopped crying). "I—"

"I don't love you, Fabio. I don't even like you. You think you're some kind of entrepreneurial genius, but you're a fucking moron." Carol's hands become claws, as if she's trying to scratch further words out of the air. "You're shallow. Do you realize that? In fact, you are probably the shallowest person I've ever met, and I've dated some *incredibly* shallow guys. My friend Mike is as complex as grape soda, and he looks like

282

David Lynch next to you. And I'm pretty certain you don't know who either of those guys are."

"I don't."

"Your life is a complete waste of time. You haven't done *one* worthwhile thing. Your *father* has accomplished something and made life easy for his lazy, indulgent children." She points at Jeff. "That man is intelligent and caring and supportive. He wants to make a difference in his community."

I turn to Jeff. "You're involved in the community?"

He shrugs. "I've been thinking about it. I guess."

Fabio is still on his knees, but now he's recoiling, not proposing. Carol looms over him.

"I challenge you do one thing," she says, "*one* thing of substance. One thing that doesn't involve spending your parents' money. But I doubt you'll do it. Frankly, I don't care. I don't want to hear from you anymore!"

Fabio is back on his haunches. His hands are folded in his lap. He's not focused on anything in particular. Carol grabs Jeff's hand and leads him back to the table. He looks as shell-shocked as Fabio. Everyone in the place is looking our direction. I squat next to Fabio.

"Are you okay?" I ask.

His voice sounds strangely detached. "I'm fine, Joe. Just fine." His eyes are glassy. "Would you please excuse me?"

Fabio stands and walks out the door. He doesn't move his arms. It's like something is broken inside. It's concerning. I give some thought to running after him and making sure he's okay. But it's cold out, and my beer is getting warm.

You can't save the whole world, right?

***

I'm not sure if it's depression about the movie or preoccupation with the case. But when I get back to my building, I don't go straight to my apartment. For reasons passing understanding, I visit Deirdre's hiding place. I move past Lars's deck (resisting the urge to throw a Molotov cocktail through the window) and approach the empty apartment. I use the secret knock. A moment later, Deirdre opens the backdoor.

"To what do I own the pleasure?" she asks.

"I thought we should talk about the case."

I follow her to the empty living room. The blinds are closed. The overhead lights are off. A single lamp lights the bedroom. We step in there. A mattress is still the only furniture.

"Not exactly living the life of Reilly, are you?" I say.

"Don't want to take chances. Street's men aren't staking out the building. But that doesn't mean I should have all the lights on and be entertaining guests twenty-four/seven."

"Must get pretty boring. What do you do all day?"

"Meditate. Keep calm and focused. That's The Discipline."

"The Discipline?"

"Something I learned a long time ago." She leans against the wall. "It *does* get boring. I suppose there are ways to find entertainment."

Deirdre looks me over. Her eyes travel downward, then slide toward the bed. The invitation couldn't be more obvious.

"I don't think that's a good idea," I tell her.

"You didn't always feel that way."

"It's how I feel now."

Yes, there was a night where I took Deirdre up on that offer. On one level, I don't regret it. In strictly carnal terms, it was fantastic. But on another level, it made me think there might be a human component to her. That was my big mistake.

Deirdre takes the rejection in stride. "Your loss." Her eyes return to me. "Where do we go next? With Grace Jelinski?"

"I'm thinking Wilryan Realty, up in Brooklyn Point. Keith, the manager, gave Grace rides to and from work. Maybe he knows something."

"How cooperative do you think he'll be?"

"Not very. Keith was pretty dismissive of Grace disappearing. He was anxious to get Mike and me out of there."

"Do you think he's hiding something?"

"I do now. When I was at Grace's place, it felt like someone had been taking care of it. The mail was picked up and the front walk was shoveled. But the interior hadn't been cleaned. Everything in the fridge had gone bad."

"Like someone was keeping up appearances."

"Exactly," I say. "Keep the neighbors or the postman from getting suspicious. Whoever is taking care of the house probably helped Grace get away. And they might know where she is. Keith is the best candidate."

"Good. I'll go with you."

Zoinks. It's not as if I couldn't use Deirdre's help. But the thought of her dealing with Keith's potential (or almost certain) truculence doesn't fill me with confidence. The last thing we need is her busting up the office and someone calling the cops. Particularly when I've assured the chief of those cops that Deirdre is dead, and I have absolutely no knowledge to the contrary. I rub my chin, looking for a delicate way to handle this. (I've already turned down sex. I don't want to antagonize her any more than necessary.)

"Okay if I do the talking? They like me up there. One of them is a fan of my column."

"Whatever you say. I'll just be the dumb muscle."

I have a hard time picturing that, but I'll take it. Deirdre walks over to the mattress and plunks down, leaning back against the wall. She closes her eyes and takes a breath. Words come out of my mouth before I give them proper thought.

"Are you sure you're all right?" I ask.

Her eyes open. "Why wouldn't I be?"

"Just something I noticed. You get quiet every time Miles is mentioned. I know he meant a lot to you. At least, that's what it seems like."

Deirdre's eyes are fixed on me, and it's not a comforting feeling. Given her profession, she's not the kind to open a vein. In fact, I know *nothing* about her (beyond her being an excellent shot and preferring to be on top). The less I know about Deirdre, the less dangerous I am to her. But it's out there now. She draws her legs up, folding them under her like a Buddha.

"I owe Miles everything," she says. "More than you realize. But he kept things from me. I didn't let it bother me. It was a reflex with him. I wanted to be the exception. I guess I wasn't." Her voice is hollow. "How can you say you loved somebody who never really let you know them?"

Someone, somewhere might be able to answer that. But it's not me and it's not here. I slide down the wall, dropping into a sitting position. "It's hard," I say. "When you avoid a thing long enough, you can't go right back to it. Even if you want to."

Deirdre cocks her head. "You speak from experience?"

287

"I guess I do." I look away. "There was somebody I was in love with. Back in high school. It didn't work out. Ever since, I haven't been a big fan of letting anybody get close. She came back into my life not too long ago. It's made me realize how much closer I feel to her than anyone else I've ever met."

"Have you told her any of this?"

"No. We talk on the phone every now and again. It's nice. I don't want to risk that."

"So, you're keeping her at arm's length as well?"

Son of a bitch. She's right. Deirdre, of all people. "I guess that's the case." I smile. "I'm not sure I should be telling you any of this."

"I *know* I shouldn't be telling you anything. But Miles is gone now. So is Emily."

"Were you and Emily close?"

"Yes. We...we worked together a long time."

"I'm sorry. I'd ask you about her, but—"

"It's better if you don't know." Deirdre pulls her legs up, wrapping her arms around her knees. "I've been wondering how much longer I want to do this. Miles wanted to get out of The Life. He never made it."

"You think you could walk away?"

"Yes. Miles had a place picked out. I know where it is. Maybe it's time to go." She sighs. "But I can't leave until the cartel is dealt with. They don't let loose ends go, either."

My phone rings. I don't recognize the number at first. But something is familiar about it. Then it hits me: Sophie Walker. Miles's aunt. I scramble to answer. Sophie's voice is tremulous.

"Hi, Joe," she says, "I'm sorry to bother you, but I wasn't sure who else to call. I tried Simon. You remember him? He was Warren's friend. But I didn't get an answer. You were the next person I thought of."

"That's okay. What's going on?"

Sophie takes a quick breath. "Someone's watching my house. Can you help me?"

CHAPTER FOURTEEN

Once a month, Fidel fucked a woman named Gwen. A friend of his ex-wife. Fucking her was a way of fucking over his ex-wife. A win-win deal, as far as he was concerned. They had a routine. Pick Gwen up at her house. Go out to dinner. Back to her place. Cocktails in the hot tub. Let the festivities begin. Sometimes, she met him at the door. She'd be wearing only a silk kimono. To hell with dinner.

Fidel parked in the alley. The house was a simple A-frame. Two stories. A wooden fence around the yard. He went through the back gate, walked to the backdoor. The lights were on. The hot tub was bubbling. He set the bottle of red wine next to it. His balding head felt the cold. Winter was coming. Albuquerque was a hell of a lot colder than Phoenix. It made the hot tub savory. Fidel accepted the change of scenery. Like he accepted the change in bosses. Accepted but didn't like. He sucked in his gut. Stepped through the backdoor.

A guy dressed in black sat at the kitchen table.

Fidel stopped. He'd left his damn gun in the car. All he had was half a hard-on. And that was going away fast. The guy in black used his foot to push out a chair.

"Hi, Fidel," he said. "Thought we should talk."

"Where's Gwen?"

"Upstairs. I asked her to wait. She's fine."

Fidel was relieved. He didn't show it. His eyes were on the guy. Sort of. Fidel had an astigmatism. People thought he had one eye on them, one on other shit. Some didn't trust that.

The stranger looked familiar. His legs were crossed. He kept an elbow on the table. Fidel could sense the violence. Couldn't see it. Couldn't make a move. Couldn't risk Gwen. Couldn't risk his own ass. He sat down.

"Who are you?"

"Miles Slayne. I've done business with your boss. Maybe you've heard of me."

Fidel had. He knew the reputation. Knew Victor was fucking with the guy. Big mistake. Not that Victor saw it. He didn't want to. Victor thought getting away with shit made you smart. Fidel knew better. It made you lucky. Until your luck ran out. Fidel's luck had run out. He was staring at the guy. Completely fucked. His heart jackhammering.

"I've heard of you," Fidel said.

"Good. You know what your boss is doing?"

"Yes."

"And you approve?"

291

"Not my place. I do what I'm told."

The guy grinned. "You can think for yourself. That's why you're alive."

"You're very well informed."

"That's why I'm *alive."*

A tinkling sound outside. Wind chimes. A thing Gwen liked. Fidel asked, "What do you need from me?"

"Victor picked a fight he didn't need to pick. He does that. Long as Victor produces, the Don will tolerate it. But it's going to bite Victor in the ass. You know that."

"What if I do?"

"I'm asking for help. Won't cost you much. I'll make sure you're protected. And paid."

Fidel folded his hands, kept them on his lap. Miles was right. Victor was headed for a cliff. Foot to the floor. Headlights out. And they were all in the car with him. But Fidel played it safe. Maybe fucking his ex-wife's best friend wasn't safe. Didn't mean he wanted to make it a habit. Or maybe sticking with Victor was the risk. Maybe Fidel was fucked either way.

"Let's say I agree," Fidel said. "What does this something involve?"

Miles took out a cell phone, laid it on the table. "Two numbers in there. One to a guy in Minnesota. If it comes down to it, you send him one message. For you, there is only the desert."

"What does that mean?"

"It'll mean something to him. That's it."

"And the other number?" Fidel asked.

"Goes to me. Victor's going to make a move against me, you let me know." Miles kept his eyes locked in. "What do you say?"

"That's all you need? A phone call and a text message?"

"Just keep your eyes and ears open. Message accordingly."

"And I can trust you?"

"Yes."

Fidel considered the phone. "You got a deal."

Miles offered his hand. Fidel took it. "Thank you," Miles said. He got up from the table, stepped to the backdoor. "Tell your girl I'm sorry. Came downstairs in her underwear, found me in the kitchen. She freaked out a little."

"I'll try to explain it to her."

"Have a nice night."

Miles disappeared. Fidel got up, walked to the bottom of the staircase.

"Gwen? It's all right. A business thing. Let's hit the hot tub."

Fidel walks to the backdoor, unbuttoning his shirt. Gwen's footsteps were on the stairs. She'd need to unwind. Wine would help.

Forgetting would help.

***

Deirdre and I make it to Brooklyn Point without being gunned down or arrested. (These days, that's a win.) I'm about to turn on Sophie's street when Deirdre puts a hand on the wheel.

"Let me out here," she says. "Then park out front. Don't look around, don't pay attention to anything. Just go to the front door and knock."

"What are you going to do?"

"You'll know it when I do it."

Deirdre shoves open the passenger door. She moves into the shadows. I ease the Saturn down the street and park in the driveway. Sophie opens the front door before I can knock.

"Thank you for coming," she says, toying with her gold necklace. "Sorry to bother you. I don't know who to call, and I wasn't sure the police would listen to me."

She ushers me into the house. I try not to track snow in. Sophie locks the front door and moves me toward the dining room table. The blinds in the dining nook have been closed.

"What's going on?" I ask.

Sophie half-reaches for the blinds. "There's a car out there, just down the street. A black Buick. There are two men, both Latino. It's been there all afternoon, watching the house."

I might know what's going on, but that won't bring Sophie any comfort. *Hey, it's an elderly lady and a humor blogger up against hired killers from a drug cartel.* "If I'm right," I tell her, "they're not particularly good guys."

"What do they…" Then it occurs to her. "Is this related to Warren somehow?"

"It might be. I think they're going to try to get answers out of you."

"About what? I don't know anything."

"I know that, and you know that. But…"

Sophie taps her fingertips on the table. "Are these people from the army?"

"No."

"What would Warren have been into if not the army?"

Hoo-boy. I'm not sure Sophie wants the answer to that. "Just know these guys are dangerous," I say. "They're not people we want to mess with."

Sophie opens her mouth to ask a question. We're interrupted by footsteps coming up the driveway. I peek through the blinds. Two guys approach. True to Sophie's description, both are Latino. They wear light black coats that don't match the weather. One has dark hair, shaved on the sides, with a scar right behind his ear. The other is tall and broad. He has jet black hair and a pockmarked face. Scar looks around while Pockmark concentrates on the front door.

"Go to the bedroom," I say. "Don't answer the door for anybody but me."

Sophie bustles off toward the bedroom. She's just gotten there when the front door gets kicked in. Scar is first through. His gun is drawn. I put my hands up and step back. Scar looks around.

"Where's the old lady?" he asks.

He's probably not in the mood for *What old lady?* "Why do you want her?"

"Fuck you."

That's about what I should have expected. Pockmark moves toward the kitchen, gun low. He flicks a look back to Scar.

"Basement stairs," Pockmark says. "And a backdoor."

"Try the backdoor first. Then go downstairs." Scar turns his attention to me. "Unless you know where she's at."

I do, but I'm not about to share that information with Scar. I say nothing and wish I'd made out a will. (I don't want the state claiming my Batman memorabilia.)

The backdoor opens, and there are footsteps in the kitchen. Scar keeps his eyes on me and calls to the next room. "You find her?" No answer. "Hey Tony, I asked you a fucking—"

"Tony isn't in right now," a familiar voice says. "How about you and I chat, sweets?"

Scar spins toward the kitchen doorway. He does it in time to take a thrust kick to the chest. He flies backward, over the coffee table, and onto the sofa. His gun clatters to the floor. Deirdre calmly scoops it up, disassembles it, and sets most of the pieces on the coffee table.

"That's better," she says. "Now we can have a proper chat."

Scar rubs his chest. "Fuck you, *punta*." He struggles to get the words out.

"Let's try to be more polite," Deirdre says. "While we still can."

Scar sits up on the sofa. One arm dangles below the level of the coffee table. He hunches his shoulders, trying to get a deep breath.

"What did you do to Tony?" he asks.

"He's fine," Deirdre tells him. "Lying in a snowbank but okay. You'll want to get him out of there before frostbite sets in."

Scar looks down. A moment later, his hand comes up. Something flies across the room. Deirdre leans back and out of the way. The thing hits the wall and sticks. It's a small knife. It must have come from Scar's boot. He dives over the coffee table at Deirdre. The two of them crash into the piano bench and onto the floor.

Scar is on top of Deirdre. He tries to get into her coat, to the gun she keeps there. I'm frozen, wondering what to do. Scar headbutts Deirdre. Twice. The second draws a cry from her. He gets the gun out of her coat. Deirdre knocks it across the floor. Scar leaps for it.

It's under the coffee table. I get there just before Scar. Before I can grasp the gun, though, he grabs the back of my peacoat and tosses me aside. I fly back, blocking Deirdre's path. Scar grabs the gun and rolls toward us.

Deirdre dives over the top of me. She grabs Scar's gun arm. They struggle. Deirdre shoves him away. Scar jumps to his feet. He's holding the gun. It's aimed at Deirdre's chest.

Suddenly, there's a crash. Followed by another crash. Turns out, the first crash is a vase coming down on Scar's head. The second crash is him hitting the floor, out cold. Deirdre grabs the gun. Sophie stands in the hallway, holding the remains of the vase.

"It's okay," she says, setting the remains on a small table. "I bought the damn thing at Goodwill. No loss at all."

***

The difficult question is what we're going to do with Scar and Tony (FKA Pockmark). If we call the police, what do we tell them? We can't reveal Deirdre's presence. Are they going to believe an elderly lady and a complete candy ass took down two killers? Deirdre gives us a temporary reprieve by tying them up and sticking them in the trunk of the Saturn (covering them with a warm blanket, at Sophie's insistence). We gather in the living room for a debrief (which is never as fun as it sounds). Sophie positions herself on the couch while Deirdre takes a nearby chair. I sit on the arm of the sofa.

"Where are those men really from?" Sophie asks.

Deirdre lets me field this one. Thanks. "They're with a drug cartel," I say. "They're looking for someone named Grace Jelinski. Apparently, Grace knew…" I look toward Deirdre, hoping she won't mind me using the name. "Warren."

Sophie looks confused. "How did they know each other? Like I told you before: I don't remember Warren ever mentioning someone named Grace."

"We think they knew each other…later."

Her eyes flick toward Deirdre. Miles had mentioned his aunt to Deirdre. He wouldn't have mentioned Deirdre to Sophie. They take each other in. I feel like an intruder. Sophie's voice is gentle.

"You knew Warren?" Sophie asks. Deirdre nods, barely. "Where is he?" Sophie asks.

"He's gone." Deirdre looks for other words but only gets out, "I'm sorry."

Sophie's face is still. "How did it happen?"

"It's a long story. I'd rather not get into it."

"How would Warren know people in the drug business? He was in the army."

"This was after he left the army," Deirdre says. "He did some…intelligence work. He ran across people like this."

299

"And you're in intelligence, too?"

"I am. Yes."

Sophie moves a finger between us. "How do the two of you know each other?"

I bob my head. "That…is an even longer story."

Sophie is willing to let it go at that. "Those men want Grace Jelinski. And they thought I knew where she is?"

"They're taking their chances on it," I say. "I think they're getting desperate. Whoever Grace is, she's making them nervous."

"And stupid," Deirdre says. "But they didn't have to go far to get there."

"I couldn't have helped them," Sophies says. "Are they really going to go around and attack people who used to know Warren?"

"If they get desperate enough," Deirdre says.

"Maybe I should leave town," Sophie says. "God knows where I'll go, but…"

"We'll call the police," I say. "They'll protect you. I, uh, I know the chief of police."

"The woman? I've heard she's on the ball. At least from people I trust. A lot of others don't like her."

A collection of racist homophobes in the suburbs. Who'd have thunk it? "I'll vouch for her," I tell Sophie.

She lets out a grateful breath. "Thank you."

"But you'll need to make the call," I say. "We'll leave the two guys here. We'd appreciate it if you didn't mention Deirdre."

"What should I tell them?" Sophie asks.

Deirdre lays a hand on Sophie's arm. "I'm sure you'll think of something."

Sophie doesn't seem convinced, and frankly, I'm not either. But I don't have a better suggestion. Sophie focuses on Deirdre.

"You were special to Warren," Sophie says. "I can tell." This gets no response. "If you wouldn't mind, I'd like to give you something." Sophie bustles into one of the corner rooms. She returns several moments later, holding a book. She offers it to Deirdre. "This was Warren's favorite when he was in high school. I think he'd want you to have it."

Deirdre hesitates, then takes the book. "*The Great Gatsby.*"

"Have you ever read it?"

"No," Deirdre says, her voice tight.

"Neither have I," Sophie says. "Warren nearly wore this copy out. You can tell by how dog-eared it is."

Deirdre blinks rapidly. She finally says, "Thank you."

We walk to the door. Sophie offers Deirdre a hug. Deirdre is slow to return it, but she pats Sophie lightly on the back.

"It was nice meeting you," Deirdre says.

"We should talk sometime," Sophie says.

Deirdre and I walk to the car. Sophie watches us through the picture window. The second we open the trunk, she disappears, probably to call the police. Our friends are awake now, and neither looks happy.

"You're going to get yours, bitch," Scar tells her.

"Not from you, sweets," she says.

She yanks Scar, none too gently, out of the trunk, and puts him in a fireman's carry. She hauls him over to the steps and drops him. She does the same with Tony. I'm glad Sophie left the outside light off so the neighbors can't get a clear look at the proceedings. Deirdre rips free a couple pieces of the blanket and gags both guys. We climb into the car and take off.

"You think everything will be okay back there?" I ask.

"Maybe. The police will be suspicious, but what are they going to do?"

"Will Frick and Frack say anything?"

"I doubt it. It's their job to keep their mouths shut. Besides, they don't want to admit a woman kicked their asses."

"The cartel will know you're still alive."

"Just confirming their suspicions, darling."

I round the corner. Deirdre looks back toward Sophie's house. She holds up the book. "You ever read this thing?"

"In college. It's a good book."

She looks it over, then tosses it in the backseat. We're quiet for the rest of the drive.

**

"Cut!" Lars says, sliding off his director's chair. "That was good. Let's do it again."

A sense of deflation spreads around the set. It's not the first one of the day. And this is only the first day of shooting.

We're in the living room of a sizable house out in the country. It's a decent setting: hardwood floors, high ceilings, a picture window looking over the desolate winter landscape. The décor is knick-knacks, old family photos, lacy curtains, etc. It's a great atmosphere, if the atmosphere wasn't so tense.

The crew isn't large, just the cameraman, the sound person, and a few others. The actors gather in the adjacent dining room, congregating around an oak table with various pastries. (The easiest way to herd actors is to direct them to where the food is.) Frankie and Kyra sit behind Lars. No sign of Fabio. I'm on a pew that must have been rescued from a local church. The script, housed in a three-ring binder, sits on my lap. I set it aside and stroll over to our esteemed director.

"You sure we need another take?" I say. "We've done ten already."

"Only ten?" Lars says, straightening his large shades. "We have to get to fifty before we even start to get close."

"Fifty?"

"At least."

He fusses with his silk scarf and straightens his beret. He looks like an off-brand Invisible Man. (If only he *were* invisible.) I hold my hands out, palms down, trying to be reasonable.

"Lars, if you try that, people will...how to put this...kill you."

"They'll come around. When they see the finished product, they'll realize how petty are their grievances. Genius will show out."

Viewed from a certain angle, genius can be defined as a collection of batshit ideas that somehow coalesce into a unique and brilliant whole. And sometimes, a collection of batshit ideas coalesces into nothing but a collection of batshit ideas. I'll let you guess which one this movie is trending toward.

"You have any idea how much time we'll need to do fifty more takes?" I ask.

"As much as we need," Lars says.

"And how much it will cost?"

"I'll refer you back to my previous answer."

I suck in some air. "There's also the small matter of the owner of this house wanting it back sometime today."

"They'll be fine," Lars says. "Now, if you could please get back to those rewrites I ordered, I have a job to do." He returns to his director's chair. "Okay everybody, let's get ready to go again."

Having been thus dismissed, I return to the pew and a script in which I've completely lost faith. I concentrate on it while Lars does take after take, exasperating everyone involved. After one of them, an actress says, desperately, "I'm not sure what it is you want."

Lars spreads his hands. "Perfection. And we'll get there. We just need another take. Maybe several."

This time, the groan in the room is audible. The actress breaks down in tears. The crew looks ready to toss Lars into the snow. I rush over and whisper in his ear.

"This would be a good time to take a break," I say.

Lars's head snaps back. "A break? We're just getting warmed up. No, no. We have to keep going. We'll lose the magic otherwise."

A hand drops onto Lars's shoulder. It's the sound guy, who is roughly six-and-a-half feet tall and nearly as wide; most of it concentrated in his chest and shoulders. "We all need a break," The Mountain says, in a voice that would make James Earl Jones sound like a pipsqueak.

The color drains from Lars's face. "I…I really…there's the momentum…"

"Now," The Mountain says.

Lars nods furiously. "That sounds good. Let's take five." Responding to a look from The Mountain, he hastily amends this. "Ten. Ten. By which I mean, fifteen."

Everyone moves away from the set as if it's radioactive. The house is out in the country, west of the Cities. The owner started observing the filming, but she eventually got bored and went upstairs. Frankie and Kyra step into the kitchen to confer. I set the script aside. Lars and I are the only ones left in the room. He walks toward me, shades off, looking at the floor.

"Hate to tell you this, brother, but you may want to take care. Chuck is looking for you."

Again, I have difficulty switching from being completely annoyed with Lars to caring about what's going on in his personal life. However, this involves my ass and the safety of same.

"Why is Chuck looking for me?" I ask.

"He thinks you're sleeping with Laura."

I'm whating with whom? "Excuse me?"

"He drew an erroneous conclusion. First, he suspects Laura is cheating on him."

"Gee, I wonder where he got that idea." I pause. "Seriously, where *did* he get that idea?"

"Laura's been a little distant lately. She gets secretive about her phone. Vague about where she's been and who's been seeing. Refuses to take a lie detector test. The usual stuff."

"A lie detector test?"

"That's what Chuck calls it. It's not, strictly speaking, a polygraph. It's closer to waterboarding. I've discouraged Chuck from using it, but he's a man of passion."

"And how do I come into this?"

"Laura mentioned in passing that she likes your column. He put two-and-two together."

"And came up with seventeen."

Lars's eyes dart about. "Chuck is a creative person. His logic, though, is…not flawless."

"But I understand his gun collection is. Has he said how he's going to handle this?"

"Something about killing you," he says, kneading his beret in his hands. "Over a three-or-four-day period."

I don't have a lot of respect for Chuck—on any number of levels—but there's always been an air of menace about him. My long-standing policy has been not to mess with him. Now he thinks I've *really* messed with him.

"Lars, this is serious shit," I say. "What am I going to do?"

"It's tricky. When Chuck is convinced he's right, he's hard to dissuade. Do you think involving the Witness Protection Program would be prudent?"

I try to think. "You've got to tell him the truth. Tell him *you* are the one sleeping with Laura."

"Whoa, whoa, whoa. Let's not lose our heads. We just need to think up a plan that will allow you to live, Chuck to have his honor satisfied, and me to keep making sweet, sweet love to his woman." He scratches his beard. "Any ideas?"

"How about *I* tell Chuck the truth?"

"That wouldn't work. He'd never believe you. He has complete and total trust in me. Which makes my betrayal all the crappier. But when nookie is involved, who's to say what's right and wrong?"

There are a few books on that subject, but I don't think they'll have a lot of truck with Lars. I admit I've slept with a few girlfriends who were not, strictly speaking, *my* girlfriend. But I haven't slept with Chuck's significant other, which makes the situation that much more frustrating. To say nothing of dangerous.

"Look, it's bad enough I've got a cartel out to kill me," I say. "I can't have Chuck on the job as well. There are only so many ways to stay safe. And I'm terrible at all of them."

Lars gives me an (intended to be) reassuring pat on the shoulder. "We'll figure it out, brother. Maybe we can pit Chuck against the cartel. We'll brainstorm later."

Chuck against the cartel would be mutually assured destruction, not only for them but the surrounding countryside. Before we can continue, the owner of the house appears. She's a stout woman in her early fifties. She wears a blue flannel shirt and jeans, and her hair is dyed blonde. She was nice enough when we first arrived, having arranged the pastry and donuts in the dining room. Now, the avuncular demeanor has been replaced by her lips being pursed and her arms being folded across her ample chest.

"It'll be dark soon," she says, her *Fargo* accent in full effect. "I was told you folks would only be here maybe half a day. You haven't even finished your first scene."

Lars gives her an airy wave. "Madam, you can't hurry art. It happens when it happens."

"Yeah?" the owner says. "I can hurry *you* or your art can happen somewhere else."

That takes some of the considerable air out of Lars. Having burned the *I'm an artist* match, he's forced to try another option: passing the buck.

"I'm afraid that's something you'll have to take up with our other producers," he says. "I was told I would have all the time I needed. If that's not workable, perhaps you and Frankie or Kyra can figure something out."

"Oh, we'll do that," the owner says. "And it'll be you getting your skinny ass off my property soon."

The owner stalks into the next room, looking for Frankie and Kyra. Lars plunks down again. A few minutes later, Kyra comes in. She stands in front of Lars, pushes up her glasses, and puts her hands on her hips.

"We have to wrap it up," she says.

Lars pops up. "We haven't gotten the scene yet."

"Are you kidding me?" Kyra says. "You have about thirty takes to choose from."

"And if we do thirty more, we might be there," Lars says.

Kyra doesn't say anything, leading me to believe she's so pissed, she's beyond the capacity for speech. Turns out she doesn't need it because the owner enters, wielding a broom.

"Last time I'm telling you," the owner says, "get all that equipment and shit and get out of here. I said I'd let you shoot a couple scenes. I didn't say you morons could move in." She puts a hand on Kyra's arm. "Please understand I'm not directing this at you, dear."

"Thank you," Kyra says, in a voice that sounds like she's passing a billiard ball.

The owner brings the broom up to Lars's chest. "Pack it up and get the hell out."

Lars scoffs. "Madam, I don't think you—"

I'm not sure what the end of that sentence would have been, since the owner whacks Lars in the face with the broom. It's not a hard smack. He catches mostly bristles. But it's enough to send him backwards, spitting and coughing.

"Ugh," he says. "Dust bunnies. And did I catch a hint of cat litter in there?"

"Probably," the owner says. "Now, get the hell out before I give you a good whack."

Lars does a masterful job of making it seem like it's *his* idea to wrap up for the day. The cast and crew are so delighted, they don't care if Lars is lying or not. (Nor are they interested in his statements about taking time off in order to recharge the creative batteries.) The house looks like a plague of locusts hit it. Within minutes, every trace of the set is gone (including, sadly, the leftover coffee and donuts). I grab my three-ring binder and clear out. My car is next to the old pole barn. I'm just about there when my phone rings. I check the caller ID as I climb into the car. It's Hank. I should have expected this.

"Fugitive Productions," is how I answer. "Mr. Polanski speaking. How may I help you?"

Hank has no time for my monkeyshines. "I seem to be getting a lot of action from the cartel these days."

"I didn't realize Brooklyn Point was becoming so multicultural."

There's a slight pause. I like to think it's Hank biting back a laugh. I'm probably flattering myself. "A woman named Sophie Walker was attacked by two men last night. She says a friend helped her subdue them. Couldn't give us a description of this friend. Said they came out of nowhere and subdued these guys."

I state the obvious. "Seems kind of flimsy."

"It would have to work its way up to flimsy. But the lady is older and pretty rattled. We couldn't get much out of her. We'll try again when she's calmed down, but I'm not optimistic."

I can't compliment Sophie on the story she came up with. But how do you explain two gunmen being captured and make sure there's little for the police to follow up on? We didn't give her much in the way of material.

"How do you know they're cartel guys?" I ask, fully committing to playing dumb.

"Jim Street looked into it. They work for Victor Merced. From what I understand, he's a mean motor scooter who had an issue with Deirdre. Angel was part of his crew."

"Any idea why they'd go after an old lady in Brooklyn Point?"

"No. That's one of the reasons I'm calling you."

"I'm not sure what to tell you," I say. "I'm glad this woman is okay, though. Did the cartel guys tell you anything?"

"Nothing worth listening to. They mostly talked about my cultural heritage and sexual preference. None of it flattering."

I wince. "Sorry about that."

"Not your fault. Unless it is."

I don't like the sound of that. "What do you mean?"

"Kind of coincidence. I'm getting cartel guys on my doorstep right around the same time you're getting cartel guys on your doorstep. And they keep turning up dead or severely beaten."

"You think I'm capable of that?"

"No. But you might be working with someone who is." A slight pause. "Is there any chance the person in my morgue isn't Deirdre?"

I'm glad this conversation is over the phone. Hank can't see how uncomfortable I am. "I suppose there's a chance," I say. "Anything in life is possible. But there are any number of reasons I'm not the one to tell you, and me not having a medical degree is just the first one."

I think that's a magnificent obfuscation. Hank says nothing in response. Or maybe it's a pause to let the suspense build again. (Harold Pinter has nothing on this woman.)

"If that's what you're going to tell me," she says. "I have no choice but to believe it. You better be telling me the truth. Or I'll come down on you with the power of God's own thunder. You understand me?"

"Seems pretty clear."

"Goodbye, Mr. Davis," Hank says.

I toss the phone into the drink holder. That was unpleasant. But it's about what I expected. There was no way to save Sophie without garnering Hank's (and most likely

313

Street's) suspicion. Can't make an omelet without breaking a few eggs and all that shit.

If only we would stop breaking eggs.

***

"You're not pleasant first thing in the morning," Deirdre says. "Have you always been like this?"

I focus straight ahead, tamping down my annoyance. "Only as long as I can remember. If you want to hear real horror stories, talk to my mother. She was the one who had to get me up for school." I stop my to-go coffee short of my lips. "Come to think of it, don't talk to my mom."

"Okay, Mr. Cranky Pants."

That halts the conversation. As much as I hate to admit it, Deirdre's right. I'm *not* great company in the morning. Must be why I'm thirty-six and not married. That reason and no other. We make our way through Brooklyn Point, heading toward Wilryan Realty. I'm not looking forward to this. Aside from getting up early, we have to go into there and ask uncomfortable questions about Grace Jelinski. I'm not sure how cooperative her co-workers will be. I'm even less sure how patient Deirdre will be. I'm holding a situational Molotov Cocktail here.

I park near the front of Wilryan Realty. For a fleeting moment, I hope Deirdre will not accompany me inside. Snake-eyes on that. She reaches for the door handle the second I put

314

the car in park. The threat level for gun violence just moved from orange to red.

The office looks much the same as the last time I was here. It's half-full and everyone seems sleepy, befitting a Monday morning in the midst of winter. A few guys perk up at the sight of Deirdre. Tracy, the employee I spoke to last time, is nearest the front desk. She quickly approaches us.

"Joe Davis," she says. "Have you found Grace yet?"

"No luck," I say. "Figured I stop by for another chat."

Tracy stiffens. Maybe she was hoping this was a social call or maybe she sees Deirdre and senses I've brought a thug this time. (Not entirely inaccurate.)

"What did you need to know?" Tracy asks.

I prop an arm on the counter. "It's kind of personal. But was there anything going on between Grace and Keith?"

"What do you mean by *going on*?" Tracy asks.

"*Going on* as in dating."

She sneaks a look at Deirdre, hesitant to take up this topic with a relative stranger around. Deirdre busies herself looking at the brochures. Tracy lowers her voice.

"Your friend there," she asks, "is she a police officer?"

"No. Just…somebody helping me with this thing." I switch to my most confidential tone. (The one I use whenever I tell Mike I'm seeing somebody I probably shouldn't be seeing. Not that I, uh, use it a lot.) "I have pretty good reason to believe Grace is in danger. I can't go into details but trust me when I say that."

Tracy gives it some thought. She doesn't throw any looks back toward the main office, so I assume Keith is out at the moment. The other employees try to look like they're minding their own business. (We know better.) Finally, Tracy leans toward me.

"I wouldn't say they were dating, exactly," she says. "Keith was interested in her, but Grace didn't feel the same way. Then he started doing this big brother thing. Being really protective."

"And Grace was okay with this?" I ask.

"She was. Oh, I hate talking about her in the past tense. Anyway, I think Grace was relieved to have Keith as a friend."

"Do you think he has any idea where Grace is?"

"No, not at all. He likes to pretend he's mad at her for disappearing and not giving him any notice. But I can tell he's worried something's happened to her."

I'll take Tracy's word on that. "If we assume Grace is hiding someplace, do you have any idea where she might be?"

"I don't. I'm sorry."

Nuts. Nobody here seems to know where she might be or why she might have run (let alone what the cartel might have to do with it). And I'm not anxious to talk to the one person who might—*might*—have an idea.

"What the hell is this?"

Speak of the devil. The harsh voice cuts through the conversation. Tracy drops her eyes. I snap a look toward the door. Keith moves toward us, undoing his scarf. I try to seem jaunty. (It doesn't become me.)

"Hi there," I say. "Keith, right?"

"You know who I am," he says. "I want to know what the hell you're doing here."

"I just needed to talk to Tracy," I say. Might as well throw caution to the wind. "Maybe I can talk to you as well."

His eyes get beady. "About Grace?"

"Yes."

"Go to hell."

It's a fair cop. Keith steps to one side, clearing our path to leave. Deirdre looks on, bemused. Hopefully, Mr. Reasonable can rescue the situation.

"I'm just trying to get some information," I say. "I want to help Grace, really."

Keith is unmoved. "Grace isn't here."

"Any idea where she might be?"

"She isn't here."

"So, you're saying she isn't here."

Deirdre looks down, smiling. Tracy snorts, fighting back a laugh. Keith eyeballs me.

317

"We have work to do," he says. "You aren't customers. Please leave."

Deirdre sets the brochures aside. "We will. When you've answered his question."

Keith spins toward her. "Who the hell are you?"

"Your orthopedist."

There's a moment where Keith falters, as if he senses this is someone he shouldn't mess with. However, he's being disrespected in front of his employees. He can't let that go. He drops his hands on the counter and faces off with Deirdre.

"Listen to me, lady—"

That's as far as he gets. Deirdre grabs the letter opener from the desk and brings the point of it down on Keith's hand. His eyes bug out, and he starts sweating. Deirdre's countenance doesn't change.

"Maybe *you* should listen, dipshit," she says. "We want to find out what happened to Grace. If that gets in the way of your little house-selling business, I'm terribly sorry. But that's no reason to be rude. Do we understand each other?"

Keith barely gets the words out. "My hand…"

"I asked you a question. Would you have the courtesy to answer it?"

"Yeah…we understand each other."

"I'm so glad to hear that. Now, do you have any idea where Grace has gone?"

"No. No idea."

"That's a shame. Okay, I'm going to take this thing out of your hand, and my friend and I are going to leave. We're doing that because you're useless and not because you told us to. I'm also going to check back, and if I hear that you've taken your Teeny Pee-Pee energy out on Tracy or anyone else in this office, I'll come back here and reinsert this thing in a much more painful area. Are we clear?"

"We are."

"That makes me very happy. Thank you."

Deirdre releases Keith's hand. He clutches it and scurries back to his office. She tosses the letter opener on the desk and turns her attention to Tracy, who's transfixed.

"If you're ever in Kansas City, look me up," Deirdre says. "You haven't had a decent meal until you've been to Joe's Kansas City Barbecue. Have a nice day, Tracy."

Deirdre steps out the door, leaving the office dumbfounded. I say nothing and follow my partner out. I catch up with her when we're halfway back to the car.

"Was that really necessary?" I ask.

"I don't know if it was necessary. It was fun. You can't let people insult you."

"That's why I generally try to insult them first."

"You have your way. I have mine."

We climb into the car, but I don't move it. We're far enough from the front door that the people at Wilryan Realty won't know we're still here.

"Did we get *anything* interesting out of that conversation?" I ask.

"Keith had a crush on Grace, and he's an asshole. Nobody seems to know where Grace is. Not exactly groundbreaking."

I tap my hands on the steering wheel. "Nobody knows. Or do they?"

Deirdre slides to one side. "What do you mean?"

"We have to assume Grace is still alive. Otherwise, the cartel wouldn't still be looking for her. She doesn't have the means to get very far. She has to be hiding somewhere close by. According to Tracy, she didn't have a lot of friends. We don't know if she had any family around. She didn't have a lot of people she could rely on to help her. But she had Keith. He's twisted at least that far around her finger."

"Should we go back in and talk to him?"

"I think that waterhole has been poisoned. But maybe we should track him. See if he leads us to Grace."

"You sure we just can't grab him and torture him?"

"Why don't we try my way first?"

That deflates Deirdre. She knows my plan makes sense, even if it isn't as fun. Just one of those things in life. The devil is in the details.

Or in my case, the passenger seat.

CHAPTER FIFTEEN

Mexico City Grill was in San Antonio. A hole in the wall joint. Clean and well kept. White tile floors, dark wood tables, open kitchen. Ranchera music on the P.A. A mural on the wall. A Mexican village, a family leaving, maybe for the fields, maybe for America. Omar Fuentes liked the place. He owned it. He was there twice a week.

Fuentes got up from his table. The staff scurried to clear it, refill his drink. He buttoned the gray suitcoat, ran a hand over the black collarless shirt. The men's room was near the back. Guys guarded the backdoor. Fuentes stepped into the restroom. Stopped to pick up a crumpled hand towel. Tossed it in the trash. Bellied up to the urinal. A guy in black stepped out of a stall. Fuentes saw the reflection in the framed ad over the urinal. The guy folded his arms.

"Evening," the guy said.

Fuentes' tone was measured. "Who are you?"

"My name is Miles Slayne."

He'd heard the name. Miles Slayne was supposedly retired. Apparently not. Fuentes went about his business. Zipped up. Turned to his guest.

"I had someone guarding the backdoor," Fuentes said.

"He'll be fine. Eventually."

Fuentes went to the sink, washed his hands. "What do you want?"

"Victor Merced's head on a platter. That sound good to you?"

"What do I have to do with it?"

"Don Pedro wants you two to make peace. I assume you've got a meeting set up?"

Fuentes ran his fingers along his close-cropped hair, brushed the gray at the temples. "Yes, we do."

"Too bad my associate and I got there first, wiped out Victor and his boys."

"A tragedy." Fuentes dried his hands. "What's your issue with Victor?"

"Let's just say it's best to get it taken care of. Something you and I have in common."

Fuentes used the towel to clean a smudge from the mirror. "If I let you take out Victor, I get blowback from the Don. He won't believe I had nothing to do with it."

"He knew Victor took out Michael. His own nephew. The Don's not stupid. He knows you make more money in peace than in war. That's why he let Victor get away with it. And why he won't make a move on you."

"I could still make peace with Victor."

323

"You could. He'll look you in the eye, shake your hand. Smile at you, even. Same smile you'll see when he sticks the knife in your chest."

A moment passed. "How do we do this?" Fuentes asked.

"Where is the meeting with Victor?"

"Holy Family Church. Here in San Antonio. Next Wednesday night."

"Deirdre and I will be there. Your guys just have to be outside. That work for you?"

"You expecting anything from me?"

"This one is gratis."

Fuentes offered his hand. "You have a deal."

They shook on it. Miles said, "By the way, tell the guy guarding the backdoor I'm sorry. Just business."

"He and I won't be on speaking terms much longer. At least, he won't be speaking."

"Tight ship. I get it."

He left without looking back. Fuentes watched him go.

***

There are times in life when you feel like an asshole. I'm having one of those.

I'm in a car with Robbie. It's not Robbie's car, so I assume it's either a loaner or a rental. (At least, I hope it's either a loaner or a rental.) I'm again wearing a trench coat and playing a role. I've added a fedora (borrowed from Carol, who got it from her dad). We're in the parking lot of The Tav, waiting for a certain Lyle Wills. The only sound is Robbie munching a hot dog.

"We going to do this whole meeting in the car?" I ask.

"No. We'll take him someplace. Follow my lead."

"It would be easier if I knew what was going on."

Robbie spills some mustard on his coat but ignores it. "Can't take the chance. You might screw something up."

"How do you know that?"

"Not my call. I'm taking orders from Stoner."

I can't believe it's come to this. Robbie and Stoner have been best friends and mortal enemies since college. Until recently, I would have testified in court that Robbie would rather have his nuts laminated than take orders from Stoner.

"The hot dog part of your cover?" I ask. "Like Brad Pitt in *Ocean's Eleven*. Too busy to sit down and eat?"

Robbie talks with his mouth full. "No. I'm hungry."

Before I can dig any further into that (not that I much want to), a car pulls up and Lyle Wills gets out. He tries to be nonchalant in making his way over to us. (His success is…indifferent.) He climbs into the backseat.

"Good to see you both," he says.

Neither of us responds, unless you count Robbie tossing down his hotdog wrapper. He puts the car into gear and pulls out of the lot. Wills leans into the front seat.

"Where are we going?" he asks.

"I'll worry about that," Robbie says. "Did you bring The Method?"

Wills holds up a manila envelope. Robbie nods. That brings the conversational portion of our program to an end. We descend into downtown St. Paul and make our way over to the Green Tree Building. It's a four-story cement structure off Mears Park, on the eastern edge of downtown. Robbie parks on the street. Our guest looks up at the plain structure.

"Is this your headquarters?" he asks, skeptical.

"It's a place we use," Robbie says. "That's all you need to know."

Robbie leads the way inside. The lobby is darkened. The place is mostly deserted (like an increasing number of buildings in downtown St. Paul). Our steps echo on the tile floor. It's creepy. We get into an elevator off the lobby and go down one floor. Robbie brings us to an unassuming office about halfway down. It contains only a small round table and a chair. The carpeting is threadbare, and the outlines of now missing pictures line the walls. The fluorescent lighting is a shock to the eyes. On the table is a small mic and a cheap razor.

"Take off your shirt," Robbie says. "I hope you're not hairy."

"Not, not all that much," Wills says, meekly taking off his winter coat and unbuttoning his shirt.

326

"Even a little is too much. You're going to have to shave your chest."

Wills doesn't look happy. I don't blame him. I have little to no hair on my chest, and I'm perfectly happy keeping it that way. Wills takes off his shirt and undershirt, revealing a mild bit of hair. Robbie hands him the razor. Wills issues a high-pitched yip as he scrapes away. Robbie examines the mic. He takes a roll of medical tape from his jacket pocket.

"You remember the plan?" he asks.

Wills closes his eyes and recites from memory. "I meet with Mike. We set the price for The Method. I hand it over. You guys move in."

Robbie turns to me. "Sounds like he's got it. What do you think?"

I'll agree with anything Robbie says. (Not normally a good policy, but here we are). "Got it to a tee."

"Hand it over," Robbie says to Wills.

Wills offers the envelope to Robbie but gets redirected to me. I take it and remove the contents, presumably The Method. I don't have a fucking clue what it is or what it's supposed to look like. I show the contents to Robbie.

"We're in business," he says. He turns to Wills. "Here's the garbage." He hands Wills a similar-looking envelope. "Griffin will meet you in the parking lot of The Tav. You make the deal and hand over the junk. Then we move in."

"Sounds good," Wills says. "You're gonna put Griffin away, right? I'm not going to have to worry about blowback?"

Robbie looks to me, since I'm supposed to be his superior. (I can agree with that much.) I give Wills my sternest look (such as it is).

"We're the federal government," I tell him. "We don't blow."

That's good enough for Wills. He puts his clothes back on, and we return to the car. We make our way back up the hill to The Tav. Robbie pulls over a couple blocks shy of the bar.

"We're gonna let you out here," he says. "You can't be seen with us before the meeting."

"I get it."

Wills reaches to shake hands. I face forward instead of taking the hand, figuring that's what someone in my position would do. Robbie does the same. A moment later, Wills is out of the car and marching toward The Tav. I turn to Robbie.

"How do we do the bust?" I ask.

"We don't," Robbie says.

"Then what was all this about?"

He flicks the envelope with his middle finger. "That. Mission accomplished."

I'm tempted to open the envelope and look at the contents again. But I saw it once and had no idea what it was. I toss the envelope on the dash.

"What's going to happen to Wills?" I ask.

"He's going to get fired."

I snap him a look. "Because of us?"

"Because of him, really."

"I don't suppose you're going to give me any details?"

"Mike can do that."

"When do you think that'll be?"

"When it's over. For now, relax. You did good."

I throw up my hands. "How did I do good? I don't even know what I did."

"That's life for you."

Great. Philosophical advice from a guy who thinks Aristotle was one of the X-Men.

He wasn't, was he?

***

As soon as I'm home, I feed the cats and hang up my trench coat. The secret knock on the front door tells me Deirdre is about to visit. She's amused at the trench coat and fedora on the coat rack.

"Working another undercover operation?"

"Deep cover. So deep even I don't know what the hell is going on."

She sits at the breakfast bar and accepts my offer of coffee. Yes, it's late afternoon, but I always need a pick-me-up this time of day. I set a mug in front of her at the breakfast bar. Deirdre cups her hands around it.

"We should get going soon," she says.

"Yet another fruitless night."

"Surely, it can't be your first."

I ignore the snark, choosing to dispense with the suitcoat and tie before taking a seat at the breakfast bar. We've been following Keith for the last few days, but we're not getting anywhere. He's maintained a straightforward routine. He works about ten hours at Wilryan Realty, then he goes home and spends the night there. My belief that Keith will lead us to Grace Jelinski is starting to waver.

"Everything quiet today?" I ask.

"I hate to break this to you, darling, but you don't live in the most exciting building."

"I beg to differ. We have all sorts of thugs and killers around here. They all seem congregate in my apartment."

"You're lucky to have Leo around."

It takes a second to attach *Leo* to *Old Man Albertson*. For some reason, Deirdre's admiration is a slight irritant. Don't ask me why.

"I didn't realize the two of you were on a first name basis," I say.

"We spent a little time together today. He's very sweet. Once you get to know him."

They must know each other pretty well because *sweet* is the last—and I mean the absolute last—word I would use to describe Mr. Albertson. Personally, I've never gotten past *crusty* and *potentially homicidal*.

"What did the two of you talk about?" I ask. "Guns?"

"Mostly. That and his time in the army. A little about his neighbors. He likes you, but he thinks you get in too much trouble. It's going to bite you in the ass. His words, not mine."

"I'll have to thank him for his concern." I sip my coffee. "Keith is still in the office?"

"That's what Tracy tells me."

Yes, we've hauled Tracy from Wilryan Realty into this whole thing. Her concern for Grace and her disdain for her boss are both assets. We asked her to clue us into Keith's movements. Deirdre frowns

"If following this guy doesn't work, what do we do?" she asks.

"Maybe we just need to speed up the process."

"How do we do that?"

"Keith is still at the office. If there's anything in his house worth finding, maybe we need to go take a look."

Geez, *I'm* the one recommending a break-in? We really are through the looking glass here. Or it's a mark of how desperate I've become.

"I'm in," Deirdre says. "Finish your coffee, and let's get going."

I pick up the coffee and start for the bedroom. If we're going to Brooklyn Park and performing a break-in, I'm not going to do it while dressed like an extra from *Dead Men Don't Wear Plaid*. Lars chooses this moment to burst in on us.

I'm used to Lars coming into my apartment and bringing a jovial air with him (even if I *do* find it irritating). This time, something is bothering him. My first clue is the old-time goalie mask propped on his head. (The kind of mask from the Jason Voorhies era.) He slams the door behind him and leans against it.

"You got problems," he says. "Chuck is after you."

"You told me that already," I say.

"No, I mean he's after you *now*. He's in the building."

Geez, if I didn't like Lars's visits before…

I stand in the hall, unsure what to do. I could run like hell, or I could reason with Chuck. Then I realize the absolute folly of that last statement. I'd be better off finding a weapon to defend myself. But beyond the old tennis racket in the closet, I don't have anything. (I don't want to put the olive oil bottle at risk unless it's completely necessary.)

"Where is he in the building? I ask.

"In the parking lot. He's gone down to his car to get a crowbar."

I wonder if I remembered to lock the backdoor. Maybe I should run out the front. Maybe I should consider another weapon. Maybe I should call my mommy.

"Lars, I'm going to have to tell him the truth," I say. "I love you—theoretically—but I'm not going to get killed to protect you."

Lars's head snaps back, causing the hockey mask to wobble. "Are you kidding me? Has our entire friendship been a lie? I always believed I could count on you. Now, at the crisis of this thing, you've cravenly decided to abandon me?"

"I do crave, and I will abandon. Sorry. But not really."

Before we can continue this debate, a loud knocking comes from the backdoor. I can only hope it's the cartel. But I don't have that kind of luck. Chuck's voice comes through.

"Open up, you treacherous bastard! You're gonna put your hands on my woman, you're going to fucking pay! You hear me?"

Lars drops the goalie mask over his face. "I think that's for you."

I'm going to have to handle this. Another pounding. I get closer to the backdoor but don't move to open it. "Chuck, maybe we can talk about this," I say.

"We're not talking! You're going to be wearing your ass for a hat!"

My father used to use that phrase whenever he was fantasizing about taking revenge on a rude customer. I always thought it was funny. It's less amusing, though, when it's my ass and potentially my hat.

"Listen, Chuck, I'm willing to let you in here," I say, "but we have to talk like civilized adults, okay? No fisticuffs or ass-hatting or any of that. How does that sound?"

There's no response. I take it as a good sign. I carefully open the backdoor. Chuck comes through it like a murderous whirlwind. He's covered in camo, right down the face paint. Goodwill John Rambo. Given that the jacket may contain any number of weapons, I'll keep that observation to myself.

"You son of a bitch!" he says, as I hustle back down the hallway. "You lousy rotten son of a bitch! You're going to pay! You think you can mess around with my woman?"

I backpedal into the living room. Lars's head swivels between the two of us. He steps in front of his friend.

"Chuck, I can't let you do this," he says. "I know you have love for Laura, and I hate that she betrayed you the way she did. She's a fine woman and spectacular in the boudoir. Or so I'm led to believe. But you can't take this betrayal out on a man who was simply led to his doom by the siren you brought into his life."

Chuck tries to get around Lars. "Don't give me any of your damn doubletalk. This son of a bitch bedded my woman and he's gotta pay. I'm gonna pull his nuts through his nostrils."

Lars stands his ground. "Chuck, that's anatomically unlikely and just plain rude. There's got to be a better way. Why don't we sit down and talk this out?"

Chuck slaps Lars's mask, knocking it sideways and blinding him. "I appreciate your concern. You're a loyal friend. Sorry about this." He tosses Lars over the futon and turns his attention to me. "You're next. You're going out that window."

I'm backed into the corner closest to the arch windows. Chuck's block head bears down on me. Normally, his eyes have a vacant look. This time, there's murderous animation there. The lights are on, but absolutely no one—at least, no one reasonable—is home. *This* is how I meet my end? Thrown out a window for sleeping with a guy's girlfriend? It isn't surprising. But I thought I'd at least have the decency to be guilty.

Just before Chuck gets to me, he's hurled in the other direction. He bounces off the arm of the comfy chair and ends up in a heap under the stools at the breakfast bar. Deirdre puts her hands on her hips.

"Sorry, sweets, I can't let you touch him," she says. "We're working on something, and I need him in one piece. I hope you understand."

Judging by the look on Chuck's face, he does not understand. However, he *does* understand this woman just

335

tossed him across the room like a rag doll. In Chuck's world that counts for something. He slowly gets to his feet.

"He's been sleeping with my woman," he says, with less conviction than he might.

"She told you this?" Deirdre asks.

"No. But I know she's sleeping with somebody. And she keeps talking about how much she likes this asshole's column. Doesn't take a genius to figure it out."

No, but apparently any idiot can do it. I'm not sure if Deirdre believes me or him. Either way, she's not moved.

"I'm afraid that's impossible," she says. "I've been around him constantly for the last several days. If he was sleeping with somebody, I'd know."

Chuck looks confused. (Then again, he always looks a little confused.) "Are you two…"

Deirdre dismisses that with a flip of her hand. "No, no. It's strictly business." She gives me a dirty look. "Apparently." She turns back to Chuck. "But it's a very intense business. I'm afraid your theory about Joe is incorrect."

Chuck pulls himself up. "Then who…"

"Another thing you may want to consider," Deirdre says, "is that this woman—what's her name?"

"Laura."

"Laura is her own person and free to make her own decisions. She's not your possession."

336

Lars pumps a fist. "Sing it, sister."

Deirdre doesn't look Lars's way. "Please shut the living hell up." Her eyes bore into Chuck. "Now, I think you owe my friend Joe an apology."

I don't, by any means, consider Deirdre a friend. But she prevented me from getting tossed out a window, which is more than you can say for Lars (someone I do consider a friend but for whom I am rapidly reconsidering that status). Chuck's face takes on the closest he's got to humility.

"You're really not sleeping with Laura?" he asks.

"No, I'm not."

Deirdre fixes Chuck with a look. "And even if he was…"

Chuck raises his hands in surrender. "I get it. I'm…sorry about wanting to shove you out the window and, y'know, making you wear your ass for a, a hat."

Lars claps his hands together. "Glad we could work this out. It's lovely that everyone is friends again. I think our work is done here, brother. Let's leave these folks in peace."

Chuck adopts a similar hangdog expression and follows Lars out. I look around the place, surprised it's relatively in order. For a physical confrontation, this was relatively painless. Deirdre turns to me.

"You aren't sleeping with that idiot's girlfriend, right?" she asks.

"I am not. But I know who is."

"Don't tell me. The less I know, the better."

Can't help feeling I'm in the same boat. That's *something* Deirdre and I have in common.

***

With that silliness settled, we're free to return to Brooklyn Point and break into Keith's home. He lives in a rambler on the west side of Brooklyn Point. I maneuver the Saturn down the alley behind the house, hoping I don't draw attention from the neighbors. It's dark, and they're all probably at dinner. There's a small parking area next to the garage, covered by an awning Keith probably bought at Home Depot. I park the Saturn out of sight. The back gate isn't locked. The backdoor is. Deirdre steps back, and I get the sense she's about to kick the door in. (I've seen my cats pounce on toys. I'm familiar with the look.) I put a hand on her arm.

"It would be better if Keith didn't know we stopped by," I say.

Deirdre doesn't look thrilled. I search the grounds, looking for a loose window or a hiding place for a spare key. Deirdre half-heartedly checks various windows she'd probably like to break. I step around one corner of the house. A fence stretches about halfway across the yard, giving me a little privacy. I spot something helpful.

A window leads to the basement. I pull at it, but it won't budge. Through the window, a collection of lawn furniture is visible in the room below. The room probably won't be accessed again for a few months. If I want to do the breaking part of a breaking-and-entering without letting the victim know immediately, this is my best opportunity. I kick out the glass in the window.

Deirdre has come around the corner. "Well done, darling. You want to lead the way in?"

I guess this *is* my job. I do my best to clear the remaining glass from the frame. There's enough room for us to get through one at a time. My winter coat protects me from the bits of glass. I drop onto a sofa. Deirdre deftly follows. We make our way through the collection of lawn furniture.

"Let's try not to disturb anything," I say.

"Says the person who broke the window."

I hate it when my high horse gets shot out from under me. Deirdre agrees to look around the basement while I go upstairs. Much like Grace Jelinski's house, there isn't much to see: a couple bedrooms, a couple bathrooms, a living room, a dining room, and a kitchen. None of them particularly large. There isn't a lot of decoration. Only a Vikings poster on the wall of the living room. (It's not even framed. The heathen.)

Most importantly, there's no indication Grace is here or ever has been. Nothing is here that doesn't belong to Keith.

There aren't even guest towels or linens. (The spare bedroom looks as if it's used for a home office.) The correspondence is piled in two trays on the desk. I carefully go through it. Just bills. No personal correspondence. Nothing that would lead us to Grace. There's a filing cabinet next to the desk. I go through it. Mostly work-related stuff. Various properties. Nothing of great interest. Deirdre appears in the doorway.

"Find anything?" she asks.

"Nothing," I say. "Keith is not only objectionable, he's completely uninteresting."

I slam one drawer shut and open another. More files from Wilryan Realty. This is more real estate than I've ever dealt with (or ever hope to deal with). Deirdre gives me a hand, pulling out some files and setting them on the desk to go through them. I stick to the cabinet. Keith seems to specialize in lake properties. The process is so uninteresting, I nearly miss a file with a name I *do* find interesting: Fitzgerald Investments.

I pull out the file. "Son of a bitch."

Deirdre tosses aside her work. "What have you got?"

"There's a property on Emily Lake that's owned by Fitzgerald Investments." I take a paper out of the file and read the address. "Outing Place." It takes a second to hit me. "Grace had a sticky note in her house with the initials O.P. on it. This had to be it."

"It would be a hell of a coincidence otherwise."

I look over the paperwork. "It was sold to Fitzgerald Investments about ten years ago."

"Miles was setting up a hiding place."

"That's what it looks like."

Her eyes remain on the paper. There's something soft in them. She's looking at Miles's handiwork. For her, it must be like gazing at an old photograph. She recovers herself. "Put everything back and let's get out of here."

I return the files to the cabinet. "Getting caught *would* be par for the course."

"Par for your course, darling, not mine."

We put away the files and get out of Keith's house the way we came in. A minute later, we're back in the Saturn, heading out to Emily Lake. No one has interrupted us.

Huh. I guess the key to successful B-and-E's is having a contract killer along. Who'd have thunk it?

***

Per my GPS, Emily Lake is about a half-hour up Highway 10 from Brooklyn Point. There isn't a lot of traffic. I try to quell my anxiety. I don't want this to be another dead end. If it is, I have no idea where to go from here.

We exit off Highway 10 and travel about ten miles along the two-lane road. It leads to a smaller country road. No traffic. After about a mile, GPS indicates our destination is on the left. A small dirt path winds into the trees. A simple

341

wooden sign proclaims *Outing Place*. I'm about to turn into the driveway when Deirdre stops me.

"Park here," she says. "We'll walk."

I'm not thrilled with the idea, but she's right. If there's a house there and someone is in it, they'll be alerted by the headlights. Best to approach on foot. I turn off the Saturn, and we start up the road. A light snow is falling. Deirdre huddles into her coat and sticks to the shadows. I try to ignore the sound of my heart beating in my ears. The driveway goes up slightly, then drops. The second we get over the top, we have a view of a cabin. It's not large, probably no more than two or three bedrooms. The blackness of the frozen lake looms beyond it. A permanent dock juts out. A circular parking area sits at the bottom of the driveway. The cabin proper is off to the right. There's a light inside.

And a blue Mustang parked out front.

I come to a halt. Deirdre looks over at me. "What's going on?" she asks.

"I've seen that car before. It was parked outside Grace Jelinski's house. I never got a good look at the owner."

"No better time like the present."

We walk down the driveway, our footsteps crunching in the new-fallen snow. It sounds like we're walking on eggshells (which, viewed from a certain angle…) A path has been shoveled around the back of the cabin. The place must have a backdoor. The shades are drawn. We can't see anyone inside. We halt near the Mustang.

"What now?" I ask.

"Simple. You go up and knock."

"Huh?"

"You heard me."

"And what are you going to do?"

"Something else."

Before I can ask, Deirdre pushes me toward the front door. Apparently, the discussion is over. I carefully make my way to the front door. I look back. No sign of Deirdre. Swell. I knock.

For a few moments, nothing happens. Don't ask me why, but I get the sense everything in the place has come to a halt. There's movement to my right, at one of the windows. Maybe someone glancing through the curtains. Another few seconds of nothing. I may hear hushed voices. I could be wrong. I knock again. Still nothing. I decide to get aggressive. I try the door, preparing to throw my shoulder against it and force it open. But the damn thing is unlocked. (I've really got to stop trying the complicated method first.)

I step inside. The living room is small and there's a kitchenette just beyond it. A door slams at the back of the cabin. I run that direction. The backdoor is just past the kitchenette. It's starting to close. I rush through it.

I'm on the shoveled path. Off to my right, someone runs around the side of the cabin. Two someones. I follow, chasing a blur. They disappear around the corner.

A cry comes from that direction. Followed by a deep groan. I round the corner. Two people are immediately recognizable. One .is Keith, who's laid out in a snowbank, holding his jaw. The other is Deirdre. Her arm is looped around the neck of a dark-haired woman wearing a long gray coat. She's limp in Deirdre's grasp. I take a shot.

"Grace Jelinski?" I ask.

She speaks in a nearly inaudible voice. "Who are you?"

"We're friends of Miles Slayne," I tell her.

Her eyes widen. The name must be a passcode with her. "Nice to meet you," she says. "I'm Grace Jelinski. I hope you know what you're in for."

I *do* like surprises…

CHAPTER SIXTEEN

Holy Family Catholic Church was tucked into a forgettable neighborhood. The meeting would be after hours. Miles assumed Fuentes had pull with the priest. Miles grew up Catholic. He knew how far a cash donation could get you.

They cased the place. It was more interesting than the neighborhood. Brick and marble, domed top, cement steps out front. The main door was oak, brass door handles. Multiple side doors, also oak. The lights in the church were off.

"How many men do you think Victor will bring?" Deirdre asked

"Not nearly damn enough."

"You'll leave Victor for me, right?"

"I'll do my best. But if I have the shot, I'll take it. That's—"

"The Discipline. I know, darling. I was trained well."

Miles's watch said nine-thirty. The meeting was ten-thirty. No sign of Victor's men. No sign of Fuentes's. Neither wanted to arrive first.

"Let's go," Miles said.

They crossed the street. Faded into the shadows. Miles picked the lock on a side door. They stepped inside. Waited. Let their eyes adjust to the dark. Miles led the way to the chapel. A bejeweled altar, curved rows of pews, artwork in the stained-glass windows. A choir loft with a grand pipe organ. The offices were probably below. Ambient light came through stained glass windows. Miles pointed to a side door across the way.

"Victor's men will come from there. Fuentes's guys will be outside, cutting off escape routes. I'll be in the choir loft." He pointed to the altar. "There's space behind there. Follow your instincts."

Deirdre disappeared behind the altar. Miles found a space beneath the choir loft, covered in shadows. He trained his gun on the side door. Waiting for Victor's men.

A door opened somewhere below. Footsteps. Whispers in Spanish. No one coming through the far door.

Something didn't add up. These were Victor's men. They weren't following the plan.

Miles stepped over to a side door, pushed it open a crack. No sign of Fuentes's men. No one to help Miles and Deirdre.

Fuentes made a deal. But not with Miles.

Miles could run. He had the opening. Protect yourself first. That was The Discipline. But there was Deirdre. Could he abandon her?

No.

Moments passed. Don't make the first move. Let them come to you. No way to get to Deirdre. She'll have to read the play.

Then all hell broke loose.

Deirdre popped up behind the altar. A Berretta in each hand. Victor's men were ready. The chapel lit up with gunfire. Miles opened fire from the shadows. Deirdre dropped. Miles couldn't tell if she was hit.

There was a hallway at the back of the chapel. Miles ducked down it, looking for cover. A small office to his right. A room for restless kids. Miles peeked into the chapel. Two men down. No sign of the others. No sign of Deirdre.

A single shot behind him. It clipped his arm. Flesh wound. Miles fired into the darkness. He dropped the floor. No return fire.

Shots from the chapel. Someone using a pew for cover. Miles pulled a second Berretta. Leaned against the wall.

A gunman moved from pew to pew. Trying to get closer. A bullet went through his skull. Another fusillade of bullets toward the altar. Miles dove into the office, gave himself cover. Deirdre was okay.

It was quiet. Miles tucked himself in a corner. Kept an eye on the door.

Two guys came through. Miles shot one in the chest. The second took cover. Miles waited. The second guy came around, firing. Something stung Miles.

Two shots. Both through the guy's head. Miles didn't fire either. The body fell sideways, out of his sight.

Deirdre slipped into the room. She crouched near the wall. Miles got to his knees.

"Nice work," he said.

Deirdre noticed the rip in Miles's suitcoat. He didn't see it. Didn't need to see it.

Blood was dampening his shirt.

***

We go back into the cabin and settle in the main room. There are, in fact, small bedrooms on one side of the cabin. There's a picture window at the front. No decorations. The place is warm, at least. Deirdre leans against the front door. Grace sinks into the couch. Keith hovers in the kitchenette, holding his swollen jaw in his bandaged hand. I sit in a chair near Grace.

She's an interesting looking woman. Her hair is dark and straight, a few traces of gray. Her eyes are brown. Her face is lined. Her blue sweater is baggy but implies a great figure. She seems numb. I keep my tone cautious, as if I'm afraid of frightening off a doe.

"The cartel is after you," I say. "Why?"

Keith steps her direction. "Grace, you don't have to tell these people anything."

Grace holds up a hand, letting him know it's okay. Deirdre pushes away from the door, letting Keith know he should be quiet. He sulks his way back to the kitchenette. Grace closes her eyes. I get the feeling she's conjuring up a memory she'd rather keep buried.

"My real name is Allison Darnell," she says. "I used to...be with Michael Santana."

"Michael Santana from the cartel?" Deirdre says.

"Yes. I was there the day...the day they killed him."

A tear slides down her cheek. Deirdre appears neither interested nor sympathetic. I'm tempted to sit on the couch with Grace, but I don't want to get too familiar. Keith takes a few steps her way, as if he'd like to step into the breach. He hesitates. I slide my chair closer to Grace.

"What happened?" I ask.

"I was at Michael's house. It was morning. We were in bed together. Just hanging out. I got up and went to the bathroom. The window looked out over the driveway. I saw a car pull up, and some guys got out. Michael's guys. Victor, Angel, a couple others. They were carrying Uzis. They only showed guns around the place when something was happening. I saw Michael's bodyguards walking away. Victor and his guns came into the house." She puts a hand in her hair. "I ran out of the bathroom and told Michael what I saw. We could hear them coming up the stairs. He told me to use the safe room. He'd talk to Victor and the guys. They wouldn't try anything. I hid. I asked Michael to come with me. He didn't do it. He had this macho thing that wouldn't let him hide."

I'm more inclined to call it a stupid thing, but I keep that thought to myself. "You went into the safe room?"

349

"But I could hear everything. Victor and his guys came in. Michael started to ask, 'What the fuck is going on?' or maybe 'What the fuck are you doing?' I don't know. He never got the whole thing out." She closes her eyes. "When it was done, they were all speaking in Spanish. I didn't catch everything, but they were looking for me. Victor didn't know about the safe room. But he knew where I lived. He ordered some guys to go over there and take care of me." She rubbed her forehead. "Just sitting there hiding while they gunned him down. I didn't do anything. Can you imagine that?"

There's a slight tremor in Deirdre's cheek. "Yes."

"They left, and I got out of there. I had to..." Grace's voice breaks. "I had to walk by Michael's body. I tried not to look. I was on automatic pilot. I knew where Michael stashed some emergency cash. I grabbed it. That was pretty much all I had. That and the clothes on my back. I found a place to hide."

"And Miles Slayne found you?" I ask.

"I found him," Grace says. "We had met once before. When he was supposed to do a job for Michael. He seemed...different. Not like Michael's guys. Not like how you picture a hitman. Anyway, I still had his card. I thought maybe he could help me."

"That's how you got here," I say.

"Yes. He gave me a new life. A new identity. Everything."

"You didn't go to the police?"

"Michael didn't talk business with me. I hadn't *really* seen Victor's guys kill him. I wasn't any good to the police. Why keep me safe?"

I'm sure my friends (?) in law enforcement might have an issue with that. But they're not here, and I'm not taking up the argument.

"Did Miles check on you?" I ask.

"No. He told me it would be better if he kept his distance. He didn't want to lead anyone to me. He said someone would keep an eye on me."

I turn to Keith. "And that was you?"

He shakes his head. "It was Simon Gray. I guess he's a friend of this Miles. He represented Fitzgerald Investments. They bought this place. They bought Grace's house. Asked me to give her a job." He looks down. "It paid pretty well."

"And you helped Grace," I say.

"Yeah. They didn't pay me to do that. I...I wanted to do that."

Grace smiles, briefly, toward Keith. "I didn't see much of Simon. Keith helped me out with most everything. But then I got word that the cartel was coming after me. That was it. I couldn't hide anymore. Sooner or later, you have to be you, I guess. Does that make any sense?"

Deirdre answers before I do. "Yes," is all she says.

"How did you know to run?"

"I got a text from Simon. On a burner phone Miles gave me. There was a coded message Miles told me about. Just one sentence. *For you, there is only the desert.* When I got that, I was supposed to hide. Keith gave me a hand."

Keith tugs at his mustache. "Nothing much. Just picked up the mail, kept the house looking normal. That kind of thing."

"I was supposed to be safe here," Grace says. "But you found me. What do we do now?"

I take out my phone. "I need to call someone."

Grace has no objection. Keith starts to say something, but she holds up a hand, backing him off. I move to a corner and bring up my contacts. Deirdre joins me. I show her two numbers I'm considering.

"You're okay if I do this?" I ask.

"Yes," she says. "I'll have to disappear, but I'll wait until they get here."

I waver over the two numbers. I finally choose the one I'm most comfortable with. Hank answers on the third ring. I speak without preamble.

"I know where Grace Jelinski is," I say. "And who she is."

Hank's voice drops to a hush. "Fill me in."

"No time," I say. "I need you to pick her up. The cartel is looking for her."

Hank's voice is tight. "Where are you?" I give her the address. She says, "See you shortly" and hangs up. I slip my phone back into my pocket.

"Cavalry is on its way," I say.

No one says anything. Deirdre takes up a position near the window and keeps an eye on the driveway. I sink into a chair. Grace remains on the couch, staring at the floor. Keith joins her. We largely stay that way for the next twenty-five minutes. Finally, we hear tires crunching on the freshly fallen snow. Deirdre straightens up.

"The cops are coming," she says.

I join her at the window. A beaten-up Cadillac comes into view, getting near the house. Alarm bells go off in my head. This doesn't look like a police cruiser, even an unmarked one. The Caddy halts near the front door. Four Latino guys get out. Victor is chief among them. They're all carrying guns. My heartrate skyrockets. Deirdre lets out a breath.

"Not exactly the cavalry," she says.

CHAPTER SEVENTEEN

Deirdre looked over the hole in Miles's coat. "Are you hurt?"

"I'm not hurt at all," he said. "Didn't you know? They can only kill me with a golden bullet."

"Is that a fact?"

Miles slipped a hand over his shirt, tried to ignore the pain. "How did you get here?"

"Staircase behind the altar. Leads to the basement and the basement leads here."

"Good work. How many of them?"

"Eight. I didn't see Victor."

"He'll let his guys do the dirty work."

Deirdre looked toward the hall. "Four down. Not bad."

Miles got up. He ignored the stabbing pain in his side. He moved to the door, got a glimpse of the hallway. Two bodies on the floor.

"There's a stairway," he said. "Leads to the choir loft. Might be more guys up there."

"They're going to have the entrances covered."

"From the choir loft, they can cover a bunch of them. Two side entrances and a backdoor. They'd have to cover all of them." He let out a ragged breath. "They're going to wait us out."

They were running out of time. Miles was running out of time. He had to get Deirdre out of there. He closed his eyes, took a breath.

"Fuck it," he said. "I was never good at waiting."

He stepped into the hall. The bullet hit him in the gut, left of his bellybutton. It knocked him down. A spider web of pain spread across Miles's abdomen. Another bullet sailed over his head. Deirdre returned fire. Pulled him back into the office.

She searched for the wound. Miles mumbled, "Gut shot."

Every move was a knife, tearing something inside. Blood pooled on the floor. Deirdre looked for something to pack it.

"It's going to be okay," she said. "We'll get you out of here."

"And do what?"

She stopped. Miles knew what she was thinking. Four gunmen left. Even if she got past them, got Miles out, where could they go? No contacts in San Antonio. They couldn't go to a hospital. The gunshot wound would be reported. No cover then. The house of cards comes tumbling down. The options were limited. And clear.

"You have to get you out of here," he said.

"I'm not going without you."

"That's exactly what you're going to do. You find a way out. I'll help you if I can. But I'm not getting out of here. We both know that."

The gun hung loosely at her side. A tremor in her cheek. "I can't do this alone."

"You can. It's not going to be easy. Just stick to—"

"I mean everything. Not alone"

Deirdre wiped her face. Miles waited for her to turn to him.

"This is what you signed up for. You stay safe. That's The Discipline." He sat up, the pain searing through his guts. "There's a cell phone in the cubby hole in my study. Hold on to it. If someone calls you on that line, get the hell out. The cartel will be coming for you. That happens, you find Grace Jelinski."

"Who the hell is that?"

"Save it as a last resort." He put a hand on her shoulder. "Make me a promise. One of these days, get out of The Life. Find that place in the Caribbean. Understand? Now get the hell out of here. I'll give you whatever cover I can."

She took his head in her hands. Held him. Then she slipped out of the room.

The shots came immediately. Deirdre fired back, moving toward the chapel. Shots from above. The choir loft.

Miles slid along the floor. Curled himself against the wall. No escape route. The basement covered. The chapel covered. The guy in the choir loft seeing all.

He got to his knees. He was off-balance, lightheaded. Unable to take deep breaths. Push through it. Weakness is a state of mind. That's

The Discipline. He got to his feet. Leaned against the wall. Grabbed the doorframe. Swung into the hallway. Found the stairs to the choir loft.

Gunfire in the chapel. Miles ignored it. He struggled to walk. Blood slickened the stairs behind him. Something vital slipping away.

The choir loft stretched away from the stairs. A railing along the front. The gunman patrolled the railing, looking for Deirdre.

Miles dragged one leg. The world tilted. He reached for a chair. Missed. Stayed on his feet. The gunman spun, fired instinctively.

The bullet hit Miles high in the chest. The impact spun him around. The marble floor came up fast.

A clear moment. Miles landed on his side. Brought the Berretta up. Fired. The bullet went through the gunman's left eye. He disappeared over the railing.

Miles sagged. The Berretta fell away. He lay on the floor. Shots somewhere below. Miles crawled toward the railing. Used it to pull himself up. He practically hung over it.

One of Victor's men hid in the pews. Angel. Miles recognized him. Angel made his move. Came out firing two handguns. Several shots. One in return. Directly into Angel's left knee. He went down, screaming. Curled into a fetal position.

Deirdre hopped up, ponytail whipping around, coat flowing behind her. She ran toward the side door. A clear path. She kicked the door open. Disappeared into the night.

Miles straightened up. His hand came away from the wound in his side. He clutched the railing. No gunshots outside. No one lying in wait. Deirdre was gone. Safe. His work was done.

Miles felt himself falling backward. He didn't feel himself land.

***

The four guys separate. Two run around back. Victor leads one toward the front. Deirdre and I step back from the window. Keith pushes away from the kitchenette. Grace sits up straight, a prairie dog sensing danger.

"What's going on?" she asks.

"We've got visitors," I say. "They aren't friendly."

Grace hops up to her feet. Deirdre draws two guns. She flips one around and holds it, butt-first, toward Keith.

"You know how to use one of these?" she asks.

His face goes blank. It looks like he's about to wet himself. He looks toward Grace, then takes a big breath. "Yeah, I do," he says.

Keith gingerly takes the gun and looks it over, perhaps trying to make sure the safety is off (or trying to find out what the safety looks like and where it might be located). Deirdre finds a spot near the front door.

"Big guy, you cover the backdoor," she says. "Kill anything that comes through it." She looks at me. "You and Grace go to one of the bedrooms."

I hesitate. "What are you going to do?"

358

"Kill as many of them as I can. It's what I do."

Keith moves to the backdoor. Grace and I hustle to one of the bedrooms. There's a big bed in the middle of the room and a closet in the nearest corner. I halt in the doorway.

"Hide under the bed," I say.

"What are you going to do?"

"Nothing intelligent, believe me."

I step back into the main room. Deirdre snaps a look at me as I close the bedroom door.

"What are you doing?" she asks.

"I want to help."

"You want to help? Let me use you as a human shield. Otherwise, you're better off in the there with Grace."

Before we can debate this any further, the window in the front room is shot out. I drop to the floor. So does Keith. Deirdre flinches, annoyed. She pumps several shots through the front window.

No return fire. My ears are ringing. Cold air rushes in through the open window. No one moves. The cartel guys are waiting, maybe letting us make the next move.

Gunshots from behind the cabin. The little window in the kitchenette is blown out. The backdoor is kicked open. One of the cartel guys starts to come through. Keith fires blindly. The guy ducks back through the door. Keith opens his eyes and gives us triumphant smile.

"Huh," he says. "How about—"

And that's the end of that. The cartel guy comes through the backdoor again and shoots Keith. It bounces him off the wall and drops him to the floor. The gun falls away. Blood trickles down his arm. He's wounded but not fatally.

Deirdre dives across the floor and fires at the backdoor. The cartel guy falls through the door and out into the snow. Deirdre pops to her knees, keeping an eye on both doors. She speaks without looking at Keith.

"Are you all right?" she asks.

"My arm…"

"Shit happens, darling. You're going to have to live with it."

A shot comes through the window, taking out the light in the kitchenette. I bellycrawl away from it, moving to the front room. A second cartel guy comes through the back. Deirdre fires a series of shots. The cartel guy doesn't get off any. He drops to his knees, then hits the floor.

Shots come through the front window. Deirdre's body spins. She falls, the gun clattering away from her. She looks over her arm, more dismayed than hurt.

Victor stands in the front doorway. His gun is loose at his side. His wolfish eyes focus on Deirdre, as if they are the only two people in the room.

"Good to see you again, Christina," he says.

"Fuck you, Victor," is the answer.

That amuses him. Deirdre sits up, keeping her eyes on Victor. Blood runs from a jagged gash in her upper arm. She was wounded in that same spot the last time she was here. A wound I had to sew up. This asshole has undone all my good work. Victor raises the gun.

"Don't think about going for the piece," he says. "You know you won't get to it."

Deirdre remains still. "Probably not."

Victor looks over the room. "Where is she?" Nobody answers. Victor's eyes drift to the bedroom door. "In there?" he asks. No reply. "Oh well. Nice knowing you, Christina."

I get to my feet and launch a tackle into Victor's midsection. I hit him hard enough to take us both to the floor. Victor, though, maintains control of his gun. He grabs me by the hair and flings to me to one side. The gun comes up. It's aimed at my face. A shot is fired.

The bullet hits the wall over my head. Victor flinches. He didn't fire. He rolls away from me, facing Deirdre, who has reclaimed her gun. Her face is contorted, snarling. I dive behind the sofa, getting out of the line of fire. Victor shoots and misses. Deirdre returns fire. The lamp near Victor explodes. He crawls toward the door, firing as he goes. Deirdre cries out. Blood appears around a wound on her leg. She keeps firing. Victor gets out the door.

Deirdre slides into the kitchenette. She takes cover behind the table. Keith scurries to join her, trying to stay out of the line of fire. Victor is positioned outside the front door.

"Miles would be proud of you," he says. "Probably break his heart to see you go out like this."

"Don't pretend you knew him."

Victor's voice is closer now. "Go get the girl."

"Go piss up a rope."

They take this as a cue to resume hostilities. Deirdre comes up from behind the table. Victor gets off the first shot. Deirdre goes down, clutching her side. Her gun again clatters on the floor. Victor steps into the room and aims at Deirdre.

"Freeze!"

This comes from outside, beyond where Victor is standing. He hesitates. The voice comes in again.

"Step back from the doorway. Put your weapon on the ground. Get on your knees and put your hands on your head. Do it now!"

It's Hank. A bit of hope rises in me. Victor steps back from the doorway, raising his hands, still holding the gun. Hank's voice rings out again.

"I said put the weapon down! You have—"

That's as far as Hank gets. Victor spins and fires. He gets off several shots before slipping back into the room. He looks annoyed but isn't breathing hard. He stops to reload. A voice comes from behind him.

"Put it down, Victor."

I look up. So does Keith. So does Deirdre. Victor turns slowly, a look of amusement on his face. Grace has claimed Deirdre's gun. She clutches it with both hands, aiming at Victor's chest. He holds a hand out.

"Good to see you again, Ali," he says. "You can put the piece down. We both know—"

And Grace shoots him in the chest.

For a moment, Victor is still standing. The hole in his chest causes his breath to come out in gasps. He drops his gun. His eyes are wide, filled with an emotion that might be new to him: fear. Then he topples to the floor.

Footsteps approach, tentatively. Deirdre is still on the floor. She'll never get out of here in time. The police will have her. If that's what I want. Isn't it?

Ugh. Dammit, Joe…

I run over to Deirdre, drape her arm around my shoulders, and help her to her feet. She grunts in pain. I guide her toward the backdoor.

"Can you move on your own?" I ask.

"I'll be fine."

"I'm sure. But we've got to get going or you're dead."

She merely shrugs in response. "Been there."

Deirdre takes the gun back from Grace. We shuffle out the backdoor. Behind us, footsteps pound into the cabin. There's a path through the woods, close to the lake. I drag Deirdre that direction. She regains her strength, taking the load off me. Just as we reach the path, she pushes me away.

"Go back," she says. "They know you were in there. There'll be too many questions."

"What should I tell them?"

"The truth. If you want. It's doesn't matter now." She takes a hesitant step, wincing from the pain. "We've got one more thing to do. I'll let you know when it's time."

"How will I find you?"

"I'll find you."

Deirdre moves slowly but steadily. I huddle into my coat and turn back toward the cabin, ready to face the police.

***

Returning to the cabin gives me my first look at the totality of what's happened. I knew about the demise of the two cartel guys at the backdoor. Apparently, Deirdre's initial burst of gunfire took out one at the front, leaving only Victor. Hank treats Keith's wound as best she can and calls an ambulance. He's in pain but otherwise okay.

As could be expected, the police have quite a few questions. Most of them are about what exactly went down, given it's unlikely Keith and I gunned down three cartel guys and left the last one for Grace. Since I've lied repeatedly to Hank, it's time I told her the truth.

"It was Deirdre," I tell her, standing outside the cabin.

Hank doesn't react, as if it isn't news to her. "Who's in my morgue?"

"A woman named Emily. An associate of Deirdre's."

"How long have you known that?"

"More than a week."

"You were helping her with all this," she says, "and you didn't bother telling me?"

"Deirdre has a way of not giving you a lot of options."

"For your sake, I hope the jury sees it that way."

A thrill of panic goes through me. I've deceived myself into thinking Hank and I are friends. But if we are, I've done more to betray the friendship than she has.

"You're arresting me?" I ask.

"Not yet. But the night is young." She slips her hands in her jacket pockets. "You got any idea where Deirdre went?"

"Into the woods. That's all I know."

"I'd love to believe that, Mr. Davis." Hoo-boy. We're on a *Mr. Davis* basis again. That does not bode well for my future as a free man. "You should probably get out of here."

I do double-take. "You're letting me go?"

"For now. Doesn't mean you're in the clear. We'll see how things shake out. But if you hear from Deirdre *at all*—and

365

I don't care if it's an obscene phone call or you catch her spying on you in the shower—you call me *immediately*. You understand?"

"I get the gist."

"Good. Get the hell out of here."

I take a step, then look back. "Thank you."

Hank hesitates, then turns away. "Don't thank me yet."

I take her advice. The walk takes me past a collection of emergency vehicles from a variety of agencies. (Apparently, every sheriff's department and Podunk PD in the general area wanted to get in on the action.) My car is parked at the end of the driveway, out of the worst of the congestion. I get out of there and back to the main road.

"Are we clear, darling?"

I damn near put the car in the ditch. The voice comes from the backseat. I pull off to the side of the road, making sure I'm not having an infarction. Deirdre sits up. I look around, hoping no police vehicles are coming. Deirdre joins me in the front seat. She's holding her side. I look her over.

"We should get you to a doctor," I say.

Her head rolls toward me. "Doctors ask questions. And we have a stop to make."

Not sure if I like the sound of that. "Where?"

"Just drive. I'll let you know."

I pull out again. Deirdre rests against the passenger window. She's not the kind to show suffering. That means her pain must be excruciating. I keep quiet. (Though, I can't help wondering if she's going to get blood on my interior.)

CHAPTER EIGHTEEN

Hell rained down on the cartel. Omar Fuentes's body turned up in the Mexican City Grill. And three other restaurants. Victor sent men after Deirdre. Their bodies were scattered all over south Florida. He hired killers from the rest of the cartel. Their heads were sent back in boxes. One had a note attached. You're next.

Deirdre left the apartment in Jupiter. She packed Miles's things, sent them to an address he'd left her. A guy in Minnesota.

Police ID'ed the bodies in the Holy Family Church. All of them were cartel. Save one. DNA indicated he was John Tuttle. No other info found.

Deirdre moved to San Francisco. She found a new assistant. Gave her the name Emily. *Emily learned quick. She was trustworthy. Business was strong. The cartel was still a nuisance. A cop named Street opened a file on her. She considered eliminating him. Decided against it. Leave cops alone. Miles taught her that. Eliminate only if necessary. And make damn sure it's absolutely necessary.*

Don Pedro ran the cartel. He was a good businessman. Wouldn't sacrifice men to a vendetta. Especially if the vendetta wasn't his. He called a meeting with Deirdre. Assured her safety. He was the only one who could make the offer.

The meeting was in Chicago. Deirdre wouldn't meet on cartel turf. Only Don Pedro and Victor would be there.

La Cucaracha was the place. Family owned. Great food. A backroom was available. The owner looked the other way. For the right price.

Deirdre sat with her back to the wall. A complimentary pitcher of sangria on the table. Chips and salsa, tostadas, sopes. Don Pedro and Victor walked in. They sat across from her. Don Pedro was in his sixties. Grey hair, slight comb-over, thin mustache. His eyes were kind and sharp. His manner was easy.

Deirdre wasn't fooled. Don Pedro was old school. Women were for fucking or charming. Both, if you could manage. But she felt at ease. He was polite. Fatherly. Probably made you feel that way right before cutting your throat. Victor just glowered. Don Pedro poured sangria. One for Deirdre, one for himself. Victor could pour his own.

"I don't care for small talk," Don Pedro said. His voice smooth and deep, "I would like this business between you and Victor ended. There's money to be made, and we can't do that if we're at each other's throats. That's fair to say, isn't it?"

Deirdre ignored the sangria. "I didn't start this. I'm not the one you have to concern yourself with."

Victor slapped the table. "Fuck you, bitch. How many of my guys you kill?"

"Sorry. I was only aiming for one. Haven't gotten him yet."

Don Pedro held up a hand, silencing them both. He turned to Victor, his eyes cold.

"We're not here for this. You understand me?" Victor shut up. Don Pedro gave Deirdre an apologetic look. "I would like to end this peacefully. Can we agree to that?"

"We can."

"No moves against each other. We all stay in business. That sound good?"

Victor's nostrils flared. "After all this shit, she's getting a pass?"

Don Pedro didn't look at Victor. "Yes, that's what I'm saying."

"But this—"

"Like the pass I gave you after Michael." Victor clammed up. "Good," Don Pedro said. "Let's eat."

Victor said nothing during the meal. Don Pedro seemed perfectly at home. They finished eating. He shook Deirdre's hand.

He said, "Maybe we'll do business together again someday."

"That would be…interesting," she said.

Don Pedro led the way out. Victor turned to Deirdre. He mouthed, "Christina." She mouthed "Fuck you." They left. She tossed her napkin aside.

***

The warehouse loft was in Kansas City. An industrial section the city hadn't gentrified. A trucking firm out of Dallas owned it. On paper. The loft itself overlooked a training area. Deirdre punched in the security code. *Walked across the training area. Took a swipe at the speedbag. Climbed the steps to the loft.*

Emily was at the computer in the corner. Honey-colored hair in a ponytail, wire-rim glasses, jean shorts, pink t-shirt. Her bare legs were crossed. She kept her eyes on the screen. Deirdre tossed the overnight bag on the bed.

"How was Chicago?" Emily asked.

"We shook hands and promised to play nice."

"You think it will take?"

"For now. Victor will bide his time. Build up his power. He's younger than Don Pedro. When the Don goes, Victor will come after us with both barrels."

"But for now…?"

Deirdre sat on the bed. "We go about our business. Work on a plan for later."

Emily got up, sat on the edge of the bed. "What about Grace Jelinski?"

"We'll worry about her when—or if—we need her."

Emily tapped Deirdre's foot. "And hope we never do?"

"That would nice." Deirdre stretched out on the bed. "For now, we forget about that stuff." She breathed through her nose, closed her eyes. "That's The Discipline."

***

Deirdre mutters the occasional direction. We're heading toward Brooklyn Point. What the hell are we going to

371

do there? Is there some mess we have to clean up? As we pull into town, Deirdre studies her wounds but doesn't seem overly concerned. I try to concentrate on the road.

"I suppose you're going to tell me it's just a flesh wound," I say.

A corner of Deirdre's mouth goes up. "They actually are." She reaches inside her coat and feels around. "The one in the side has an exit wound. It hurts, but it won't give me trouble."

"You're not hurt that bad?"

"I'm not hurt at all. Didn't you know? They can only kill me with a golden bullet."

The neighborhood looks familiar. We round onto a street. I finally recognize where we're going. Simon's house is on the left. The light is on in the kitchen. I'm assuming the occupant is at the kitchen table, a rapidly emptying whiskey bottle in front of him. I park on the street.

"What do we want with Simon?" I ask.

"Just a word. You can stay here."

"I don't think I will."

She sighs but says nothing. We start toward the house. The footing is secure, so there's no risk of Deirdre falling due to her bad leg. She grimaces as she goes up the two steps to the backdoor. It's locked. She puts her good shoulder to the door and drives it open. Hi, honey, we're home.

Sure enough, Simon is at the table, drinking. The bottle is nearly gone. The sight of Deirdre and his partially splintered door causes him to hop to his feet.

"What the hell is going on?" he asks.

Deirdre holds her gun at her side. She speaks calmly. "Let's not make a scene, okay?"

Simon sits down, though he nearly misses the chair. There's a bruise under his right eye, though Deirdre hasn't touched him. Yet. She raises the gun. I step toward her.

"What are you doing?" I ask.

"You sold out Grace," Deirdre says. "Didn't you?"

His eyes get wide, giving the game away. If he lies to Deirdre, he's a dead man. On other hand, the truth isn't going to get him far.

"How do you know he sold out Grace?" I ask.

"Process of elimination, darling. Who knew about the cabin? Keith, Simon, and then us. The cartel didn't follow us there. If they had, it wouldn't have taken almost forty-five minutes for them to attack. If they followed Keith or if they got the location from him, they would have beaten us there. They didn't get it from us. They didn't get it from Keith. That just leaves our friend here. Right, sweets?"

Simon's jaw works, but he doesn't say anything. His mouth wants the perfect lie, but his brain is flashing the *Out of Order* sign. He sags in his chair.

373

"That's right," he says, his voice small. "They came here and…" He puts a hand to the bruise. "I didn't have a choice."

"We always have a choice, darling."

I point toward his eye. "You were lucky to get away with just a bruise."

"They mostly worked the body," he says, shifting uncomfortably. His eyes fill. "I sentenced someone to death."

"Grace is okay," I tell him. "She's with the police right now. The cartel guys aren't going to be a problem."

Relief floods him. It lasts as long as it takes Deirdre to level the gun at him. I hold up my hands.

"You don't need to do this," I say.

"He betrayed us."

"Because he was getting his ass kicked. Grace is safe. Victor's dead. It's over."

Deirdre blinks back some of the pain. "You know how I feel about loose ends."

Moments pass. Simon slumps in the chair, reconciling himself to his fate. Maybe welcoming it. Deirdre keeps the gun steady. I can't stop her. She closes her eyes and takes a breath. She lowers the gun.

"You caught me at a good time," she tells Simon. "Turns out I'm going to make a change in my life. Live and let live. Or something like that."

Simon is about to wet himself (assuming he hasn't done so already). "Thank you," is all he can get out.

Deirdre grabs the bottle of whiskey from the table and limps toward the door. "Do better."

She steps through the remains of the door and moves painfully down the stairs. I follow her. She chugs some whiskey. I catch up to her.

"If you're not going to a doctor," I say, "let's at least get you back to the apartment."

She pulls her hair out of the ponytail. "You go ahead. I'm going somewhere else."

"Where is that?"

"I'll keep that one to myself, darling." She stops and looks back at me. "Thank you."

She starts to limp away. I let her go a few steps.

"What are you going to do?" I ask.

Deirdre doesn't answer. She moves down the street. I'm tempted to run after her. But I don't. Instead, I stand in the snow. Slowly, she disappears into the darkness.

EPILOGUE

"I believe you'll find the view to your liking," the manager said. He opened the door, let her into the bungalow. "You will have easy access to the beach. All the accommodations should be to your satisfaction."

The bungalow wasn't large. It was as much as she needed. Plush couch. A glass coffee table. A wicker chair. Shag carpeting. A secluded patio. A path to the beach.

She moved gingerly. The pain in her side wasn't bad. The rest would take a while. Some people asked about it. She'd vaguely mention a car accident. Change the subject.

The manager didn't ask questions. He was pleasant looking. Fifties. Flecks of gray in his hair. Perfect English, slight hint of French.

She stepped onto the patio. The temp was in the eighties. The ocean rolled gently against the shore. A tang of salt. The sun caressing her. Tension in her neck and shoulders. Maybe that would go away. Time would tell. Time.

She returned to the living room. The manager's hands were folded in front of him. His deep tan showed off his bright white teeth.

"It's lovely," she said. "I think I'll be very happy here."

"Excellent. And your possessions will be arriving soon?"

"I have only a few things. They'll be here in a couple days."

"Very good." He gestured to a phone on a small table. *"If you need anything, feel free to call the front desk. We'll be happy to help."*

"Thank you." She took a small envelope from her bag. Held it out. *"Would you mind mailing this for me? I'd do it myself, but—"*

"That's quite all right. I'll be glad to do it."

He took the envelope facedown. Didn't look at it. He left.

She slipped off her sandals. Walked to the patio. Put up the umbrella on the small table. Sat in one of the chairs. She took off her sunhat, tossed it on the table. She took a book from bag. The Great Gatsby.

The occasion called for something. She went back inside, picked up the phone on the small table, called the front desk. She ordered a bottle of white wine.

"Of course," the woman said. "I apologize. I don't have your name yet."

"Christina," she said. "Christina Newson."

She hung up. Returned to the patio. Looked toward the ocean. The unending horizon. She opened the book.

***

"It's a matter of vision," Lars says, pulling his IPA close. "I have vision and many of you do not. That's why I'm best qualified to take this on."

I'd make some crack about his vision being colorblind, but he'd probably get some fool idea about shooting the movie in black-and-white. We're at The Tav, having completed another day of filming. Today, Lars offended our leading lady by coming up with yet another sex scene. It went without saying this would involve full frontal nudity. He said it anyway. The leading lady left to call her agent (an agent we're not entirely certain she has). I take a healthy sip of my Grand Brewing Maibock.

"You think Mandy's going to quit?" I ask.

Lars adjusts his shades. "The choice is hers. She can be bold and have the greatest moment of her career, or she can shrink and return to doing theatre in glorified boiler rooms."

"Decisions, decisions," I say.

As per usual, Lars ignores me, tossing his scarf over his shoulder. The Tav is hopping. I look out the window next to our high-top table. The weather is warming slightly. March will be here soon, and spring will follow.

"Fabio wasn't at the shoot again today," I say. "You have any idea what's going on?"

"He's not essential to the process. I don't pay much attention to him these days."

I used to understand the merits of ignoring Fabio, but now I'm concerned. I might be able to get an answer to that question, though. Carol gets a Cosmo from the bar and makes her way over to our table. She ignores Lars and turns to me.

"How did the shooting go today?" she asks.

"Same as it ever was," I say.

Lars spins toward Carol as she takes a seat. "The key to leadership is having the long view. If people are quibbling, you gaze at the stars above their heads and know that one day they'll understand. It's like when Donald Sutherland and Elliot Gould wanted to fire Robert Altman during the filming of *MASH*. It took some time, but they finally—"

Carol is looking at me. "Did anyone quit?"

"Jury's out on our leading lady," I say.

Lars waves this off. "She'll be back. It's like Elliot Gould in *MASH*. After the movie came out—"

I speak to Carol. "Fabio's been missing from the set. I wonder what's going on."

Carol flips a hand. "I'm sure he's fine. Probably just pouting."

"At least he's out of your hair."

She frowns. "Him and Jeff both."

It takes a second to hit me. "You guys broke it off?"

"We did," Carol says, sadly. "After what I said to Fabio, Jeff started wondering what I would say to *him* if we ever broke up. I didn't have an answer. He said we should take a break."

"For how long?" Lars asks.

"I'm not sure," she says. "But he changed his phone number and didn't tell me the new one. I'm thinking it's going to be a long one."

Lars and I exchange a look. Carol pounded Fabio into the ground *and* got her boyfriend to break up with her. Talk about going scorched earth. Time to find a new subject.

"How are things with Chuck and Laura?" I ask. "And you?"

"I'm afraid that's over. The whole shooting match. The engagement, the affair, all of it."

Carol sets her Cosmo aside. "What happened?"

"Chuck felt he couldn't trust Laura. It was better to break things off and move on."

"He's not coming after me?"

"You're in the clear," Lars says. "So am I. From now on, Chuck will focus his energies on getting revenge on Laura."

"What kind of revenge?" I ask.

"He didn't say. Knowing Chuck it will be more than sugar in the gas tank or a flaming bag on her front doorstep. I can't blame him. Chuck has been hurt."

"And the fact you contributed to that hurt…?" Carol asks.

"Is neither here nor there," Lars says. "That she gave in so willingly to my animal magnetism proves she had the evil gene the whole time. I take no responsibilities for the wanton actions of that fallen woman."

Carol rolls her eyes. "You make it sound like you gave her The Clap."

Lars rubs his beard. "Let's not rule anything out."

I drain the rest of my beer and signal Tina, the bartender, for another. She's on top of it, as the staff at The Tav always is. I get the feeling I'm going to need a lot of these.

Our conversation is interrupted by shouts of laughter from a table on the other side of the bar. I assume it's a collection of college bros talking about dude stuff. Turns out I'm right. But I know this collection of bros being dudes. I went to college with them.

"Be right back," I say.

I shoulder my way through the crowd. Mike, Robbie, Stoner, and T.J. are draining a pitcher, clearly not their first. Mike throws his arms wide as I arrive.

"Hey, lookee here!" he says. "It's our unindicted coconspirator."

The others hoist their beers. I wonder if this will get anybody's attention. (Not that I mind being the center of attention, but I don't want people thinking I'm part of any conspiracy these guys would unfold.)

"I guess whatever the hell you were doing was successful?" I ask.

Stoner leans back in his chair. "It was. We thank you for your help."

I plunk down at the table. "Then can you finally tell me what the hell was going on?"

Everyone looks to Stoner for approval. He gives them a regal nod.

"Teej, why don't you get us started?" he says.

T.J. takes a micro-sip of his beer. "As you know, I've been at my company for a while now. I developed a method that would make our manufacturing more efficient and take us to a whole new level in the market."

"What is this method?" I ask.

T.J. frowns. "Joe, are you genuinely interested in what my company does and how it works?"

"Not really."

"Then suffice to say it's a good method. We can call it…well, the Method."

"Fair enough."

"I showed it to Lyle, my boss. He loved it. He loved it so much, he took the only copy and claimed it was his work."

"Seriously?" I say. "What an asshole."

"That's what I thought," T.J. says. "I told Stoner. That's when he hatched the plan."

Stoner lays an arm on the table. "The situation seemed to call for a Spanish Prisoner."

I hold a hand out. "And what is a Spanish Prisoner?"

Mike takes over. "It's pretty simple. You bring a guy into your confidence. Give him the idea there's a threat to something, and you're the only one who can help him. Sooner or later, you get the guy to give you something to hold on to."

"And once you have it," I say, "you're not likely to give it back."

"Exactly," Mike says. "Makes it easier when the something didn't belong to the mark in the first place."

"How did you pull this off?" I ask.

Mike knocks back some beer. "I found the guy at a bar he likes—thanks for the intel, Teej—and I started chatting him up. Just about sports, investments, shit like that."

"You know about investing?" I ask.

"No. On the bright side, neither does he. I convinced him we could use The Method to make him a fortune. Sell it to the competition and live like kings. I even showed him how to open an account in the Cayman Islands. He completely bought it. Along the way, I gave him a package to deliver to a friend. Told him it was a rare book."

I sit up. "That was what he delivered to Carol's place."

"Exactly."

"But it wasn't a rare book," I say. "It was just an old dictionary."

"Sure, it was," Mike says. "We knew the dumb son of a bitch would look in the package. Once he realized it wasn't a rare book, he started to realize I wasn't on the level."

"Wait a minute," I say, "you *wanted* him to know you weren't on the level?"

Stoner fields this one. "Absolutely. Then he'd have to put his trust in somebody else."

"And who would that be?" I ask.

Robbie hoists his drink. "Thank God the feds were on the job."

I rub my face. "That's what we were doing?"

"You got it. I approached the guy, said we'd been investigating Mike for a while. We were closing in, and his attempt to grift Lyle out of The Method was the perfect excuse. He just had to help us nail Mike's sorry ass to the wall."

"Wait," I say, "how did I come into this, vis-à-vis Mike's sorry ass?"

"Kind of a mistake by me," Robbie says. "I mentioned my supervisor, and Lyle was anxious to meet him. Guess he wanted to make sure I was legit."

"Imagine that," I say,

"Anyway, we brought you in," Robbie says, "and you did the job. We had the guy convinced we were going to run a sting on Mike and use The Method as bait."

"And what happened with the bust?" I ask.

"Nothing," Robbie says. "Dumb son of a bitch gave us The Method, so there was nothing else to do. He was supposed to meet Mike in the parking lot of The Tav. Lyle showed up. Mike didn't. We left him there with his dick in his hands."

I scratch my head, unsure of my role in this dubious venture. "Okay, you've got The Method back. But you scammed your boss, Teej. Aren't you going to get blowback over that?"

"I might," T.J. said. "If he was still my boss."

T.J.'s whole manner is a little strange. His face normally projects anxiety and constipation. Now, he looks almost relaxed.

"Lyle got fired for stealing The Method?" I ask.

T.J. bobs his head. "More for trying to sell it to our competition. But whatever got us there, right?"

Mike jumps in. "That account I set up for him in the Caymans? That was legit. So was the money I transferred. It came from one of the competitors. At least, that's how it looked."

"And where did you guys get this money?" I ask.

Stoner waves a hand. "Don't worry about it."

Knowing Stoner, any number of criminal gangs and terrorist organizations might be involved in the raising of these funds. But I'll stay out of it. (These organizations have my pity.)

"You got The Method back," I say. "But what about your new boss? Can you trust him?"

"I hope so," T.J. says. "He's me."

Wow. An incredibly guilty man has lost his job, and a moderately guilty man has taken his place. As a wise young lady once said, funny how two wrongs sometimes make a right. I lift my glass.

"Here's to you, my friend," I say.

That provokes a round of toasts. I have to hand it to them. My college buddies might be idiots, but they're really good at this sort of thing. I'm not sure if society is better off for it, but I'll contemplate that another day.

Meanwhile, I should be getting back to Lars and Carol. It's not good for them to be alone for too long. When I get back to the high-top. Lars is lecturing Carol on something (likely his own genius), and she is rapidly downing her Cosmo. She seizes on me when I slide onto a stool.

"Have you heard from…our friend?" she asks.

"Nope. She's disappeared again."

"Permanently?"

"Who knows? If not, I'll probably be the first to find out."

"What about Jim Street?" Carol asks. "Any trouble there?"

"Haven't heard yet. I guess no news is good news."

Lars is about to address the situation (oh joy), but something catches his eye. Frankie enters the bar. I almost didn't recognize her. Her hair is clipped back, and she wears wire-rim glasses. She doesn't look happy. Lars springs from his seat.

"My good lady," he says, bowing deeply, "I am truly honored to—"

Frankie holds up a hand. "Can we cut the shit, please?"

Lars returns to his seat. "Consider it cut. What can we do for you?"

I jump in before Frankie can answer. "Where's Fabio? Is he okay?"

Frankie squares a look at Carol. "No, he's not."

Carol opens her mouth, likely to ask, *What did I do?* Then she remembers *exactly* what she did. "What happened?"

"He took all that stuff you said seriously," Frankie tells her. "He decided he was wasting his life, and he should do something about it. He's going to become a painter."

A collective cringe circulates the table. Frankie glares at Carol, who tries to maintain some optimism.

"I'm sure he'll be great at it," she says.

Frankie flicks her an annoyed look. "No. He's going to suck. He's my brother, and I love him. But he has absolutely no talent. He's got money and a big mouth. That's why he's the perfect producer. *Was* the perfect producer. He quit."

There's that other shoe I was waiting for. Carol looks out the window, maybe contemplating her own guilt (and rationalizing it away). I drop my face into my hand. Lars remains impassive.

"Are we going forward with the film?" he asks.

"Yes, we are," Frankie says.

Lars rubs his hands together. "Excellent. I've got some great ideas for another sex scene."

"I said the movie was going forward." Frankie points at me and Lars. "I didn't say you two were going forward."

I've got a curious mix of chagrin and relief. Lars, on other hand, nearly falls off his stool, grabbing the table to steady himself.

"You...you are implying...that my—*our*—services are no longer needed?" he asks.

"I'm not implying it at all," Frankie says. "I'm telling you flat out. Hit the bricks."

Frankie turns to go. Lars leaps off his stool. His sunglasses drop to the floor. He tries to strike a jaunty pose, leaning against the table. And mostly missing.

"I believe you're making a mistake," he says.

"I'm not," Frankie says. "Lars, you were a lot of fun in the sack. I thought maybe we could do a booty call or something in the future. But as a director, you're a perverted moron. The more I saw you direct, the less attractive I found you. You and your buddy can both move along."

Lars's face falls, but he recovers and raises his chin in a haughty pose. "I will remind you, madam, that the idea for the film was *ours*."

"And the money to make the film is *ours*," Frankie says. "We'll give you a *story by* credit." She turns to me. "Sorry, Joe. I still think you're cute. Maybe if you weren't so tight-assed and went horizontal with me when I offered, things could've been different."

"That thought will keep me up nights," I say. Maybe two or three. Certainly no more.

Lars puffs himself up to his considerable height. "I really don't want to bring lawyers into this."

"No, you really don't," Frankie says. "If you read the paperwork, you have no rights to the movie. You weren't going to share in the profits. You have no intellectual claim to anything. We could fire you at any time. And since Fabio signed over his rights to me, that means *I* can fire you at any time. And that's what I'm doing."

Lars holds his hands out. "I'm begging you to reconsider."

"Lars, come on. Don't make a scene."

But that's exactly what he does. He drops to his knees—crushing his shades—and clasps his hands in front of him, begging Frankie to give him one more chance, to not take his dream away, to have pity on a poor soul such as his (that last one is a direct quote). Frankie looks as if she's stepped in a pile of dog poo (which, viewed from a certain angle...) She's finally able to get around Lars and out the door. He follows her on his knees, still begging. He only stops when the door hits him in the face. He remains there a few long moments, then stands and slouches back to the table. Carol puts a hand on his shoulder.

"Sorry, Lars."

He takes a deep breath. "Can't be helped. Y'know, Joe, I was thinking of another idea we could work on."

"Unless it involves me running you over with my car, I'm not interested."

Lars folds his arms on the table. "Bugger."

***

I'm home an hour later. The erector set of decks and stairs are wet with melting snow. I'd like to say I'm finally relaxed, with this thing over and Deirdre located God-knows-where. But I'm still inclined to look over my shoulder. It may be a long time before I can unwind. If ever.

When I get to my deck, James Street is waiting for me. He wears the usual black coat and scarf, this time with a gold suit and a white collarless shirt. I've been expecting this visit. I stop at the edge of the deck.

"Here to arrest me?" I ask.

Street's smirk has returned. "Relax, Slick. This is just a visit."

I nod toward the backdoor. "Buy you a beer?"

"Sounds good."

We step inside. The cats approach, sniffing around Street's legs, wondering why I didn't clear a visitor with them. Street sits at the breakfast bar while I grab two bottles of Grand Maibock out of the fridge and pour them into pint glasses. (Hey, it's late, but that's no reason to behave like a heathen.) I set them on the breakfast bar.

"You're not arresting me?" I ask. "Does this only apply to this visit?"

"Well, I won't be arresting you over the thing with Deirdre. At the rate you're going, though, I'm sure you'll give me another reason."

"If the cartel doesn't get me first."

"Don't think you have to worry about them. From what I gather, Victor Merced was kind of a loose cannon. They have disavowed all knowledge of him. *Victor? What Victor? You must have us confused with another cartel.*"

"*We're The Respectable Businessman's Social Club.*"

"Exactly."

I tamp down my relief, hoping my détente with the cartel is permanent. Now, I just have to wonder about the détente with Jim Street.

"Should I ask why you're not arresting me, or should I just count my blessings?" I say.

"Got a note from…our friend. She made it clear you didn't have a choice in helping her."

"She can be pretty persuasive. If *persuasive* is the word I want."

"Whatever the case, you're in the clear. Besides, it's not my concern anymore. I've closed the file on Deirdre."

I almost choke on my beer. "You have?"

"It's time to let that go. After everything that's gone down, I'll bet she's out of the game. And if she is, she's no concern of mine."

"I'm surprised. I got the impression you were obsessed with Deirdre. Like…"

"Ahab and the whale? How did that work out for Ahab?"

"Good point."

Street holds up his glass. "To Deirdre."

"To Deirdre."

We chitchat for a while, which is unique because I don't know a lot about Jim Street. He doesn't open up a lot now. But he does have a greater appreciation for hockey than

I would have expected. He finishes his beer and declines my offer of another. He stops at the front door.

"If you hear from Deirdre," he says, "you *will* let me know. Right?"

"Of course."

Street gives me the old smirk. "You've gotten better at lying, Slick. I'll give you that. Thanks for the beer."

He disappears out the front door. It's a fair cop. I've lied to Jim Street often enough that I can't feel too insulted about his accusation. I lock the front door, then step over to the arch windows and look down at Summit Avenue. Street climbs into his sports car and takes off, bound for whatever Batcave he lives in. I've just turned away from the windows when the phone rings. It's Lisa.

"Stately Wayne Manor," I say. "This is Stately speaking. How may I help you?"

"Thought I'd make sure you're still among the living."

"Still here. For my sins."

I plunk down in the desk chair. Lisa's voice is a little businesslike. I wonder if she's still at the office. Or if she's waiting to be asked for another research favor.

"Is everything okay over there?" she asks.

"Better than it was."

"Good. I've been worried about you. Not knowing what was going on."

"I'm sorry about that."

"It's okay."

"No, it's really not."

I know Lisa's dying to ask me, but she's trying not to. Maybe she doesn't *always* want to be a reporter. Maybe not with me. Maybe I'm flattering myself.

"You think you'll be able to tell me one of these days?" she asks.

"Today seems as good as any."

"Are you sure?"

"With you? Always."

I open the right-hand top drawer of my desk and dig out something buried at the bottom. It arrived in the mail yesterday. A postcard showing a tropical vista: ocean, palm trees, sunshine. The postmark was New Orleans, but the picture clearly isn't New Orleans. There's a handwritten message. *Enjoy your winter, darling. Maybe we'll meet again.*

"Are you still there?" Lisa asks.

I return the postcard to its hiding place and kick up my feet. "Still here. I can tell you about it. But it has to be off the record. Is that okay?"

"With you? Always."

I find myself smiling as I close the drawer and give Lisa the whole story.

Randall J. Funk is the writer of the Joe Davis Mystery series. He has also been an actor, director, and playwright. His plays include *The Hound of the Baskervilles, The Mudslinger Party*, and *Bring Me the Head of Dominic Papatola*. He teaches Composition at Arizona State University and is currently enrolled in the MFA Creative Writing program at Augsburg University in Minneapolis. He lives in St. Louis Park, MN, with his daughter Bea.

www.ingramcontent.com/pod-product-compliance
Lightning Source LLC
Chambersburg PA
CBHW070200120726
47909CB00001B/184